"HAL, THIS IS WORSE THAN WE THOUGHT," THE PRESIDENT SAID

"We don't know how they did it, but a lot of the information the Chinese stole has to do with the Slingshot Project."

"I remember hearing about that—a protective shield of missiles designed to react to incoming enemy missiles while they're still off the coast and take them out before they reach our shores."

"It's a hard system to beat. But if the Chinese have gotten hold of our technology, they could press a button and shut us down.

"All we can do is to try to find their secret base and wipe it off the face of the earth. Zero options on this one, Hal. No prisoners. Tell your men to end this once and for all."

DON PENDLETON'S
MACK BOLAN.®
STONY MAN™
DRAGON FIRE

A GOLD EAGLE BOOK FROM
WORLDWIDE.®

TORONTO • NEW YORK • LONDON
AMSTERDAM • PARIS • SYDNEY • HAMBURG
STOCKHOLM • ATHENS • TOKYO • MILAN
MADRID • WARSAW • BUDAPEST • AUCKLAND

First edition October 2000

ISBN 0-373-61933-2

Special thanks and acknowledgment to
Michael Linaker for his contribution to this work.

DRAGON FIRE

Printed in U.S.A.

DRAGON FIRE

PROLOGUE

Djin Shu's fate had been sealed the moment he attempted to betray his beliefs for money. His reasons at the time had been far from altruistic. He had seen and had been seduced by the lure of the nation he had come to rob. When he first set foot on the shores of America, culture shock, which he had been warned to ignore, attacked from all sides. The noise, color and the vibrant life-styles of the Americans had, regardless of his severe indoctrination, overwhelmed him.

Djin Shu was thirty-two years old. He had been born in Shandong Province, the second son of a peasant farmer, and at school had shown great promise. He had learned English quickly, becoming fully proficient in the language in record time, and when he had moved to university in Beijing he had been singled out for special attention for his grasp of technology and computer skills. Before his twenty-second birthday Djin Shu had been recruited into a department of the government which, due to the nature of its covert operations, was known only to a select few. Djin, aware of the great honor that was being bestowed on him, devoted his existence to the State. He accepted without question any and every assignment placed before him by his masters and, with the acute sensitivity of a born survivor, never once asked why. He simply did what he was told to do.

All went as planned. Over a number of years Djin operated for the State Agency, traveling widely, always under the scrutiny of his masters. The paranoid hierarchy of the agency trusted no one. Not even its most faithful disciples. Djin was never aware of being under observation, though he often suspected it might be happening. He was too involved with his work to pay much attention, and as time slipped by, he let the thoughts drift to the back of his mind until they were nothing more than flitting shadows.

His missions took him to Europe, most notably to Great Britain, where he masterminded the acquisition of military information regarding missile systems being developed by Britain and the U.S.A. That information, returned to the State Agency pool, became integrated into the Chinese defense strategy and enabled them to prepare countermeasures that would keep them ahead of their rivals. It was because of Djin's success that he was considered and finally chosen as an important part of a long-term operation designed to siphon off technological information and even examples of hardware relating to the U.S. Defense Program.

China's intention was clear and simple. They wanted to build a full-scale replica of the U.S. Defense Network Control Facility. It would be as sophisticated as the U.S. original, using the same technology with the same purpose, and if successful it would allow the Chinese to break in and take command of any U.S. military functions. The scheme was breathtaking in its sheer size and complexity. The cost would be enormous, but if it worked the payoff would be phenomenal. The controlling agency, with foresight, spoke covertly to its counterparts in North Korea, offering them a stake in the project; and the North Koreans, who needed some kind of boost to prop up their crumbling Communist regime, agreed. There was to be a cost-sharing between Beijing and Pyongyang. To finance such an undertaking meant allying themselves with less-than-scrupulous groups who would aid in bringing in much-needed currency. To this end the Chinese made overtures to the criminal Triads based in Hong Kong. The Triads, always on the lookout for new ways of making money while courting the favor of their overlords on the mainland, fell in with the scheme immediately.

China's toleration of the Triads became almost brotherly. The Triad bosses, though content to follow Beijing's lead, were ever watchful. They were well aware how the smiling face of the Dragon could change in an instant. Benevolence became outright savagery the moment the Dragon decided to change its strategy. Over the years the Triads had survived and even thrived during British rule in Hong Kong and the Territories. They had learned how to stay one step ahead. To use their enemies weaknesses and exploit them. They saw no reason why things should change now. The Triads, as did the mainland Chinese, ruled by fear and dominance of their underlings. They inspired loyalty by using scare tactics and, if the need arose, physical violence and intimidation. Those same tactics still applied. At the moment the Chinese needed the Triads. So the bosses put out the word. Accept the offers, but stay alert. Watch for signs. The Chinese weren't to be fully trusted yet. Until the Triads had the full measure of their new masters they would play a patient, observational, waiting game.

Once the Triads became wary partners, the Chinese used them for a variety of functions. They were aware that Triad influence ranged far and wide, even to the shores of America. It gave them an opening for easing in their agents, using the routes the Triads used often to enter the country illegally. The U.S.A. was a vast place, with many borders, and although entry was monitored closely, it was impossible to spot everyone.

It was by one of these routes that Djin Shu came to America. His entry into the country was at night, coming ashore from a rust-bucket freighter that had docked in San Francisco.

Rain slanted down out of a misty, clouded sky. The dockside was wet and cold, and Djin Shu's first view of America was far from rosy. He spent the next hour being driven around in a battered panel truck, peering out the rear window at a gaudy, neon-lighted landscape of endless streets and huge cars swishing by. The sights and smells of this new, vast land unsettled him. Even though he was in the company of his own countrymen, he felt out of place. Djin Shu failed to recognize it at the time but he was already becoming disenchanted with his position in life, and those unvoiced concerns were soon to show themselves.

Within a week of his arrival in America, Djin Shu was at work developing the strategy that would enable him to feed gathered information back to China. His task was made considerably easier by the fact that the Americans were a trusting people, only too eager to share the wonders of technology with anyone who showed interest. It was only after the discovery of

wholesale technology thefts that found a new home
in China that the Americans brought down the shut-
ters, and the free-and-easy access to many secrets was
shut off. By then the damage had been done. American know-how was aiding the possible enemy. The
extent of this information transfer took time to filter
through. When the U.S. government realized just how
much information had been spirited away, it was
shocked. Years of laborious development, of experi-
mentation, was now in the hands of a foreign power,
and one that—as yet—remained a thorn in the side
of the Americans.

At first, Djin Shu saw America's open culture and
the freedom of its people through disbelieving eyes.
The way that they lived in their vast, rich country
amazed him. During infrequent breaks from his work,
he was able to walk the streets in comparative safety.
He saw the gleaming cars; the stores racked high with
goods; food in plenty; a nation of people reasonably
happy with their lot.

And Djin Shu became jealous. It was a surprise to
him. He had imagined himself devoted to the cause
for the duration of his life. Dedicated to the way of
the PRC until breath faded from his body. Yet here
he was, in the land of the enemy, not only envying
but wanting to be one of them. He saw what the
Americans had, remembered how life was back in
China, and from that moment he began to edge away
from the years of indoctrination. His time in America
had not only given him a taste of their freedom and
the freedom of choice they had as a right, it had in-
fected him with its seductive freshness. Alone in his
room at night, religiously transcribing the information
that was fed to him from the various sources within

the Chinese cell working for him, Djin's mind was on other things, in particular the riches available in America. He had heard the expression "money talks." It didn't take Djin long to realize he possessed the means by which he could bring some of that money to him.

There was another reason—a beautiful Chinese woman named Jenny Yeo. Djin Shu had met her during one of his infrequent trips into the city. To be truthful *she* had met him. However the introduction had been managed, Djin Shu didn't care. He was instantly captivated by her youthful beauty, her grace and her intelligence. She responded to his every suggestion, following his every move, and within a short time Djin Shu was contemplating a move that would not only divorce him from his past but would provide them with the financial means to make their escape.

His existence up to then had been a mere shadow play, something with little substance outside the relentless pursuit of technical knowledge and endless days spent encrypting that knowledge. What had seemed so important to Djin Shu paled into insignificance as he contemplated his life with Yeo. Nothing mattered to him now except their being together. Her utter devotion to him, and the time they spent together in her tiny apartment, convinced Djin Shu that nothing else mattered to him. As they lay in each other's arms and talked of their life together, Djin Shu revealed his plans to her. He had already admitted his true identity to her, explaining that his old life was behind him. He only wanted her and the life they could build together. She listened and accepted his scheme as the only way they could move on from their present situation. Djin Shu's infatuation was so extreme he never once considered her unquestioning acceptance of his revelations as a little too convenient.

Djin Shu planned carefully over the following few weeks. First he contacted an Iraqi associate he had dealt with before, who had expressed interest in any technical information that might become available. Previously Djin had ignored the request. Now the lines had shifted and Djin, realizing that the kind of information he was handling would come in very handy to the Iraqi weaponry researchers, made his choice. He began to collate a dossier of advanced missile processes that would be viewed by the Iraq government with pure joy as heaven-sent. Since the Gulf War and the actions of the UN inspection teams, much Iraqi research and development had been stalled, and in some cases wiped out. Despite the disruption by the UN, now that they had thrown out all the inspection teams, the Iraqis were making frantic efforts to get themselves back on track. But they needed information. Their development teams were sadly lacking in up-to-date information, and were scouting the black market for cutting-edge technology. What Djin had safely stored on a computer disk was current and applicable. It would advance the Iraqi missile program by a significant leap.

As an extra bonus, with a thought to the future, Djin Shu also compiled disks and printouts of more stolen information. This was all placed in a locked attaché case and left in a locker. Yeo kept the key.

Djin's contact was sent a disk that contained just enough information to whet the Iraqi appetite. With his contact on the hook, Djin was able to bargain. He was aware that the amount he was asking for would allow him to break away and live extremely comfortably. As far as the Iraqi buyer was concerned, it was a drop in the ocean when compared to what they would actually gain. The information would eliminate years of research, so the actual cash saving by purchasing it ready to use would be phenomenal.

It was a sound deal all around. Djin would receive his payment in cash, which he would deposit in a number of accounts he had already opened in American banks, and his Iraqi contact would walk away with the information disk in his pocket.

The time and place had been arranged. The Iraqi would bring with him an expert, armed with a laptop computer so he could check the disk's authenticity. After that it would be comparatively easy for Djin to slip away and begin his new life.

In the planning it had all seemed so easy, and at first the arrangements had clicked into place.

Djin had prearranged time away from the base house, using the pretext that he was going to attend a computer exhibition in San Francisco. That hadn't seemed to cause any concern within the group. Djin was well-known for his addiction to computers, and his fascination was viewed as enthusiasm for his work. On the morning of the visit he had taken time to do a little work before setting off, so as to set the pace for the day. Even though he was going somewhere else he would attend to the day's needs first. At ten o'clock he left the house and walked to the nearest taxi stand where he took a Yellow cab. Djin sat back as the vehicle pulled away from the curb and merged with the traffic, heading for the exhibition center, which was a forty-minute ride away.

He didn't, however, make that journey. He had

asked the driver to take him to a different destination. Twenty minutes later he walked into the lobby of a hotel, checked in for the reservation he had made a few days earlier and took the elevator up to the third floor. Once in the room Djin made a telephone call, connected for him by the desk, and spoke to his Iraqi contact, confirming their appointment. His visitors were on their way.

Djin sat on the edge of the bed. He reached inside his coat and took out a manila envelope. He removed the two floppy disks and sat staring at them. The disks were identical, except for the colors of the printing on the labels. One was in red. The other blue.

The blue disk held the information he was selling to the Iraqi. The red label identified the disk that, in reality, held only a small amount of data. Once loaded it would work perfectly until the program reached the encrypted section that could only be opened via a password. If anyone tried to access beyond that data block the program would simply inject a virus into the computer database and wipe it clean. It was nothing more than a simple device Djin had created to use if he thought there was any kind of double cross taking place.

He wasn't fool enough to believe the world was awash with honorable people. The Iraqis were just as capable of cheating *him* as he was of deserting his own society.

The thought crossed his mind to call Yeo, but he immediately thought better of it. They would stay with the plan they had devised. He wouldn't contact her, nor she him, until a week had gone by. In that time she would relocate to Los Angeles and wait for him, taking the attaché case and the additional data.

Once he had conducted his business with the Iraqi he would vanish, moving around for the following few days to hide his tracks, leaving his former employers none the wiser as to his whereabouts.

Or so Djin Shu thought. With the blindness that seems to come hand in hand with deception, he imagined that he had created a righteous departure, one that would allow him to lose himself in the vast American landscape. The Asian community was large and diverse, so it wouldn't be difficult for him to blend into that landscape. He would act low-key. Nothing that would arouse suspicion. Due to the diligence of his ex-masters, he was equipped with a superb set of credentials that would pass the most careful scrutiny, right down to his Social Security number and family background. All this had been created for him by the department back home. It had been given to Djin Shu so that he could walk the streets of America with impunity. Now those very same documents would help him to become part of American society.

The error he had made was in thinking he had no need to look over his shoulder. His excellent work record and the manner in which he conducted his business had made Djin Shu comfortable. He had long since forgotten about the people in the background, those who stood aside and watched, listened, made careful note of everyone he saw. Everywhere he went. They were, as he had been, part of the distrust that was built-in to members of his society. It was the Communist doctrine that had children spy on their parents and report any nonparty activity. Toeing the party line became more important than any one person's freedom to think or act as an individual. It wrecked the idea of self and turned a nation into a collective that thought only about the sanctity of the all-important state.

In reality, though Djin Shu deluded himself into believing his importance allowed him more personal freedom than those around him, he was under close scrutiny, mainly due to his blossoming relationship with Jenny Yeo. His meeting and subsequent meetings, were recorded and detailed, sent in reports back to Beijing, where the controllers ordered a full security blanket that would encompass both Djin and Jenny Yeo. The information unsettled the shadowy men in Beijing. Even though one of their most reliable operatives, he had allowed himself to become involved with a U.S. citizen and immediately compromised his position. He was no longer to be fully trusted. His work would be allowed to continue but every move he made had to be placed under the spotlight.

When it became plain that Djin Shu was planning a defection, after selling information to another country, his fate was sealed. Plans were made to eliminate him. The fact that he not only wanted to desert his post, betray his country and sell information vital to the project being created meant his life was over as far as the PRC was concerned. They could no longer trust him. So he had to die before real damage could be done.

Intelligence work identified the buyers as Iraqis. The date and time of the exchange were established, and only hours before the rendezvous was to take place the Iraqis were warned off in no uncertain manner. When there was a protest, two of the Iraqi team were snatched from their hotel and killed. The message told the Iraq administration that they were playing with fire. The ruthless determination of the PRC was well-known. They didn't bend to threats, or negotiate. With bad grace the Iraqis stepped out of the game and left Djin Shu to his fate.

He made his way to the place where he was to meet the buyers. It was a busy place, so Djin Shu felt safe. He remained so up to the moment he realized that the Iraqi buyers weren't going to show. Alarm bells rang inside his head. Djin Shu began to retreat, searching for a safe haven. He suddenly felt naked and exposed.

The SFPD cruiser that turned the corner at that moment seemed to offer him sanctuary. Djin Shu made for it, waving his arms and shouting to attract attention. All thoughts of the future were dismissed. His promised life with Jenny Yeo was forgotten in the instant he attracted the attention of the police officers.

Djin Shu took three steps in the direction of the cruiser before his world exploded in a blinding flash of pain. He felt only a stunning impact at the back of his head, bright light, followed by utter darkness. Djin Shu stumbled and fell, crashing to the ground, his dying body jerking in spasms.

He wasn't aware of the police officers standing over him, nor the spreading pool of his blood spidering out from under his shattered skull. He died on a San Francisco street, the freedom he had desired snatched from him as swiftly as his life ended.

CHAPTER ONE

Stony Man Farm, Virginia

"Any questions?" Hal Brognola asked as he completed the mission outline to the assembled Stony Man teams.

Carl Lyons leaned forward. The expression on his face told Brognola that the Ironman wasn't in a good mood. He had noticed during the briefing that the man's expression had been getting grimmer with each passing minute.

"You can explain to me how a mess like this can happen. How the hell do the Chinese get their people into the country and then walk off with information about our missile systems?"

"It isn't as simple as that, Carl," the big Fed began.

"The hell it isn't. You've just taken twenty minutes to tell us exactly that. If it wasn't that simple, we wouldn't be sitting here waiting to go on a mission."

Brognola sighed. He had been expecting something like this, and that expectation had come through Lyons's question. If the truth be told, he would probably have been of a similar mind if he had been asked to put his life on the line, taking into account the background to the upcoming mission.

"There's no questioning the fault here," Barbara Price said, breaking the silence that had followed the Able Team commander's outburst. "The administration has accepted there were mistakes. We made it too easy for outsiders to come here and gain access to information. The Chinese in question came as workers in various technology-based industries. Some on exchanges, others as genuine employees. Now it appears that a percentage of them were actually infiltrating sensitive information and siphoning it off to their control cells. These cells were passing the information back to Beijing, where it has been used to update Chinese technology. What we didn't realize until recently was the existence of organized cells in the U.S., entirely devoted to gaining this information."

"So what were the security agencies doing all this time?" Lyons asked. "This is what they're around for. Or have I got that wrong, too?"

"No," Brognola said. "The various agencies have accepted they were caught off guard. Technology has become so widespread it's hard for them to watch every offshoot. Government contracts are being handled by companies also doing private work. Universities have access to updated technology that can have direct links with defense applications. It's all held in computer systems, and let's face it, we all know that computer programs can be accessed by dedicated programmers."

"One of the problems has been our willingness to share our knowledge with others," Yakov Katzenelenbogen pointed out. "America has a reputation for being generous with its wealth. We give too easily sometimes, and these infiltrators have made use of that generosity. In truth we've made it too easy for them."

"You can say that again," Lyons snapped. "To the point where a Chinese physicist can download sensitive information into his laptop and supposedly take it home for the weekend."

Brognola cleared his throat. "I don't deny that was one hell of an oversight. Look at it from the other side of the coin. That Chinese had been working with the company for eight years. He was a renowned researcher in his field. He had helped develop that particular piece of work. It wasn't the first time he'd taken work home."

"Only this time he sent it all the way to China. Information that will give the Chinese a big hand up the ladder. Now they'll have technology as good as ours."

"He has a point, Hal," David McCarter said from the far end of the conference table. "Look what happened in England not so long ago. Similar thing. The Chinese walked away with technology that put the British navy and its submarine missile capability into question. We had egg on our faces for months. The White House was really pissed off because a lot of that technology originally came from America. We'd let you down and all that. Now if I was a cynical bugger, I'd be saying, 'Now who's got a red face?' But I won't."

Lyons scowled at the Phoenix Force commander. Not because McCarter was being his usual sarcastic self, but because the Briton had spoken the truth.

"One fact that has come out of all this," Price said,

"connects Djin Shu, the Chinese who was killed in San Francisco, with the British affair David just mentioned. We now have proof that he was in Britain at the time of their leaks."

"This gets better all the damn time," Lyons said. "Has everybody been walking around with their heads up their asses while the Chinese steal our technology? Hal, what's the President got to say about it?"

"A lot. He's not a happy man. The way this has come out just when things are on the balance with China doesn't help the peaceful coexistence policy."

"A tad late for that," T.J. Hawkins mused. "And what does peaceful cooperation mean when the Chinese are shaking hands in the front yard while all our secrets are being shipped in by the back door?"

"Nobody said it was a perfect setup, T.J.," Katz said. "This sort of thing goes on all the time. Espionage and diplomacy are strange bedfellows, but it happens. The Chinese are past masters at subterfuge. They have a lot at stake. An emerging nation of millions, most of whom are still living in a peasant culture. A small percentage of the country lives in the cities, but by our standards it's an existence we left behind before the Second World War. The Chinese economy is pretty unstable because they still cling on to the old Communist doctrines. Five-year plans. Ten-year plans. We all know how they turn out. But the Chinese have two things in abundance—people and time. They are, for the most part, a very patient culture. They'll stick to something for a decade quite happily, where we would want a result in six months. They have to because they don't have the technology to overcome slight problems."

"So they steal it?" Gary Manning said. "No worse, I suppose, than the jobless kid who sees the shiny car you've worked hard for and takes it. It's the easy option."

"Hell of a difference between a car and missile technology that could wipe out a country," Calvin James commented. "China is doing it because it can't take losing face any longer. Am I right or am I right, Katz?"

"In the context of Chinese culture I'd say you are. Look back over history. There was a time when China led the world, culturally, scientifically, philosophically. China was a civilized nation when the rest of us were barbarians. Now things have changed. We have the wealth and the power, the ability to create all things. China has fallen behind, and it doesn't like it. The fact they have a repressive regime in power doesn't help. Old men perpetuating outmoded ideals that are simply holding the country back. And that's how it will stay until they alter their ways and get rid of the Marxist dogma that keeps them in the Dark Ages."

"So stealing our technology is going to do that?" Lyons asked. "Somehow I don't see one helping the other."

"I agree, Carl," Katz said. "The problem with a nation like China is, to a certain extent, territorial. Look at the map. China is the largest nation in the area. But it is surrounded by smaller, wealthier nations—Japan, South Korea, even Taiwan. They've all embraced the new age, created solid manufacturing bases, and they are benefiting from it. North Korea, more or less China's only ally, is in the same straits as China. It's a country on the brink of collapse—starvation, practically no manufacturing base to speak of, bankrupt economy, a leader with a grip of terror on the population, backed by his military. China must look at this and realize it is slipping farther behind. It wants to be the U.S.A. of Asia, the power base. But that isn't going to happen. Oh, it's trying. Building tourist attractions and the like. But it won't haul the country out of the mess it's in.''

"So? Are they planning on starting a war to cure their problems?" Lyons asked sharply.

"China needs to assert itself. To regain some its former status in the area. Military superiority has always been a matter of pride for the Chinese. Yes, they outnumber us as far as manpower goes, but that isn't going to mean very much. China's air force and navy are poorly equipped. Everything is years out of date. They don't have the money to buy new equipment in the amounts they require. Nor do they have advanced development capabilities. So they go for the easy option. Find out where the best technology is and steal it. Bit by bit. Here and there. Make up a list and gain access to the information. Send it back to China so their research people can collate it and create instant, up-to-the-minute hardware. No need for years of research. That's all been done by us. They benefit from that, and we end up with the Chinese facing us down with our own weapons technology."

"Is this all about saving face?" Rosario Blancanales asked. "Do the Chinese need that so badly they'd go to all this trouble? Or are they setting up for some kind of strike capability?"

"Most probably a little of both," McCarter said. "The Chinese are big on flexing muscle. They want to be boss in Asia. They see the U.S. as a threat.

Domination through finance. Through political intrigue. Uncle Sam manipulating the Pacific Rim nations for its own ends. China is being pushed to the back of the stage, and I'll bet it doesn't bloody like it.''

''The string-pullers in Beijing need something to keep the people happy. They'll believe having China back on the world stage as a power to be reckoned with could help settle some of the unrest.'' Katz inclined his head as he thought over what he just said. ''I don't believe that it'll keep the people happy. They're more concerned with having a bowl of rice to eat than waving a flag because China has produced some new military hardware. The problem is that the government has full control of the media in China. They only broadcast what they want the population to hear. Television is nothing more than a means of getting their message across. Remember, China is a big country. People living in the interior have little contact with the outside world except through the media. So the many are controlled by the few, and it's the few who have their hands on the infrastructure. They decide everything.''

''Nothing new there,'' Rafael Encizo said softly. ''What we need to know is what the Chinese intend to do with the stuff they've got from us. How are they going to use it?''

Brognola shrugged. ''We're not entirely certain. Washington has its think tanks working on that. One idea is the Chinese are duplicating our systems and using them against us. Sounds logical enough. Whatever the reason, the fact that they've gone to a lot of trouble to steal it means they have something in mind that isn't going to be good as far as we're concerned.

This leakage of information goes back six, eight months. Enough time for the Chinese to have put some of the technology to use. Our job is to neutralize whatever they have. Find out where it is and take it out of commission.''

Price leaned over the table and passed out files to each of the team members.

"Phoenix, you're booked on a commercial flight to Hong Kong. We have a British agent you'll liaise with. He has some information that could be helpful. It should give you somewhere to start. The British still have their connections out there. People who were in place before the handover. They're still doing the job. They have contacts in the area. Your cover stories are in the files. Nothing exciting. Just a group of businessmen on vacation, taking in the sights. Hotel reservations are in there, too. You can't go in armed, because it's a commercial flight. So your contact will help you with that.''

"No other way?" Hawkins asked.

Price shook her head. "We can't get you in by military airlift. Not to Hong Kong. Sorry, guys.''

"Be nice to check out Hong Kong again," McCarter said. "Haven't been there for awhile.''

"Oh, bloody marvelous," Manning said, mimicking a plummy English accent.

McCarter shook his head. "One of the saddest things is a Canadian trying to be funny.''

Manning grinned at the Briton.

"So what have you got for us?" Lyons asked tetchily.

Price ignored his sharpness as she answered him.

"The Chinese set up here. The fact that Djin Shu has been killed tells us the Chinese aren't squeamish about doing a little housecleaning. Even so, they must still have their organization in place. SFPD has been instructed to treat Djin's death as a random murder. Keep it low profile so we don't scare anyone off. If the Chinese believe they haven't been compromised, they may still be operating. We want them out of business. So Able can start in Frisco. Check in with the SFPD. They've been asked to cooperate."

San Francisco, California

BY THE TIME the delayed flight touched down at San Francisco International Airport and Able Team disembarked, Carl Lyons's mood was even darker than it had been when they left Stony Man Farm. During the flight, the weather had changed abruptly. The latter part of the journey was uncomfortable, and the aircraft had been put in a stack on its arrival. They had circled San Francisco for almost an hour before landing and had emerged from the plane into driving rain that swept across the tarmac.

As he walked down the steps, Hermann "Gadgets" Schwarz nudged his partner. "Just don't ask him whose turn it is to pay for lunch at McDonald's," he said.

Rosario "The Politician" Blancanales smiled, turning up the collar of his jacket against the driving rain. He hoped Schwarz kept his remarks to himself. Not that he didn't appreciate his teammate's humor. It just wasn't appropriate at the moment. Lyons, in one of his darker moods, was even less prone to taking a ribbing than usual.

It wasn't the best way to start a mission, especially one that looked like it had all the signs of turning into something of a fiasco. Stony Man hadn't been able to provide much intel, which meant Able Team was walking into this one cold. And in more ways than one, Blancanales thought as he felt the rain creeping under the collar of his coat.

At the rental agency they were subjected to more delays when the woman behind the desk couldn't find their reservation. Someone at the Farm had arranged the car for them, but it didn't immediately come up on the computer screen. Lyons stood silently at the desk, shoulders hunched. Blancanales, struggling to maintain a dignified silence of his own, crossed over to the vending machine and bought a coffee. Schwarz buried his head in a brochure.

After a couple of minutes the woman located the reservation. "Sorry about that," she said in apology, reddening with embarrassment when Lyons refused to cut her any slack.

"These things happen," Blancanales said, stepping in to ease the woman's discomfort. "It's been a bad day all around. Rough flight, and we were stacked up there before we could land in *sunny* California."

The woman, pretty and blond, flashed him her best smile. "Let's hope things get better, huh?"

"Thanks for your help," Blancanales said. He scooped up the paperwork and the car keys. As he turned, he caught Schwarz's eye. They left the office and stood under the canopy, scanning the line of parked rentals. Blancanales checked the registration number on the key tag.

"That's the one," he said, pointing at a bronze Bronco 4x4.

"At least the damn car's a decent size," Lyons acknowledged.

As they sprinted across the lot, Blancanales tossed the keys to Schwarz, who activated the infrared locks. They piled inside, and he turned the key. The engine roared to life.

"Okay," he said. "Everybody happy?"

"Just drive the damn thing," Lyons snapped.

Schwarz wheeled the 4x4 out of the parking spot and headed for the exit. In the rear seat Blancanales was studying the map he'd picked up from the rental desk.

"Take a left," he said.

"You sure?" Lyons asked.

Blancanales grunted. "If I can route us out of the jungle in Central America, I'm damn sure I can get us to our hotel in San Francisco."

"You know," Schwarz remarked, "I reckon he has a point."

"Can we get the Smothers Brothers gags over with?" Lyons said tautly. "I'm not in the mood."

"Well, that's a real shame," Blancanales said. "We sat up all night working on a new routine."

Lyons didn't respond so Blancanales sat back, shaking his head in frustration. The drive to the hotel passed in silence.

Both Blancanales and Schwarz knew when to let things drop. Lyons in a foul mood was on a par with a snappy tiger. It just wasn't worth testing the water.

They pulled into the hotel's parking lot, grabbed their luggage and made their way inside. Stony Man had booked their rooms, and this time there was no problem. The three Able Team commandos went to their rooms and freshened up before meeting Lyons in *his* room for a council of war. Lyons was on the phone with the San Francisco Police Department, talking to the officer in charge of the Djin Shu homicide.

"Look, pal, don't give me a hard time. You have your orders, and so do I. If you read yours, it says I'm in charge. Now we can do this easy or we can do it hard. Your damn choice, so make up your mind. Whichever it is, we are coming down there within the next hour, and I want everything you have on this case. *Everything*."

Lyons banged down the receiver.

"Local hassle?" Blancanales asked innocently.

"Cops," Schwarz murmured, flicking through a brochure that extolled the delights of San Francisco.

"*What?*"

Schwarz glanced up at Lyons's snap.

"Nothing."

"So what's the plan?" Blancanales asked quickly.

"You heard me tell that cop. We're going to head down to the station and go through everything they have on this Djin guy."

As FAR AS Jimmy Yip was concerned, the stakeout had been a total waste of time and effort. For one thing stakeouts weren't his thing. Yip was homicide. So what was he doing sitting on his butt outside a fleabag hotel?

Because Lieutenant Dakin had assigned him was why. Dumb-ass Dakin who didn't know a drug bust from a kick in the nuts. The man had no vision or tactical sense whatsoever. If he had, Yip would have been on his home ground, working the murder case he and his partner had just taken on, not dusting the seat of the parked panel truck. Two days he'd been doing this, and the result was a big fat zero.

Yip reached for the foam coffee cup resting on the dashboard. He stared into the steaming dark brew, then took a sip. The only decent thing about this stakeout was the coffee his partner Stan Loomis supplied. The two cops worked well as a team. Loomis was in his forties, a powerfully built, easygoing cop who was one of the best shots with a handgun that Yip had ever met. He was also one of the most patient cops, in Jimmy's experience, when it came to stakeouts. The boredom of long, often fruitless hours didn't bother Loomis one little bit.

"Hey, Jimbo, let me know when you want some more," Loomis said as his partner picked up the cup of coffee.

Only Loomis called him *Jimbo*. Only Loomis was allowed to call him Jimbo. Others had tried to use the nickname and had immediately regretted their error. Yip wasn't a large man physically, but he had the reputation of possessing a volatile temper when aggravated. Jimmy Yip on a rampage wasn't something a person ever wanted to see a second time.

Taking a long swallow from the cup, Yip leaned back in his seat and concentrated on watching the front of the Argyle Hotel, willing something to happen. He was almost hoping for some kind of action, anything to relieve the tedium of the day.

"Jimbo, you are letting the situation get to you again," Loomis said, seated at his right.

Yip sighed. That was the only thing about Loomis that bugged him. The man had perception, and he knew that his partner was tensing up.

"Maybe I'm drinking too much of this coffee," Yip suggested.

"Nah, it isn't that, pal. You're hating every minute of this, and it's getting to you."

"Stan, how do you put up with this all the damn time? I know you and stakeouts. You could sit in a car for a week and never make a sound. What is it with you? You know what? I think you died and came back as a stakeout dummy."

Loomis chuckled at that, then offered Yip various remedies for combating the inactivity.

The voice coming from the com unit on the seat interrupted Loomis's narrative. Yip picked it up and heard the brittle tones of Dakin.

"That you, Yip?"

"How do you do that, Lieutenant? I hadn't even spoken and you knew I was Chinese."

"Cut the clever stuff. You and Loomis are wanted back here right away. If you take a look in your mirror, you'll see a Ford pickup. Yellow. Markowich and Sturmer are in it. They'll be taking over the stakeout as of now."

"We're on our way," Yip replied, grinning from ear to ear as he started the engine and pulled away from the curb.

"Happy now?" Loomis asked, grabbing the coffee cup his partner thrust at him.

"Ecstatic, man. Ecstatic."

As they rolled along the street, Yip was trying to figure out what was so important that it had caused Dakin to pull them off the stakeout.

He knew the moment they walked into squad room at the station. Through the glass front of Dakin's office, he could see Captain Russo. He was Dakin's superior and from the unhappy expression on the lieutenant's face, he had suffered one of Russo's famous tongue-lashings. Probably because he had pulled Yip and Loomis off the homicide investigation and sent them on the stakeout.

"Jimbo, I know what you're thinking, but for Christ's sake don't say anything. If Dakin thinks you're gloating, he'll make it personal."

Yip turned to stare at his partner. "*Me?* Gloat? Not in my nature. But it feels good just seeing that look in Dakin's eyes."

Russo, a big man with thick, steel-gray hair, rapped his knuckles on the glass and beckoned the two detectives. As they approached the office, Yip saw three strangers.

"Close the door, Stan," Russo said.

Yip moved to stand to one side of Dakin so he didn't have to look him in the eyes. He took a moment to size up the three visitors. They looked at ease, almost casual, but there was an air of quiet authority about them that made the young detective pay close attention.

Russo stabbed a finger at Yip. "This is Inspector Yip. Our best man where Chinatown is concerned. He knows it well. He's done some good undercover work there in his time, and he's your best bet for finding the woman. His partner is Stan Loomis. Don't let his looks fool you. He's an untidy son of a bitch, but he's got a nose for sniffing out information from the most unlikely situations."

Yip nodded at the trio. The hard-looking blond man barely acknowledged him, while the other two smiled back. He studied the sullen guy. Whatever his problem, Yip decided to leave it unasked. The man had a no-nonsense look about him.

Russo cleared his throat. "I took you off the stakeout because I want you back on that homicide you were handling and to liaise with these people. They're from the Justice Department in Washington, and they'll fill you in. I want cooperation from both of you on this. No crap about jurisdiction. As far as you're concerned, these guys call the shots. They can, if they want, shut us out and take over completely. But I have assured them that there will be no need. There's already been enough of that around here."

Russo didn't name names, but Yip picked up on the glance the captain threw in Dakin's direction as he spoke.

"You two will work with these people, and you will answer directly to me. Understand? To me and no one else. Until I give the word, you're on this full-time."

Yip glanced at Loomis, who remained impassive.

"You can use this office for the moment while you get to know one another. Lieutenant Dakin and I have a few things to clear up. We'll do that in *my* office."

Dakin trailed after the captain, his slight build dwarfed by Russo's bulk. Everyone in the office watched until they vanished from sight.

Yip closed the door, turning to face the three strangers. "Jimmy Yip," he said by way of completing the introductions.

"Jake Collins," Schwarz said, showing his Stony Man ID that had him as a Justice Department agent.

He pointed at Blancanales. "That's Henry Dutton. The other guy is the boss. John Shelby."

"Nice to meet you," Loomis said.

"Now that we know who we all are," Yip said, "what can we do for you? I heard something about a missing woman?"

Schwarz nodded. "That's part of it."

Carl Lyons moved to sit behind Dakin's desk. He cleared the top, then spread out the contents of a buff folder.

"The dead man is Djin Shu. He was assassinated two days ago. Shot through the back of the head from a distance."

"With a 7.62 mm slug from a Galil sniper rifle," Yip added.

Lyons nodded.

"Our Triad sniper again," Loomis commented.

"You recognize the shooter?" Blancanales asked.

"Oh, yes," Yip said. "This guy has worked in the area before, and in L.A. The 7.62 mm is his trademark."

"Likes to advertise, does he?" Schwarz asked.

"More of a symbol of his skill," Yip replied, "and a way of saying, 'Look what I can do and walk away.' The Triads are a very image-conscious group. They consider themselves a superior breed, long on tradition, and they show defiance by being open about their work."

"We're talking about a bunch of gangsters here, aren't we?" Lyons asked. "Is it respect they want?" Yip regarded the man, weighing Lyons's attitude. There was something about the man that told the detective he was entirely capable of going up against the hardest and not breaking a sweat.

"The history of the Triads goes back a long way. They were originally formed in A.D. 36. They were a Buddhist cult then. In the eighteenth century they moved into politics. They were involved in the Taiping rebellion in 1851, and Sun Yat-sen's republic in 1912. Since then things have changed for the Triads.

Criminal activities have taken over. When an organization has been around for as long as the Triads, traditions are going to be formed and held on to. Remember we're talking about a Chinese organization. We always have been strong on tradition. Ceremony. We don't always take to rapid change. And for the Chinese, rapid is a few hundred years. Walk through Chinatown and you'll see what I mean. The electronic age alongside the wisdom of old China. Come back in a hundred years, and Chinatown won't be much different.''

Lyons glanced at Loomis. "Does he always answer a question with a lecture?"

Loomis shrugged. "He can't help it. It's a Chinese tradition."

Even Lyons had to smile.

"Okay. Djin Shu, as it turns out, was an illegal immigrant sent over by the Chinese to gather information and send it back to Beijing. We don't know the exact details of the main event, but Djin was taken out by a sniper here in San Francisco. A local SFPD cruiser got to him straightaway, but he was dead. They found papers in his pockets, and a photograph of a woman named Jenny Yeo. Her address and phone number on the back. The cops also found a couple of computer disks in his pocket, and there was a locker key he had hidden on him. It was found during the autopsy. It was identified as a bus-depot locker. When the local cops opened it, they found a package addressed to this Jenny Yeo and also a number of computer disks. After studying them, the cops realized they were looking at sensitive information and passed the ball to Washington. Which is where we come in.''

"Jenny Yeo?" Loomis asked.

"Our information from the SFPD indicates she has disappeared," Blancanales said. "She might just be scared because of what happened to Djin Shu. On the other hand she might have more information he passed to her. If we've figured that out, so may the Chinese the man worked for."

"So we could have local Triad people out looking for her?"

"She's going to go to ground," Lyons said. "Thinking along the lines you were going, I'd say she's probably somewhere in Chinatown. With her own people. In a place where she won't stand out."

"You want us to go look for her?" Yip asked.

Lyons nodded. "You can take Collins and Dutton with you. I'll borrow Loomis, and he can drive me to Jenny Yeo's apartment for a look around."

Yip nodded. "Okay. Let's go, guys."

Blancanales and Schwarz followed Yip down to the basement where they climbed into his battered Dodge. The car was in need of a paint job. Three of the hubcaps were missing, and the rear window had a crack in it. The interior was just as untidy.

"I know what you're thinking," Yip said as he started the engine. It turned over with a low, deep pulse of sound. "But listen to that engine, man. Is it sweet or what?"

"Sounds good to me," Blancanales said. "Is this a department car or yours?"

Yip laughed. "It's mine. The department paid me to soup it up."

"They pay for the interior trash, too?" Schwarz asked.

"I get expenses for lunch, so I guess the answer is

yes. Hey, look at it, guys. Would you steal this heap?''

He drove out of the basement garage and onto the street. It was still raining, but not as heavy. Yip cut back and forth through the streets with the casualness of someone familiar with the city.

''Just so I know, are you guys armed?''

''Yeah,'' Blancanales said.

''Too late to find out in the middle of a firefight. You know what I mean?''

''No problem. So, Jimmy, you a native of San Francisco?''

''Me? No. I'm from L.A. Transferred here four years back. It's okay. Apart from dicks like Dakin.''

''What's the deal with him?'' Schwarz asked. ''He gave us a hard time when we turned up. Wasn't going to cooperate. No way he was about to turn over evidence. Until your boss Russo showed up and read him the riot act. Then your name came up, and Dakin said he had you on a stakeout. Russo nearly threw him out the window. Something about you wasting time on stakeouts when you should be on the Djin Shu homicide.''

''Dakin is the department Jonah. He has his own agenda when it comes to his career. He's out to prove something. Trouble is, he does it by stepping on toes. The guy is too wrapped up in his own glory that he can't see what he's doing. He wants Russo's job, but he won't get it by pissing the guy off. Russo is too well thought of. The other thing, well, Dakin doesn't like the way I operate. He expects me to toe the line. His line. But I can't work with those kind of restrictions. Russo knows that, and he gives me a free hand. Just to get at me, Dakin pulled me off the homicide investigation and put me on some dumb-ass stakeout a rookie could have handled. I guess I have to thank you guys for making it easy for Russo to find out where I was and pull me and Stan out.''

"You could have called Russo yourself and told him.''

Yip shook his head. "I couldn't do that. Dakin is my superior. Okay, so he's a dick-head, but I answer to him. I don't go over anyone's head like that. Brings me down to Dakin's level.''

Schwarz glanced at his partner and saw Blancanales smile. Jimmy Yip was all right.

"So how do we find this woman, Jimmy?'' Schwarz asked. "We are in your hands.''

Chinatown

JIMMY YIP PARKED his car outside a restaurant whose gaudy facade was painted in scarlet and gold, replete with writhing-dragon symbols, and framed by pulsing neon lights. The name of the establishment was written in huge Chinese characters above the window, the letters in black over vivid green.

"No disrespect, guys, but let me do the talking. They know me around here. Trust me. If I say you're okay, no problem. But it'll save time if I ask the questions.''

Schwarz and Blancanales nodded and followed Yip inside. The restaurant was just starting to fill for the midday meal. Yip threaded his way among the tables to the counter at the far end of the low-ceilinged room. A mixture of steamy aromas wafted through the swinging door leading into the kitchen.

"Lunch breaks part of this assignment?" Blancanales asked.

"Are they ever?" Schwarz replied. "Maybe we can get takeout."

Yip had attracted the attention of a broad, squat Chinese clad in a black tuxedo. The man kept looking in the direction of Blancanales and Schwarz, his face impassive. Light bounced off his black, slicked-back hair. He reminded Schwarz of a heavy out of an old black-and-white B movie. In reality he was probably an ordinary, polite guy, who just happened to look stern.

When Yip rejoined them he nodded and led the way back outside. He paused beside his car.

"Mr. Yat suggested we go have a word with Mrs. Choy. She might be able to help."

Back in the car, Yip pulled away from the curb and they threaded their way along the busy street, where crowds pushed their way off the sidewalks and crossed without hesitation. The area was alive with people, noise and smells. Music floated out of windows, the singing resonating with that distinctive pitch associated with traditional Chinese song. It was a sound you could hear in any Chinese community anywhere in the world. Like their food and the tantalizing odors that were part of it, the Chinese were never separated from the characteristics that made up their culture. They would embrace the good things of the new world, but were never isolated from their traditions and rituals.

Yip eased off the main street and negotiated a narrower, though still-crowded thoroughfare. He eventually brought the car to a halt outside a dark-fronted building flanked by a Chinese herbal shop and a mah-jongg parlor.

Leaning over the rear of his seat, the detective grinned. "Now you know why I asked about you guys being armed."

"*Oh*," Schwarz said. "It's that kind of neighborhood?"

"Not on the tourist map for sure."

"What is this place exactly?" Blancanales asked as they made their way in through the beaded entrance.

"Kind of a refuge for anyone who can't make it in the regular world," Yip explained. "Mrs. Choy is kind of like a do-gooder. Likes to help. She's run this place for years, since her old man died. He was a businessman. Story goes he was the meanest mother this side of Scrooge. All he did was make money. Wouldn't spend more than a penny he didn't have to. When he died it all went to Mrs. Choy, and she moved into this place and decided to help people. Kind of retribution. Mr. Choy would have hated this place."

They crossed the lobby and reached a reception desk. Chairs were scattered around the area, most of them occupied by Chinese who looked like they were on the edge. The warm air was heavy with incense.

A slender Chinese woman, dressed in a dark Chinese tunic and pants, came to greet them. She listened as Yip spoke to her, then she backed away and disappeared through a door at the back of the desk.

"Mrs. Choy is in today," he explained. "If she'll see us, we might get an answer."

The woman was back within a minute. Nodding and smiling, she indicated that they go through.

The detective led the way. On the other side of the door they found themselves in a large, well-lighted office. It was ornately decorated, the carpet under their feet thick and soft. Rich paintings hung on the walls. Dominating the far wall was a large black desk, its expansive top bearing a number of telephones and a large, beautifully sculpted dragon supporting a desk lamp.

Seated in a huge, soft leather chair was a slender Chinese woman of indeterminate age. Her black hair was pulled back from her face, and her almond eyes regarded the visitors with a cool stare.

"Mrs. Choy, it is kind of you to see us," Yip said.

"Jimmy, you know my name is Angela. How many times do I have to tell you?"

Yip relaxed. He turned to introduce Blancanales and Schwarz.

Angela Choy smiled.

"Something wrong?" Blancanales asked.

"If your name is Henry Dutton, I'm Charlie Chan."

"Oh?"

"A dull name. Not for a man like you." She glanced at Schwarz. "Same goes for him. So, Jimmy, tell me who these men really are and why they're working with the SFPD."

Blancanales nudged Yip. "I thought you worked undercover?"

"Mrs. Choy knows who I am. She spotted me first time I walked in this place. I told her the truth and since then we've got along fine."

"We help each other, *Henry*," Choy said. "Now why don't you all sit and you can tell me what you need."

Jimmy explained about Jenny Yeo and the need to find her quickly. Blancanales and Schwarz showed their fake ID. Choy studied them carefully, then glanced up.

"The photos are fine, but those names."

When Yip mentioned a possible Triad involvement, the woman's dislike of the Chinese gangsters was obvious.

"Damned lunatics," she said. "They should have stayed in Hong Kong. Problem is, they see a new market opening up and they go for it like leeches."

"Do you have much trouble with them around here?" Schwarz asked.

"Not really. I don't make money out of this place, so what's in it for them? They leave me pretty much alone. It's a kind of mutual hatred. So I have to be careful who I deal with and who I talk to."

"Meaning us?" Blancanales asked. "The last thing we want is to cause you any problems, Mrs. Choy."

She stared at him with those striking eyes. "Mrs. Choy? Come on, *Henry,* you can do better than that."

"Angela, I'm serious. We're talking about the Triads. There's already one man dead, and I don't want violence falling on your head because we've been talking to you."

"I understand what you're saying, but this woman sounds as if she needs help more than I do."

Choy picked up one of her telephones and quickly dialed a number. Schwarz noticed that all her telephones were old rotary-dial types. He hadn't seen any in use for some time. It was a nice touch, he thought. In keeping with the surroundings.

The woman spoke to someone on the other end of

the line, then paused, gently tapping the receiver with one long, manicured finger. She listened as someone spoke, nodding slowly. Finally, she replaced the receiver.

"There has been a young woman staying at the Blue Stone Hotel. Her presence has not gone unnoticed because she is not from Chinatown. It appears she arrived two days ago."

"That fits in with our timetable," Blancanales said.

"Is she still registered?" Yip asked.

Choy nodded. "She stays in her room most of the time and has food delivered."

"If she knows Djin is dead, she'll be scared to move," Schwarz said. "The sooner we get there the better."

Blancanales stood. "How did she register?"

"As Linda Bey," Choy replied. "Do you think she is the one you are looking for?"

"We'll soon find out," Blancanales said. "Angela, thank you for your help."

"You are very welcome, *Henry,*" she replied, her mouth curving in a smile. "I hope you find this girl."

CHAPTER TWO

The moment Blancanales and Schwarz followed Jimmy Yip into the Blue Stone Hotel, they both picked up the prevailing mood of tension. Without saying a word, the Able Team duo took up defensive positions, staying where they could cover the entire lobby, desk and stairs.

Yip had already gone ahead, before either man could warn him, and he was halfway across the area before he became aware that he was suddenly alone. He turned, sensing something might be wrong, and immediately saw that Dutton and Collins were checking out the area. The detective reached under his jacket for his shoulder-holstered Beretta. Something made him glance at the motionless figure of the desk clerk. The man, a thin, gaunt-faced Chinese with long black hair, faced Yip with an expression of pure terror frozen on his face. The only things that moved were his eyes. As Yip locked on to him, the clerk allowed his eyes to flicker down. He repeated the gesture.

Damn!

The detective realized what the terrified man was trying to say to him. There was someone waiting below the level of the desk. Yip cursed himself for missing the obvious.

"Behind the desk!" he yelled and launched himself toward the floor. He hit on his shoulder and rolled, breaking his fall with his outstretched left hand. His Beretta was out now, the muzzle tracking on the desk. Yip saw a dark-clad figure rising, a stubby shotgun clasped in his hands. The weapon boomed, sending a spread of shot across the empty space where Yip had been standing seconds before. The detective didn't hesitate. He tipped the muzzle of the Beretta, caught the shotgunner in his sights and pulled the trigger three times. The sharp rap of the bullets came hot on the tail of the shotgun's explosion. The gunner behind the desk flipped backward as the 9 mm rounds took him high in the chest. He slammed into the rear wall, the shotgun bouncing from his slack fingers. He tried to stay on his feet, but the trio of slugs took their toll quickly and he stumbled sideways, slumping to the floor behind the desk.

"He got friends?" Blancanales yelled at the clerk.

The man nodded. "Second floor. Room 16. Looking for a woman."

"Great," Schwarz grumbled.

He took the stairs two at a time, with Blancanales close behind. Yip stayed long enough to check the shotgunner—the man was dead—then followed.

As Schwarz hit the second-floor landing, turning along the corridor indicated by the plaque bearing room numbers, he heard a crash, followed by a man's angry curse. He pounded along the hallway, counting off the room numbers. Ahead of him an armed man stepped out of a doorway. He saw Schwarz and Blancanales, then ducked back inside the room, shouting in Chinese. Someone replied, and the first man stepped out of the room again. This time he had an Uzi in his fists and he leveled it and fired.

Schwarz was already on his way to the floor, Blancanales dropping to his knees. They took aim together and triggered closely spaced shots into the gunner's chest. The force of the rounds spun him, his face rigid with shock. Blood began to spread across the front of his blue shirt, staining his tie as he sank to his knees, then fell facedown, hard.

Blancanales moved ahead of his partner, reaching the door to the room. It was wide open, and inside the room a slim, dark-haired Chinese woman was on her knees, a man's hand on the back of her head, pushing it down. A pistol in the man's hand was angling toward the back of her skull in preparation for a killing shot. Blancanales didn't hesitate. He leveled his Beretta and fired on the move, two shots coring through the gunman's skull. The impact snapped his head around as dark spray erupted from his battered cranium. He toppled away from the woman, bouncing off the edge of the room's single bed before crashing to the floor.

The woman remained where she was, paralyzed by the sounds of the shots. Blancanales crossed to her, knelt on the carpet and put an arm around her trembling shoulders. She jerked away, crying out in fear.

"Easy now," Blancanales soothed. "It's over. They won't be bothering you again."

The woman stared up at him, her face pale.

"Who are you?"

"Friends," Blancanales said. "Jenny Yeo?"

"Yes."

Behind him Schwarz appeared in the doorway. He

pulled his cellular phone from his inner pocket and speed-dialed Lyons's number.

"We found the woman," he said when Lyons answered. "Just in time. She had some visitors. Not very sociable types, if you get my drift. But they're out of the frame now. She's okay. We're out of here as soon as we can.

"The woman's room has been taken apart. Whoever was here was definitely looking for something."

Schwarz broke the connection, then glanced at Jimmy Yip, who was surveying the room and the two dead Chinese.

"The guy by the door is Hano Ho. He belongs to the Snake Clan Triad. Now those guys are hard mothers. Into drugs in a big way. Don't know the other two. Could be they're imported guns."

"We'll get that checked out later," Blancanales said. "First we need to get Jenny away from here. Pack her stuff and let's go before we have more visitors."

Jenny Yeo wasn't carrying much luggage. One piece seemed important. She hugged a locked attaché case tightly as she was ushered from the room and down the stairs, through the lobby and out onto the street when an SFPD black-and-white rolled to the curb.

Jimmy Yip crossed to the car, showing his ID. He spoke quickly to the uniformed cops before joining the others. Blancanales was in the rear seat with Jenny Yeo, while Schwarz stood beside the car, his gaze taking in the street and its occupants. Once Yip reached the car, Schwarz slid into the back alongside Yeo.

"Let's go," Blancanales said.

The detective eased the vehicle along the street, making a left turn at the first intersection.

"You guys know where we're going?" Yip asked over his shoulder.

"We were depending on you for that," Schwarz said.

"No problem. We have a number of safehouses."

Jenny Yeo spoke for the first time since they had left the hotel. "Who do I say thanks to?"

"Justice Department," Blancanales said. "And the San Francisco PD."

He showed his ID. Yeo studied it carefully.

"I could have it blown up to a larger size," Blancanales suggested.

"After the way things have happened the past few days, I'm not in my most trusting mood."

"We understand," Schwarz said.

Yeo smiled at that. "If only you did."

Schwarz leaned back and glanced at Blancanales, who gave a mystified shrug.

CARL LYONS SAT on the edge of the couch in the middle of Jenny Yeo's apartment surveying the wreckage. Someone had gone through the rooms and systematically trashed the whole place. Every place where something might be concealed had been opened, ripped apart, shattered, shredded. Carpets had been stripped from the floors. The bed's mattress had been slashed open, as had every cushion and pillow. The small kitchen had been left in a state of complete disarray, with food packages torn apart and their contents strewed about the floor. Nothing had been left untouched. The thoroughness of the search had even included sealed cans of food. A sharp knife had been used to puncture and expose the contents before they had been dumped in the sink.

"You get the idea someone is a little paranoid about this whole affair?" Loomis asked.

"Maybe they've got something to be paranoid about," Lyons suggested. "The information Djin Shu had on him is worth a lot to somebody. If there's more, they must be pretty desperate to get their hands on it."

"Yeah, I guess so," Loomis agreed and went back to his quiet inspection of the apartment.

His unobtrusive presence made it easy for Lyons to accept the big cop. Loomis was one of those people who were handy to have around. They got on with the job, didn't gripe about every damn thing, but as sure as night followed day, Stan Loomis would be there if trouble turned up. He was the perfect partner. Solid, dependable, and he only talked when there was a need.

The odd thing was that Lyons felt himself slipping back into his old role as a cop so easily. Sitting quietly, observing the mayhem that had been wreaked on Jenny Yeo's apartment, he found he was looking at it through the eyes of a cop. He was checking out the scene of the crime inch by inch, looking at this, then moving on. Going back to look at some item a second time, for the simple reason that it had held his attention. Only when he was satisfied did he turn his gaze on something else. Lyons didn't scan the room quickly, expecting to gain his knowledge on first view. Rather, he drew it in piece by piece, absorbing the whole with care and refusing to hurry the process.

He and Loomis had been in the apartment for almost an hour. Neither man showed any inclination to admit defeat and leave. They each took a separate room, stayed with it, then moved to the next, until, hopefully, something fell into place. But there were no guarantees. No rule in the book that said the scene had to yield its secrets. Where Carl Lyons and Stan Loomis were concerned, however, determination and tenacity were akin to their blood types, a natural part of their makeup.

"Whoever did this took their time," Lyons said. "They went through this apartment room by room. No panic. No rush."

"Like they felt safe?"

"Yeah."

Loomis perched on the edge of the table. "Like somebody had things covered?"

"Protected."

Loomis nodded slowly. He was turning things over in his mind, working through the options with methodical precision.

"Safe from who?" he asked tentatively, his words offered in such a way that he was almost priming Lyons, asking for confirmation of thoughts running through his own mind.

"We're talking something big here," Lyons said. "The people Djin Shu worked with have a strong organization set up. They couldn't afford not to have insurance from someone local. Someone who could run interference if things jumped track."

"Makes sense. Okay, let's move it on from there. If we're talking local protection, it's coming pretty close to home." Loomis caught Lyons's steady gaze. "This leading where I think it is?"

"Maybe," Lyons replied. "Fit the pieces together. Djin Shu gets killed because he's doing some insider trading. His organization had to have looked ahead in case that kind of thing happened, if anything slipped out. If it did, and the local police became involved, the bad guys are going to want to be kept aware. Just like what did happen. The SFPD gets the nod from Washington that the situation is delicate, and they tell them to keep a tight lid on it. No information leaks. Now that was the word."

"But next thing we know, a Triad hit team has been sicced onto Jenny Yeo and her apartment gets trashed," Loomis stated.

"Could that be because we showed up? Took over the investigation and panicked someone in the department?"

"So the snitch tipped off the Triads to clean house right away."

"And you and Jimmy Yip were moved sideways. Away from the Djin Shu killing and given a by-the-numbers stakeout."

Loomis sat upright, anger darkening his face.

"Dakin! That fuck!" He rounded on Lyons. "Now I see why he hauled Jimmy and me out of the investigation so damn quick. He wanted us out of the way while he covered his tracks."

"He didn't like it when I pulled rank and took the case out of his hands," Lyons said. "It doesn't prove all that much."

"Hell, it makes sense," Loomis retorted. "Too much damn sense."

"Let me make a call," Lyons said.

He went to the wall phone in the kitchen. As he reached for it, Lyons paused. He decided against using it and took out his cell phone. As soon as he was connected to Stony Man, he made two requests.

"Check into the background of a SFPD lieutenant called Dakin. Ray Dakin, and get the Bear to scan the phone line of a Jenny Yeo. San Francisco number." Lyons read the number off the kitchen telephone. "Give me a call as soon as you get anything."

Signing off, Lyons went back into the living room.

"Let's go," he said to Loomis. "It's time we found out what the others have been up to."

SFPD Safehouse

THE HOUSE WAS a single-story, wood-and-stone building, which stood in isolation in the hills overlooking the Bay. By the time Lyons and Loomis arrived, the others were well settled.

Blancanales and Schwarz were talking to Jenny Yeo, while Jimmy Yip made sandwiches and coffee in the well-equipped kitchen.

"Just like home," Loomis said, poking his head around the kitchen door.

Yip shook his head. "I've seen your kitchen, Stan," he said. "It doesn't look anything like this."

"I tidied up since you were there last."

"Do I look like I believe you?" Yip asked.

Loomis shrugged and wandered back into the living room where Lyons had taken Blancanales aside to talk to him.

"I'm afraid your apartment is a mess, Miss Yeo," Loomis said. "Somebody was looking for something and being really thorough about it."

"If they are the same people Shu was involved with, I'm not surprised," Jenny replied.

"And would you know who they were and what

Djin Shu was doing?'' Lyons asked, breaking away from his conversation with Blancanales.

Yeo stared at him as the realization hit her that no one in the room knew a thing about her background. She debated the implications of telling them the truth or concealing her reasons for becoming involved with Djin Shu. In the end she decided that cooperation might serve her better than trying to hide her intentions.

''I was assigned the task by my people in Hong Kong. My name *is* Jenny Yeo. I belong to a prodemocracy group opposed to the Chinese government and its regime. Part of our strategy is the infiltration of the PRC's covert military operations on the mainland or anywhere else they base themselves. We have been working against this particular cell for some time now, trying to infiltrate it. My part was to establish contact with Djin Shu to try to gain his confidence. It seemed to have worked too well, because he turned against his own people and made plans to defect. Selling stolen American technology to the Iraqis was intended to fund our plans to go away together.''

''But his people found out,'' Schwarz said, ''and had him removed.''

''Yes. When Shu was killed I didn't know what to do. He'd given me additional information, saying it would bring in more money for us.'' She shook her head. ''Whatever else I might have wanted from Shu, his death was not part of it.''

''The people he worked for don't take kindly to betrayal,'' Lyons said.

Anger darkened the woman's face as she faced Lyons. For a moment it looked as if she might strike him, but her body slumped back in the chair.

"You're right, of course. He had betrayed his trust. His beliefs. Now he's dead because I promised him something I had no intention of honoring."

"Don't feel bad about it," Blancanales said. "Djin Shu was an enemy agent. He was stealing American secrets and sending them home to China so they could develop resistance to our defense systems."

"Now his people are trying to kill you," Lyons reminded her. "This has got nothing to do with feeling sorry for Djin. But it has a lot to do with whatever you have in that attaché case."

Yeo reached down and pulled the case to her, stared at it for a moment, then pushed it into Lyons's arms.

"Take the damn thing. I don't want it anymore."

Lyons carried the case to the table and placed it there.

He activated his cell phone and called Stony Man. When Barbara Price came on the line, he updated her on the situation, adding that they had an attaché case possibly containing sensitive material.

"We need a pickup. This is for you guys to deal with. Have it checked in case it's been booby-trapped. Djin could have arranged a surprise if it fell into the wrong hands."

"Give me a location, and we'll have someone pick it up. What's next for you?"

"A couple of developments we need to move on. Right now we sit tight until this case is on its way to you."

"We'll move on that. I'll call once I have it set up."

"Make it fast. Our situation isn't as secure as we thought."

"Oh, by the way, that information you requested on Lieutenant Dakin has come through. I don't know how much the SFPD pays its staff, but our friend Dakin has been making big cash deposits in offshore banks. The Bahamas. He opened a couple of accounts within the past three months. Since then, he's made regular deposits. He's either incredibly stupid, or vainly arrogant because he made the deposits in his own name."

"Having met him, I'd go for the second option. I had a feeling something like that might show," Lyons said. "What about the other matter?"

"Aaron ran a trace and found out there's been a tap on Jenny Yeo's apartment phone for the past few weeks."

"Okay. We'll hang on for your call."

Lyons put his cell phone away and rejoined the others.

"Jenny, we found out someone has been tapping your phone for the past few weeks. Did you make arrangements with Djin over the phone?"

Yeo nodded. "Yes. He had to make all his calls from pay phones out of his workplace. We thought we were being careful. Looks like we were wrong on that, too."

"Stan, that matter we discussed. Appears we might have been right."

Loomis had his temper under control now. He simply nodded in recognition of what Lyons was saying.

"Someone like to tell me what all the mystery is about?" Jimmy Yip asked.

"You might not like to hear this," Lyons said.

"So try me."

"We're pretty sure Ray Dakin has been feeding information to the opposition. He's been depositing large cash amounts in offshore accounts."

Yip glanced across at his partner. "You think so?"

"These people seem to have some good intel, Jimbo, and it explains why we were pulled off the Djin case and sent to stakeout city."

Yip shook his head. "Son of a bitch!" He paused for a brief moment, then said, "Shit! You want to know something else about Dakin?"

"Spoil my day," Lyons said.

"He also knows the locations of our safehouses. Which ones are in current use."

"Hate to tell you this, folks," Blancanales said from where he had been standing, keeping lookout through one of the windows, "but so does someone else, and I know for sure they haven't come to get subscriptions for HBO."

Lyons moved up beside him and saw two cars blocking the exit to the drive. A number of armed figures were fanning out as they approached the front of the house. One of them was talking into a transceiver, most likely contacting others covering the rear.

"This is great," Yip said. "Just great!"

"Hey, Jimbo, where's all that cool?" Loomis asked.

"Ask me later and I'll show you."

"You guys, with me," Lyons snapped at Yip and Loomis. He didn't need to check Blancanales and Schwarz, who had already moved to cover the rear of the house.

"Hey, what do I do?" Yeo asked. "Stand here and look helpless?"

"Can you handle a gun?"

"You're kidding, right?"

"Anyone got a backup gun for the lady?"

Loomis produced a .38 Colt revolver from a hip holster. He passed it to Yeo, who broke the cylinder, checked the loads and flipped the action shut again.

"Hey, these guys look serious," Schwarz called. "I see shotguns and SMGs."

The first shots rang out, steel balls from a shotgun ripping through the front door, sending wood splinters flying across the room. The only casualty was the sleeve of Loomis's jacket. The rip in the fabric seemed to anger him more than anything else, and he might have rushed the door if Jimmy Yip hadn't caught his arm and dragged him up against the solid wall beside the door.

Glass shattered from the rear of the house as another blast from a pump-action shotgun destroyed the patio door. The answering shots came from 9 mm Berettas, which both Blancanales and Schwarz were carrying.

The opening shots were a prelude to an all-out attack. The house rocked to the concerted volleys blasted at it from both front and rear. There was little the beleaguered occupants could do until the shooting died down. The interior by that time was littered with splintered wood and glass. Somewhere glass tinkled sharply as a shard fell from a shattered frame. Outside, harsh orders in Chinese were hurled back and forth. Then came the clatter of hard-soled shoes running across the ground.

A savage kick sent the bullet-riddled front door

crashing open. A dark suited figure stood framed in the doorway, SMG blazing as he hosed the interior.

"Son of a bitch!" Loomis muttered. He fisted his Beretta in both hands as he swung it up to cover the shooter, placing a pair of quick shots into the man's chest.

The attacker fell back, control of his SMG lost as he stumbled in bloody confusion. The muzzle arced down, a line of slugs tearing at the carpet, chewing into furniture. Behind him a second man dragged the wounded shooter aside, pumping shot after shot from a shotgun, stepping up to the doorway and arcing the muzzle left and right.

Carl Lyons, down on one knee, triggered his massive .357 Magnum Python and drilled a hollowpoint in the man's right knee. The power of the bullet blew the shooter's leg wide open, tearing a big hole on its way out. The guy went down, screaming, before Lyons's second shot took him between the eyes and laid him on his back.

To the left of the door, a shadow filled the already glassless window, the man's weapon up and ready as he took a step over the low sill. He was tracking Loomis when Jimmy Yip fired twice. His first round caught the guy in the shoulder, holding him back long enough for Yip to trigger a second, more accurate shot that opened the side of his neck, tearing his main artery. The shooter fell across the sill, screaming, clutching at the bloody wound in his neck and thrashing about like a netted fish.

AT THE REAR of the house the Able Team duo was holding off the rush that had followed the frontal assault. The kitchen, by this time, was a shambles. The initial burst of firing, apart from taking out all the glass in windows and patio doors, had also torn into cupboards and utensils, sending crockery and food containers flying.

Blancanales had been the first to move as the shooting died down, knowing exactly what would happen. He had his 9 mm autopistol in both hands, the muzzle constantly tracking back and forth as he waited for their attackers to show. The first guy came through the window over the sink, scrambling in with reckless abandon, slipping awkwardly on the broken glass strewed across the drain. He got no farther than that. Blancanales leaned out from his cover behind a floor cabinet and triggered a fast burst into the intruder. The 9 mm rounds cored through the bridge of the guy's nose, angling up into his brain. He lost all control and collapsed on the drain, his blood dripping over the edge and onto the floor. The Able Team commando scooted around the edge of the cabinet and grabbed the SMG out of the dead man's loose grip. He scanned the magazine and found it was full, then checked to see that the weapon was cocked and ready. He used the weapon on the next guy at the window, blowing him backward with a face full of 9 mm slugs.

Schwarz had caught sight of shadows around the edge of the patio doors. These shooters, now aware that rushing in too fast was a big mistake, were taking their time. One covered the other as they moved in. The tip of a barrel appeared at the edge of the patio door frame. A shoe came down on shattered glass, making only a slight sound, but it was enough to alert Schwarz. He pressed against the side of the wall beside the patio door and waited until the gunner was partway through. The Able Team warrior reached out with his left hand, gripping the obtrusive gun barrel. He yanked hard, pulling the shooter off balance. As the man came toward him, unable to use his weapon, Schwarz leaned around him and put two hard shots into the shooter's partner. The man fell back into the shrubbery, leaving Schwarz free to ease his gun back and jam it hard into the side of the first shooter. He dropped the hammer twice more. At point-blank range, the twin shots cored the shooter's body, shattering ribs and cleaving organs before they emerged from the other side.

LYONS HAD NO TIME to consider any options as more shots erupted from outside the house. The attackers had a simple strategy—open up with everything they had, then rush the building. As with the first attack, this second group repeated the moves, and the defenders held their positions, knowing that the procedure would be the same as before.

A heavy body crashed through what was left of the front window. At the same time a second shooter, his SMG clattering noisily, attempted to breach the front door.

Jenny Yeo found herself confronted by the man who burst through the window. She got off a single shot, the .38 slug tearing a ragged furrow across his left cheek, before he swung the butt of his shotgun and caught her on the side of the head. The blow spun the woman off her feet. Even as she was falling, the shooter half turned, his shotgun following through, and he fired as Loomis came into his sights. The single shot ripped across Loomis's right side, shredding his clothing and opening a raw wound over his ribs. Loomis fell back, still trying to raise his weapon. He collided with Jimmy Yip who wrapped an arm around his partner, supporting him as he brought up his own handgun in a swift movement, leveling and firing. The 9 mm slug took the shooter between the eyes and he collapsed to the floor in a tangle of limbs.

As this was taking place, Lyons confronted the shooter coming in through the front door. The man's forward momentum took him a couple steps past Lyons. He twisted wildly, triggering the SMG, sending a 9 mm volley in the general direction of the Able Team commander. Lyons had already dropped to the floor, bracing his fall with his left hand and pushing his Colt out and up. He pulled the trigger, drilling three closely spaced shots into the shooter's thick torso. The impact of the .357 Magnum slugs put the man down hard.

An eerie silence descended over the house once the gunfire stopped. Then Loomis groaned, more out of protest at being shot than acquiescence to the pain he was feeling.

In real time the firefight had lasted less than a minute. To those involved it seemed longer. In the slow return to reality the realization of what they had experienced took on a greater significance than the event itself. Yip, kneeling on the floor with his arm around his wounded partner, still had his handgun in firing position. Blood from Loomis's side had covered his hand and soaked the sleeve of his jacket.

Only feet away, Yeo was curled up on the carpet, her face badly bruised with an open gash over her eye. She was semiconscious. In the rush of combat, events transpired so quickly that it took the human mind a while to assimilate them. Things were done in the heat of the moment that could remain a mystery to the individual for some time after.

Carl Lyons pushed to his feet, his gun up and ready as he moved to check each of the downed shooters, kicking weapons out of reach just in case one of the dead made a recovery. Sometimes unwary survivors ended up shot because they hadn't removed a weapon from beside someone they thought was out of the game. That was on Lyons's mind as he disarmed and thoroughly examined each of the attackers.

Blancanales and Schwarz, who had inspected their own casualties then checked outside the house, reappeared.

"Two cars. Both empty. No sign of any other visitors," Blancanales reported.

"Call in," Lyons said. "We need medical assistance and a cleanup squad."

Blancanales took out his cell phone to make the call.

"You okay?" Schwarz asked Yeo as he helped her to a seat.

She nodded slowly. Schwarz left her long enough to find the bathroom. He came back with a large towel for Yip to place over Loomis's side and a smaller one he had dampened with water for the woman's face.

"Ambulance is on its way," Blancanales said.

Lyons knelt beside Loomis. "How's it going?"

"I had worse." Loomis grinned suddenly. "It's not every day I get a cuddle from Jimbo here."

"Next time I'll leave you to bleed all over the carpet."

"Somebody is running scared," Loomis said to

Lyons. "I figure Dakin is the one to lead you to them."

"I was thinking along those lines myself," Lyons replied. "It's time we got him moving."

"Maybe I can help," Yip said. "If we've guessed right and Dakin *is* the contact man for the Triad, he'll be waiting to hear how this hit went down. Am I right?"

"I'll buy it," Lyons agreed.

"So I call him and make out things didn't go too well. I'll disguise my voice. I'm angry and blame him for the mess. Demand we meet to sort things it. Only you can be waiting when he turns up."

"What have we got to lose?" Schwarz said.

"Let Dakin choose the meeting place," Lyons suggested. "It should make him feel more secure."

"You can call him on this," Blancanales said, holding up a cell phone he had found on one of the dead shooters.

Yip checked the phone, going through the stored numbers. He made a soft exclamation when he came across a familiar number.

"Look at this." He showed the readout. Underneath the number were the initials *RD*.

"Anybody who says this is a coincidence is going to upset me," Yip said as he pressed the speed-dial button and waited as the number connected.

When the call was answered, Yip gave the thumb's-up. Then he launched into an excited tirade in Chinese, going on for almost thirty seconds before he relaxed and lapsed into agitated English. His tone was angry.

"You promised they would not expect us. We have dead people. We pay you to make certain this does

not happen. Maybe I come down to your office and
we sort it out. *No!* This is not good, Dakin. Meet?
Yes. We meet now. Where? I know that place. Two
hours. Be there, Dakin, and do not try to trick us.''

Yip cut the connection.

''He's scared. That son of a bitch will need to
change his pants before he leaves to meet us.''

''Where?'' Lyons asked.

''Fisherman's Wharf,'' Yip replied.

CHAPTER THREE

Fisherman's Wharf

Blancanales leaned against the railing, seemingly intent on watching the activity taking place below him. Some yards away Schwarz was studying the shrimps on his plate as he sat at a table outside a seafood restaurant. Carl Lyons was farther along the strip, out of sight. Dakin would have to pass him to reach the rendezvous point, and once that happened he would be within the triangle formed by the Able Team trio. They had arrived well in advance of Dakin, taking up their positions and settling in for a long wait.

Before leaving the safehouse, the Stony Man team had seen Loomis placed in an ambulance and taken off to hospital. Jimmy Yip had reluctantly agreed to escort Jenny Yeo to a location fixed through Stony Man, where Hal Brognola had his own people waiting. The attaché case went with Yip, to be handed over on arrival. Once the case and Yeo were in safe hands, the detective was to be allowed to go to the hospital to be with Loomis.

With the details arranged, the Stony Man combat team had been able to leave for their rendezvous with Ray Dakin.

Lyons saw the cop arrive and park his unmarked car. Dakin seemed confident, almost brazen, as he strolled along the boardwalk, but as he passed Lyons, the Able Team leader saw that the police lieutenant's face was glistening with sweat. The man appeared calm on the outside, but in reality he was a mess. His connection with the Triad had taken an unexpected, nasty twist, and despite his usefulness to them, Dakin had to have known the Chinese gangsters weren't to be treated lightly. Which was why he was there. His greed had put him in bed with the Triad, and once committed there was no walking away and pretending it hadn't happened. His only course of action now that his deal had soured was to tough it out.

Dakin reached the arranged spot, directly outside the seafood restaurant where Schwarz was seated. He stood awkwardly, trying to appear cool and relaxed. But he wasn't succeeding. More than once he reached up to run a finger around the inside of his shirt collar, which suddenly seemed too tight for a comfortable fit.

The tourists milled around him, moving back and forth along the boardwalk. Dakin scanned them, seeking his Triad connection, unsuccessfully.

He did recognize Schwarz when the Able Team warrior stood and moved in his direction. For a fleeting moment Dakin stared at Schwarz, realization clouding his face with anger. He knew he had been drawn into a setup. He turned abruptly and began to walk away, only to find Blancanales in his path. Quickly making another change of direction, this time back the way he'd come, he was confronted by Carl Lyons standing in his way.

Able Team moved in, converging from three points and cutting off Dakin's escape.

"Give me an excuse to shoot you," Blancanales said as he reached Dakin first. "Please give me an excuse, because I really would like to."

"You wouldn't," Dakin said. "Not with all these witnesses."

"All of a sudden he's a lawyer," Schwarz said. "By the way, you are going to need a damn good one."

"Might not get that far," Lyons contributed. "As far as I'm concerned, he doesn't have to get as far as jail."

"No," Blancanales said. "Not another one. Last time it took us weeks to get you cleared. I'm not going through all that again. This one is delivered alive."

"Goddamn, you can't pick me off the street like some criminal!"

"Dakin, that's exactly what you are. The worst kind. You sold out your country for money," Schwarz reminded him. "And while I think about it, that cash you deposited offshore has been frozen. Even if you walked free right now you'll never get any of it."

"Face it, Dakin, we've got you dead to rights." Lyons even smiled as he fell in beside the cop. "The money. Cell phone off a dead Triad member with your number and initials stored in the memory. Conspiracy to murder. Colluding with known criminals. Treason. Mister, you are going down, and for a long time."

As they walked along the boardwalk, Dakin became very quiet. He was weighing his options. He knew the finality trying to shoot his way out would bring. His cop's mind tried all the permutations he could think of and abandoned them all.

"What about a deal?"

"You don't have a thing we want."

"The guy manufacturing computer chips for the Chinese?"

"This guy is good," Schwarz said. "He makes it up as he goes along."

"Goddammit!" Dakin yelled. His outburst attracted attention, heads turning to see what all the noise was about.

"Easy," Lyons warned. "Don't play games with us."

"No games. I mean it. I can give him to you."

When they had reached the rental car, Lyons unlocked it. Dakin was put in the back, Blancanales and Schwarz flanking him. Lyons fired up the engine and drove away from the wharf, cutting back toward the city, then out to the freeway, taking them along the winding coastal road. No one said a word for the next fifteen minutes. Dakin, aware of the delicacy of his situation, remained silent as Lyons pulled off and took the car up a narrow back road. They traveled for close to a mile before Lyons slowed and stopped. He cut the engine, twisting around in his seat to face Dakin. The big Colt Python was in his hand. The hammer went back with a hard sound.

"Don't fool yourself into believing I won't kill you here and now if I get shit from you. Talk to me, Dakin, and keep your eyes on this piece. It could be the last thing you ever see."

TWENTY MINUTES LATER Carl Lyons was on his cell phone talking to Barbara Price.

"I believe him. The guy is too scared to make up stuff like this. Run some checks and see what you can find."

"What's your next move?" Price asked.

"Not a deal until you come back. We'll head back to Frisco and hand Dakin over to the Feds."

"Hal's informed the Frisco office and they'll rendezvous with you. Oh, by the way, your cop friend Loomis is off the danger list. He was lucky. A few busted ribs and a lot of missing blood, but he'll make it."

"How about Jenny Yeo?"

"We have her safe. The attaché case is on its way back here. Once we take a look, it should give us a clearer picture of what the Chinese have been up to."

"Talk to you later."

Stony Man Farm, Virginia

"SILICONE CHIPS!"

Everyone looked up as Huntington Wethers shouted. He grinned sheepishly at his own outburst.

"You want to explain?" Carmen Delahunt asked, swinging her chair around.

"It's what we should have been looking for all the time," Wethers said. "Okay, we know the Chinese have been stealing information. Blueprints for the construction of defensive and offensive systems. They can buy a lot of what they need on the open market. Hardware and the like. But what they can't just go out and buy are the chips to make the systems work. They can build whatever they want, but if they don't have the chips to make it operate..."

The silence stretched on after Wethers stopped talking. It was so obvious even Wethers felt foolish having to explain it.

"The man is right," Delahunt agreed. "The Chinese don't have the homegrown technology to develop the kind of stuff they need for this setup."

"So they go where the original chips were developed and work from there," Akira Tokaido said.

"Which is where Alexander Delmont comes in," Aaron Kurtzman said. "Able Team came up with the goods, getting that name from Dakin."

"Let's run some checks on Delmont," Delahunt suggested, "and see where he's been going, who he knows."

"Sounds like I missed something," Barbara Price said as she entered the Computer Room, sensing the excitement. "Come on, guys, give."

"Able Team came up with a name from that crooked cop. Dakin fingered an Alexander Delmont as the guy who has been manufacturing the chips and circuit boards for the Chinese," Kurtzman explained. "It's something we should have homed in on earlier—the fact that the Chinese are going to need silicone-chip technology to operate their systems, and they don't make them in China."

"So we're looking at the U.S. market?"

Kurtzman nodded. "Yeah."

"Any update from Phoenix Force yet?"

"Not since the last time you asked. I figure they're a little busy right now." Sensing her unease, Kurtzman turned and put a big hand on her arm. "They'll be in touch when they can. We always get these quiet times as soon as the business starts."

"Yeah, I know. It doesn't make it any easier. Knowing they're out there but not how they're doing."

"Barb, you can't carry it all on your shoulders. When the guys are in the field you let them go. If you don't, you can't do your job."

"I know. Maybe I'm getting too close."

"No. What you do is *care*. That's fine as long as it doesn't take over from what you should be doing."

"That won't happen. But I can't stop myself worrying about them."

"Don't ever change that. As long as those guys have at least one person worrying about them they're not alone."

Bispo, California

IT WAS EARLY the following morning when Able Team arrived in Bispo, the small Southern California town where Alexander Delmont had his laboratory and manufacturing unit. Bispo was a growing town on the edge of the desert, a small community with big ideas. The local town council, in association with the bank, had initiated a development park, building units and providing comfortable surroundings and amenities.

Delmont Electronics had been one of the first companies to set up shop. The business had grown, and the town had provided most of the workforce. Delmont himself had become well liked and established in the town affairs. He contributed to all the local charities, attended every civic function and the town as a whole would have been shocked if it had been aware of one of Delmont's practices. Outwardly Alexander Delmont was a successful entrepreneur. His products were widely sought, his development team one of the finest around.

Bispo's adopted son had feet of clay. He was a man so deep in debt he would never clear it. Delmont was an addicted gambler. For most of his adult life he had stumbled from one financial crisis to another, using his charm and guile to get additional money to keep his business afloat and his debtors satisfied. He managed to do both, always presenting a solid front whenever he was on stage. Over the years he kept the balls of his life in the air, juggling expertly and never dropping one of them. He never married because he didn't want the encumbrance of a wife he would need to keep happy and away from his gambling. But he did have a string of affairs.

The latest of these was a young woman who had caught his attention during one of his secret trips to Las Vegas. She had been at the blackjack table on his arrival, and during his reasonable winning streak she had made herself known to him. Delmont, flattered by her attentions, responded. They spent the next two days and nights together, and by the time his visit was over, the woman left with him. Delmont was a happy man. He was leaving Vegas with a beautiful girl on his arm and almost three times as much money in his pocket as when he had arrived. Back in Bispo, he established the woman in his ranch-style house outside of town and for the next few weeks life was good.

What Delmont didn't know was that the woman— Tina Maris—had been placed in Vegas with the sole intention of getting to know him. Tina, thirty-one years old, had been hired by an American contact for the Triad organization working for Colonel Li Cheng. Her assignment was to work her way into Delmont's favor, then his home. Her aim was to find out everything she could about Delmont both personally and financially. She did this so well that by the end of the third week the Triad had a complete dossier on Alexander Delmont.

Using the expertise she had gained over a long number of years, Maris got into Delmont's private safe and his computer system. She located financial statements, outstanding loans, the cache of IOUs he had run up. During her investigation, she found that Delmont had used his electronics knowledge to install a sophisticated TV/video setup in the house that recorded what went on in the bedroom. She found numerous tapes that showed Delmont engaged in sexual activities with a number of women. There were also some that showed him with young men. Delmont, it seemed, liked to sample the pleasures on both sides of the fence. In her usual thorough way, Maris contacted her employer and, while Delmont was away for a few days, she had the collection of tapes and all his documents copied. By the time Delmont returned, Maris had left the house, and he never saw her again. There was a sealed envelope waiting for him on his office desk the next day that detailed exactly what had been found in his house, and that someone would be contacting him within the next twenty-four hours.

Those hours were the longest of his life. When the call finally came, it was a relief to learn that the price of silence was his cooperation in the manufacture and supply of chips and circuit boards to precise specifications. No questions asked, and as a gesture, his new employer guaranteed to pay off any and all of his gambling debts, as well as destroy the evidence of his carnal deviations.

Delmont accepted the offer instantly. He was a man of low morals, so the proposed offer, which would in fact release him from the heavy debt that had hung over his head for too long, was too tempting to refuse. He was also smart enough to realize that they had him exactly where they wanted him. There was no guarantee, whatever they said, that they would honor their full deal and actually destroy the copies of the videotapes. There was nothing he could do about that. He had to trust them because he simply had no choice.

Within the following two days significant things happened. Delmont began to receive calls from his debtors acknowledging payment. It confirmed that his new employer was honoring that part of the deal. At the end of the two days he received a visit from a Chinese who presented him with a computer disk on which Delmont found the design and specifications of the chips and circuit boards they required. He was given a completion date. If he met the date, his tapes would be returned and he would also receive a substantial cash bonus for his trouble. The messenger left once he had made certain that Delmont understood both the requirements and the terms of the deal.

Delmont spent the rest of the day and far into the night going through the disk, establishing the expectations of the objects he would be creating. The parameters allowed for any error in the manufacture were virtually nil. Delmont realized that the technology behind the creation of the devices was of the most high standard, and it was only in the last few hours of a long, exhaustive night that he started to realize just what he was looking at. He had undertaken classified contracts before, so he knew something about the configuration of military applications. And this was what he was looking at. Something that was to be used in a military set up, in either a defensive or an offensive role.

The realization failed to shock him or to cause him alarm. Military hardware was a diverse market. Not only that, it was big business. Those who could create and build sold their goods to those who could afford to buy. The friend of this day was the enemy the next. Lines of conflict ebbed and flowed. This month you funded this group. If they turned on you, the funds could be easily diverted to the other side. Where politics were concerned the easy way through the mess was often solved by a shipload of arms sent to the leader who could offer the right kind of deal.

Delmont had sat with the disk in his hand, a smile on his face. The disaster of the past couple of days looked like it might turn out not to be a disaster at all. If he played this out to the end, he might come out the winner.

That thought was the beginning of the end for Alexander Delmont. When he actually turned the thought into action, the hammer had already started to fall. He hadn't taken time to understand who he was dealing with. If he had he might have survived. As it was, his innate arrogance led him down the road of his own destruction.

His time arrived on the same day Able Team came to Bispo seeking him.

Shortly before they drove along the main street, heading for the development park, another car had preceded them. It came to a stop outside the unit where Delmont's company was situated. Three men climbed out. All were Chinese. Dressed in smart business suits and carrying leather attaché cases, they might have been interested clients coming to observe the operation of a profitable venture.

One man remained in the car behind the wheel, and a keen observer might have noticed that he kept the engine running. No one did, and even if they had it wouldn't have caused much concern.

The three Chinese went inside and spoke to the young female receptionist, asking to see Mr. Delmont. Within a few minutes they were led to his office and went inside.

"Coffee?" Delmont asked.

The leader of the trio shook his head as he sat to face Delmont across his wide desk. His two companions remained standing.

"We have little time, Mr. Delmont. You know why we are here. Is the consignment ready?"

"Most of it," Delmont said.

"I do not understand."

"Mr. Lim, this is a precise business," Delmont said. "You must appreciate the difficulties I have producing merchandise of such extreme quality."

"Let me understand what it is you are saying, Mr. Delmont," the Chinese said. "The consignment, which we all agreed would be completed today is not ready? Is that really what you want to tell me?"

"It isn't what I wanted to tell you, Mr. Lim, but it is what I have to tell you. Apart from three boards the consignment *is* ready." He indicated a small carton, sealed and sitting in the corner of his office. "There it is."

"And the final three?"

"I need more time," Delmont said, smiling indulgently.

The man called Lim took a few moments to reflect on Delmont's words. He had been dealing with this American since the arrangement had started and in that time had come to understand Delmont's character. The man was what the Americans called a con artist. He cheated and lied his way through life. He gambled with money that wasn't his to gamble with. His moral character was unsavory, as the videotapes had proved, and though he had conceded to the demands placed upon him via coercion, he was still trying to trick them into paying him more money. He waited until Delmont spoke again just to prove to himself that he had assessed the man correctly.

"This is a difficult time, Mr. Lim. An expensive time. I hate to bring this up, but I'm trying to get you your goods. There needs to be a further cash transaction to obtain the final raw materials so I can complete the work."

Lim smiled. It wasn't for Delmont's satisfaction but merely his congratulating himself on being right. Delmont had remained true to his character. Despite the delicate position he was in because of his indiscretions, he still had the temerity to try to steal more money. And from the Triad. It was that fact that condemned Delmont. His opinion of his own worth had allowed him to try to bluff the Triad into parting with more money.

Lim turned to one of his companions and spoke in his own language, asking the man to collect the neat package sitting in the corner of Delmont's office. When the package was in the man's hands, Lim turned back on Delmont.

"Three of the boards are still not ready. You require more money in order to complete them. Have I left anything out, Mr. Delmont?"

Delmont gave a nervous laugh. "Only the amount of money I need."

"Of course." Lim reached up to stroke his broad chin. "Time for you to be paid in full, I believe."

Lim stood and stepped to one side. As he did, Delmont was able to see the third man who had been bending over to open his attaché case. The Chinese straightened, his hand holding an automatic pistol with an unusually long barrel. Before Delmont could make any kind of protest, the man holding the gun aimed and fired. The gun made a soft sound, not loud enough to penetrate the closed door of the office. Delmont was pushed back into his executive-model leather chair as the first slug cored his chest. The shooter kept pulling the trigger until he had one bullet left in the magazine. He angled the barrel up and placed the final shot in Delmont's head. The empty shell casing fell to the carpeted floor, clinking as it struck one of the others littering the carpet.

Lim gestured sharply. The man holding the package opened his case and placed it inside. The shooter reloaded his pistol, holding it at his side as he moved to the door.

The door itself opened a fraction of a second before the shooter touched the handle. The secretary who had shown the three men into Delmont's office stood in the open doorway, her gaze instantly drawn to the shredded and bloody body of her employer. More blood dappled the wall behind his chair. To her credit the woman didn't scream. She took a single step back, then turned and ran for the main doors leading out to the parking lot.

She never made it.

The shooter, annoyance lining his face, stepped out of the office and raised his gun. He fired twice. Both heavy slugs hit the secretary between the shoulders, throwing her forward against the glass doors. She hit them hard, slithering awkwardly to the floor, legs and arms twitching in spasm.

Lim snapped at his companions, and they ran for the main doors.

The shooter reached them first and had to drag the body of the dead woman away because she was lying across the threshold.

"THAT LOOKS LIKE THE PLACE," Blancanales said as Schwarz rounded the bend in the feeder road.

Swinging the car across the road, Schwarz saw there was a car parked in front of the unit. It was sitting there, waiting, a hint of smoke trailing from the exhaust. He wondered why the driver had stopped there instead of parking in the lot at the front. There were plenty of spaces, especially in the spots marked Visitors.

Instead of parking, Schwarz drove past the waiting car so they could all get a look at the driver sitting behind the wheel.

The three of them recognized the driver as Chinese.

"I don't believe in coincidence this early in the morning," Lyons snapped, unleathering his big Colt. "Not when the Triad's involved."

"Girl inside the doors, guys," Blancanales yelled. "I think she just got gunned down."

Schwarz stomped on the brakes. The car rocked to a halt and Able Team piled out in a rush.

"I'll take the driver," Blancanales said, swinging to the right and eyeing the parked car.

The driver had already dropped the car into reverse. He hit the gas hard, and the heavy limousine swerved across the road, bumping up the curb on the far side. The driver struggled to keep control, lost it and stalled the car. He fumbled with the key, trying to restart the vehicle but had forgotten to put it into neutral. Cursing in Chinese, he freed the handle and kicked open his door, half falling as he scrambled out, clawing at the gun holstered under his jacket. The weapon snagged, then came free and the driver searched for his target. He loosed a couple of wild shots at Blancanales's weaving figure, missed and ducked behind his door.

Blancanales ran around the front of the car. He could see the driver's feet below the level of the door. Raising the barrel of his Beretta, he triggered a 3-round burst, then moved, widening the arc, so he came in around the edge of the open door. He kept the Beretta on track, then found he didn't need it. His shots had gone through the door and struck the driver in the chest with enough force to put him out of action. As Blancanales rounded the door, the driver slumped forward, his gun on the ground, his chest a ragged mess where the already misshapen 9 mm slugs had chewed holes into his body. The front of his white shirt was a glistening mess.

LYONS WAS A COUPLE of steps ahead of Schwarz when the doors to the unit burst open and the Chinese shooter sprinted toward him, raising his weapon at Lyons.

The big ex-cop dived below the barrel, hearing it go off with a cough which told him the weapon was suppressed. The thought was fleeting, dissolving almost instantly as Lyons concentrated on taking out his target. He came out of the shoulder roll on one knee, catching the shooter off guard. The Chinese hadn't been expecting a fast reaction and, by the time he altered his aim, his target had pulled the trigger twice. The powerful Magnum slugs ripped into and through the gunner's body, blowing out the back in a bloody spray. He dropped to the ground instantly, all sensation gone from his lower body.

Schwarz, never once taking his eyes off the other two men, locked on to the guy carrying the heavy attaché case. The Chinese pulled a gun with surprising speed and began to fire in Schwarz's direction. He didn't bother to take the time to aim. It was panic shooting, but dangerous nevertheless. Schwarz two-fisted his Beretta and stroked the trigger twice. The first 9 mm round hit the target just below the left shoulder, spinning him sideways so that the second hit was through the side of his body, angling into his chest cavity with enough velocity to puncture his heart. Bleeding internally the wounded man went down on his knees still triggering his own gun. The slide locked back on an empty chamber just as Schwarz got a third slug into him and put the guy down for good.

Lim, seeing his two companions go down, drew his own gun as he backed off, retreating inside the building. Four doors led from the reception area—

Delmont's office, the male and female rest rooms and the locked door that led into the production area. That door operated on a keypad and could be opened only by someone knowing the combination of numbers.

Lim tried both rest rooms, which had no windows. He ran into Delmont's spacious office. A floor-to-ceiling window looked out onto a small garden, but the window didn't open. It was a sealed unit, made of thick, shatterproof safety glass. He fired a shot at it, hoping it might shatter, but the bullet merely starred it before ricocheting across the room.

Lim turned and made to leave the office. As he stepped into the reception area, he was confronted by the blond American who had taken out his assassin.

"Put down the gun," Lyons advised.

It sounded foolish to Lim, because *he* knew and the American knew that was the last thing he was going to do.

He raised his pistol, firing before he had his target because he dared not wait any longer.

Lyons was ready. He fired two shots directly over the target's heart. Lim fell back against the reception desk, his eyes glazing over from the onrush of pain. He didn't suffer for too long, because the severity of his wounds abruptly closed down his system.

ALEXANDER DELMONT WAS pronounced dead on the scene by the paramedics. The young secretary, possibly due to the field dressings she got from Able Team, didn't lose as much blood as she might have and survived.

All the Chinese were dead.

By the time the local police arrived, Lyons had already talked to Stony Man and Hal Brognola was intervening on their behalf. Yet time was something they couldn't afford to waste, and Lyons said as much to Brognola when the big Fed came on the cell phone.

"Hal, get us clear of this mess. We need to get back home fast. We've got a package here, and I've got a feeling the crew at the Farm isn't going to like what they find. If the Chinese are so desperate to get their hands on this stuff, what else have they got? And we need to locate the clearinghouse for this group. Put that out of action once and for all."

"Has the local top cop arrived yet?" Brognola had asked gruffly.

"Just now," Lyons informed him. "You'll love this guy, Hal. He's the size of a small mountain and he's dressed like an extra from the Roy Rogers TV show."

Once he had handed the phone to the cop, Lyons crossed to where Blancanales and Schwarz were checking out the car the Chinese team had arrived in.

"Anything useful?"

Blancanales didn't answer. He was checking out the glove compartment and the registration.

"He gone dumb, or what?" Lyons asked.

Schwarz shrugged. "I think he's on the trail."

"Oh," was all Lyons said, and left Blancanales to his work.

CHAPTER FOUR

Guangdong Province, China

Colonel Li Cheng stood motionless on the wide balcony of the summerhouse overlooking the wide lake that edged the estate. Cool winds carried the scent of the many flowers that filled the carefully tended, peaceful garden below the balcony. The silence at the summerhouse was overwhelming. It gave him a sense of timelessness, that he would live forever. The inner calm it brought to him allowed him to deliberate on the great plans he was commanding. Here, away from the rowdy turmoil of the outside world, he became as one with the universe. His thoughts stood in perfect clarity. He could almost see them as a panorama of events before his eyes, things he had done and, more exciting, things he only dreamed about. Yet, here in this isolated place, where time ceased to race by, Li Cheng dreamed his dreams as if he were a boy again, playing in the dust outside his parents' house in that tiny village clinging to bare hills. Then he had imagined children's dreams. Now, as a man of incredible power, when he was here in his solitude, he could do that very same thing again. And no one was ever the wiser.

Then he picked up the merest whisper of sound behind him, accompanied by the scent of angels. He cast aside his adolescent dreams for the adult fantasy that had become reality.

"Wei, I thought you were still asleep," he said, turning to stare into the eyes of the woman he worshipped.

Shun Wei, a tall, lithe young woman who was without question a beauty of great renown, returned his smile. She approached him, bending to kiss his cheek. It was one of nature's playful tricks that had created Li short, with powerful shoulders and chest. It gave him a stocky appearance, though it was something he used to great effect. Despite his lack of height, he was an impressive figure when in uniform and taking control of situations. Yet for whatever reason, kept inside her lovely head, Shun Wei worshipped him and was his greatest ally.

"You know I can't sleep if you're not there," she said.

"When I am there sleep is not what you look for."

She laughed, reaching out to stroke his cheek. "A woman who sleeps with a dragon must expect fire, my love."

He watched her cross the balcony. Her walk was controlled, as were all her moves. She moved with graceful ease, never wasting a step. Clad in a simple white nightdress of cool cotton, with her mane of shining black hair tumbling halfway down her back, she was at that moment the most desirable of creatures as far as Li Cheng was concerned, and he would have willingly sacrificed the whole of China for her. His inner thoughts manifested themselves in a physical reaction, and Li turned away until his lustful hardness calmed itself.

"Come and sit," Shun called from the breakfast table. "You have a busy day ahead. A good breakfast will help."

Now she was the thoughtful wife, concerned for her man. The night before she had been a fiery tigress, ever demanding, never sated. Li joined her at the table and waited until the cup of tea was placed before him.

"There may be problems with the project," he said.

She paused, a slice of fruit almost to her full lips. "Why?"

"Djin Shu's death has aroused the Americans' interest. It appears he may have left behind evidence of what he was doing. If it's true, then they will know what we have."

"So what can they do? They accuse, you deny it. They can't prove a thing."

"Rumor has it that a team of U.S. Government agents have been digging into Djin's past. They are in San Francisco, looking for that woman he was ready to betray us to."

"It is a man's weakness. His love for a woman. It makes him do strange things."

Li glanced at her and saw she was smiling her quiet little smile, the one that always seemed shrouded in mystery.

"I don't know what you mean," he said lightly.

"Come back to bed and I'll remind you."

Li put down his cup. "This could be serious for us. If the Americans dispatch one of their covert teams, they might come looking for us."

"Here? On the mainland? How could they?"

"The Americans will know that we will deny any knowledge of technology thefts. There would be total denial. In that case, how could we make any complaint if one of these teams actually located the project and damaged it? Beijing would not like it. But what could they do?"

"The answer is to stop these Americans if they come," Shun said as if it were the most simple task in the world. "Get Xan Hung off his lazy behind and get him to send out those Triad thugs he controls. Stop these Americans before they are able to find out anything."

"That possibility has already crossed my mind. Hung is one of the people I'll be talking to. I may be very late tonight."

"Then we had better make good use of the time we have before you go." She stood and drew the nightdress over her head, dropping it to the floor.

She stood waiting, one hand outstretched to him, and didn't move until he joined her. Taking his hand, she led him back inside the house.

AN HOUR LATER, when Li's car arrived, he was ready and waiting. He stepped outside and went directly to the vehicle. Someone opened one of the rear doors and Li climbed in, pulling the door shut behind him as he sank into the well-upholstered seat. The car moved off with barely a sound.

"Good morning, Colonel."

Li nodded his head.

"Talk to me, Wang."

Jun Wang, a slender, effeminate man in his early-thirties, cleared his throat. He was always a little nervous in Li's presence. The only saving grace was that so were all the other people within the colonel's sphere of influence. He had a fearsome reputation. He was a man of few emotions, cold almost, but the power he wielded made him someone to respect and never challenge. Some had tried and had suffered for it.

"Have you made your decision about the offer from Pyongyang?"

Li Cheng continued to stare out of the car window as it sped along the dusty road. He was watching the peasants working in the field, up to their knees in brown water. The routine of their lives never changed, he thought. Over the centuries the Chinese peasants had lived and worked these rural areas, planting, harvesting, living and dying in their thousands as the world developed around them. Men flew to the moon and back, yet the Chinese peasants simply carried on planting their rice.

He sometimes envied the simplicity of their existence, the simple philosophy of life that determined that they be content. Never wanting more than they had now or would ever have in the future. But then his mind would rebel and he would argue against that. The people of China deserved more than a primitive existence. Why shouldn't they be allowed to enter the new millennium? To have a share of the bounties that the world had on offer? It would take decades to educate them into the electronic age, but they did deserve the chance to enjoy what man had achieved.

It was partly because of his desire to better his fellow man that Li Cheng labored to bring the project on-line. It needed to happen. *It had to happen.* It was one of the levers China could use to push herself into the light of the new age, away from the shadows where she had stood for so long.

Though Li was an advocate of the Communist doctrine that had ruled China since 1949, and a disciple of its policies, he was acutely aware that in many respects the road the country traveled was becoming stonier with every passing year. The many multiyear plans, with fixed goals, hadn't worked. Industry hadn't improved. China's manufacturing base was still firmly fixed in the old ways. Instead of great electronic manufacturing processes, the masses still produced the greatest amount of China's output. Millions of workers, existing in primitive conditions, created China's exports. The country's expertise wasn't being channeled into the right areas. So China was still looked upon as a nation a step behind the technology of the modern age.

Nowhere more so than in her military capabilities. China's strength, still, lay in the fact that her military might was based on men. Millions of them. An overwhelming number, perhaps, but in truth not a statistic that would insure domination if the need arose. China's military machine was clumsy and archaic. Air force and navy were encumbered by outmoded equipment. The sophistication of the West was beyond China's capabilities. It didn't have the means to produce the sleek, dedicated machines needed to insure recognition as a world player. And this left the Chinese frustrated and not a little bitter. Until it could match the West in weapons and technology, China would always have to play second fiddle in the power game. In its own territory—Asia and the Pacific Rim—China needed to be able to do more than simply bang an empty fist on the table in times of tension. She needed a hammer to hold in that fist.

So the project came into being. Colonel Li Cheng had developed the strategy. If China couldn't create its own modern systems, then it would go where they were and acquire that technology, by any means. Once the country had the information, China would use one of its strengths—that of duplicating someone else's work. Over a period of two years, Li went looking for his people, assembling his teams, and then sent them out to beg, borrow or steal what China needed. And it proved to be a fruitful harvest. Using guile and innocent curiosity, coercion and out-and-out stealing, China took what it wanted. Li's growing department assessed, refined and built many of the systems being employed by the British, the Europeans and especially the Americans.

Chinese operatives were placed in American companies, universities and, in some instances, military establishments. Their work ranged from researchers to office cleaners. They were patient people, willing to lay dormant for months until they were able to gain access to the small area of information they required. With the cooperation of the Triads, the passage of information was handled quickly and discreetly, allowing the project to move from the drawing board to actuality.

The island chosen for the project's site was isolated and sparsely inhabited. The fishing community that had existed on the island acquiesced to Li Cheng's demands with little resistance, especially after he had used his military force to demonstrate in graphic terms the price of resistance. Li didn't fool himself into accepting their words of loyalty to the cause. His explanation that the development on the island was for the security of China as a whole might have been taken on face value and without a murmur. They might have been simple people, but they weren't foolish enough to overlook the fact that Li's armed special force was on twenty-four-hour patrol, watching and listening, making sure that the message was fully understood. The colonel needed their presence to show anyone from the outside that the fishing community was still on the island. It was no more than a flimsy cover for his activities. He didn't anticipate any interference. The island was well within Chinese territorial waters, so visitors weren't expected or tolerated.

When Xan Hung's construction workers arrived on the island and immediately began the job of opening the caverns below the surface, Li became aware that there might be another security problem that needed addressing. The workers, all on Xan's regular payroll, were told to maintain silence about the contract they were on. At first this rule was obeyed, but weeks later two of the workers, on a weekend break in Hong Kong, became talkative. They had spent too much time drinking. When news got back to Li, he was furious. His immediate reaction was to contact Xan. A day later both men were dead. They were found in different parts of Hong Kong. Each man had been shot through the back of the head, a single shot from a high-powered rifle fired from a distance. The news was quietly leaked back to the island workers. There was no more loose talk, and the project construction went ahead without interruption.

Installation of electronics began. Equipment arrived from the mainland. More came in by sea. Additional equipment was flown in by helicopter.

The defection of Djin Shu to the arms of American capitalism came as something of a surprise to Li Cheng. He knew of Djin, had seen the information he had sent home during his time in Great Britain and then later from the United States. There had been some valuable information submitted. The man was an excellent team coordinator and knew how to get the best from his people. But then, gradually at first but worsening with surprising speed, Djin's deliveries began to falter. It was as if his mind wasn't on his work. This disturbed and angered Li. The project was at a critical stage. There wasn't the opportunity for any delay. He sent orders to America for Djin's overseers to pay close attention to him. The colonel wanted to know what had happened. It took time before the reason came through. It seemed that Djin Shu had become attached to a woman, a young Asian-American named Jenny Yeo.

Li could hardly believe what he read. Djin Shu infatuated with a woman? It was entirely out of character. Not that the man shouldn't have those feelings. Li himself knew the personal agony of infatuation. But his affair was kept strictly apart from his work. Djin, it appeared, was allowing himself to be drawn away from his primary task by this American woman. Li sent orders to the U.S. Djin had to be distanced from this Jenny Yeo, and he didn't care how they did it.

The news Li received next sent him into a rage. Djin's handlers had learned that he had secretly been negotiating with a group of Iraqis, offering them highly classified information that would have aided their missile program. The colonel could hardly believe what he was hearing. It seemed that his agent had lost all control and was so involved with the woman that he was prepared to betray his country and abandon his principles. When his rage had subsided, Li contacted Xan Hung and arranged for Djin to be eliminated. It was the only course of action. The man had become a liability. In his state he was capable of anything, including the betrayal of the rest of his team, which could easily lead to discovery and the loss of vital information. His death would put a stop to that happening, and would also serve as a sharp lesson to any others who might be harboring similar thoughts.

Xan Hung dispatched his exterminator, and the job was quickly done.

There were, however, complications. The American police had got to Djin Shu's body first and had collected the computer disks that held the information he had been about to sell. The U.S. government then became aware of what Djin Shu had been doing. Their reaction had been to send in one of their covert teams. Also, the woman Djin had been involved with was still alive, and it appeared that she still had possession of information he had stolen. Attempts were being made to regain control of that information, but success still evaded them.

Li sighed. So many things to deal with. He pulled himself back to the moment and found Jun Wang waiting for a reply.

"Yes, of course. Pyongyang wants to know if they should go ahead with the missile construction. Tell them yes. I want those missiles on site within the month. Not next month, or the week after. But by the end of this month. If the Koreans want the protection the project will offer, then they must fulfill their end of the deal.''

Jun nodded. ''I will speak to the director today.''

The helicopter flight to Li's island took under an hour. The aircraft banked as the pilot began the descent. The colonel leaned to peer through the window. Below him the island rose out of the blue sea, a dark shape relieved by very little greenery, making it look barren and empty to the casual observer. If the onlooker had paid close attention, he might have seen the recent signs of activity, areas where the thin topsoil had been disturbed during construction. Finished on the surface, the current round of activity was taking place under the ground, in the extended caverns that were being turned into Li's master control facility. Here, where only caves had existed, concrete-lined passages linked various levels. And within those reinforced steel–and–concrete caverns the intricate constructions were being created that were soon to become the heart of the project.

Li Cheng's dream was finally close to becoming a reality. His project, transferred from drawings on paper to stark reality, had taken more than two years to come this far. Within the next few months it would be up and running, and once that happened Li Cheng would be able to present Beijing with a means to control the destiny of China. Only his genius had been able to devise the plan and put it into operation. It had taken long months of meticulous planning to bring together all the required elements—the vast amount of materials and people, the meetings and the discussions with the North Koreans, bringing them under the protection of the project once it became

operational. Their contribution would be the manufacture of the missiles required to arm the project.
Similarly, Li had spent many days and nights locked
in heated bartering with the Triads in Hong Kong.
The wily criminal groups, well aware that he needed
their clout both at home and in America, had struck
hard bargains. The colonel had finally hammered out
the fine details and, from those discussions, he had
become allied with the powerful and ruthless crime
syndicate. As far as Li was concerned, he was using
them. Let them have their dreams. In the future the
tables might very well turn against the Triads, but for
now he would use them and the influence they
wielded.

LI CHENG STEPPED OUT of the helicopter the moment
it landed, lowering his head against the dust stirred
up by the spinning rotors. He went directly to the
camouflaged entrance to the project. One of the
armed guards standing just inside snapped to attention
the moment he appeared. The colonel nodded and
strode onto the elevator that would descend eighty
feet to the main chamber below. Jun Wang stood beside him, sweat beading his face. He didn't like the
thought of being so far underground, nor did he like
the elevator ride. If he hadn't been such a good administrator, Li would have disposed of him long ago.

They stepped out onto the smooth concrete corridor, Li's boots clicking sharply as he walked quickly
the length of the corridor and turned to the door of
his office. It was starkly decorated, with a black desk
facing the far wall, which was composed of thick
glass and afforded him an unrestricted view of the
main operations room.

At the moment it was in a state of controlled confusion. Although the giant viewing screens were in place and the computer banks and control boards installed, nothing was actually working. Technicians in white coats were busy installing various pieces of equipment. Cables snaked across the floor and hung from overhead conduits. Leaning forward, Li touched a button on the pad sunk into the top of his desk and sound filled the office. He could hear the noise of the construction below, the chatter of voices as the technicians called out instructions to one another.

"Are they on schedule?" Li asked.

Jun nodded. "Half a day ahead, actually, Colonel."

"Good."

Li activated the buttons on his display one by one. From his office, TV cameras located inside and outside the project allowed him to check out almost every section of the installation. He could even move the cameras.

One of the telephones on his desk rang. He picked it up and heard the soft electronic hum as the call connected via the satellite link. Moments later he heard a familiar voice. It was one of his American-based agents.

Jun couldn't hear what was being said, but the change in Li's expression told him that he wasn't receiving good news. The one-sided conversation went on for some time until the colonel uttered a curt acknowledgment and replaced the receiver. It took Jun a little while before he summoned the courage to ask the question.

"What has happened, Colonel?"

Li retained his calm. He swung his chair around to face Jun, clearing his throat before he spoke.

"That was Po. There has been a serious setback. When Lim went to collect the circuit boards from Alexander Delmont, there was some kind of incident. Needless to say a firefight with some American agents took place. Delmont is dead. So is Lim and both his men. More worrying is the fact that it appears the completed circuit boards are now in the hands of the Americans."

"This is very bad, Colonel. Without those boards we will not be able to activate the systems."

"Po had other news. Earlier, one of our teams went to recover the data Djin Shu had left with his woman. They were met with resistance by a protection squad. The team did not survive."

Jun Wang began to pace around the office. The colonel didn't interfere. It was the man's way of dealing with stress, and it also gave him the chance to consider the options.

"Very well. If the Americans have recovered the information Djin left behind, they will be able to work out what we have taken from them. Now that they have the circuit boards manufactured by Delmont, they will realize that we are actually building the systems. From our perspective, that means the pressure to complete the project increases. We have lost valuable time due to the Americans getting their hands on the boards. It means we must start again."

"It took us time to get Delmont to agree to help. Mainly because of the gambling debts and the video evidence we had against him. Where are we going to find another Alexander Delmont?"

"There is no need, Colonel," Jun said, waiting for

the hammer to fall as soon as Li realized what he was about to propose.

"Makura?"

Li's expression hardened. "You know my feelings about the man."

"But you also know he is the perfect choice."

"Perfect is not a word I associate with Kobashi Makura. I understand your reasoning, and in that respect I know you are right. But Makura is like an unexploded bomb. He's irrational. An extremist in yevery sense of the word. His views are so radical no one will go near him. He is a total madman."

"Everything you say is right, Colonel. In his defense I have to say that there is no one who can come anywhere near him when it comes to creating computer hardware. The man is a genius. Flawed. Eccentric. But a true genius. He is the only man who can build what we want within a reasonable timescale."

Li pushed away from his desk and went to stand at the window, staring at the construction below. In his heart he wanted to say no to Jun, but his head told him that if he wanted to meet his deadline, then extreme measures were called for. No one could deny that employing Kobashi Makura was extreme.

"Can you locate him?"

"Yes, Colonel. I will need to meet him personally. He refuses any other kind of invitation."

"Whatever you have to do, Wang. Only remember this. Tell him no more than you need to. Until we have him secure, I do not want him given the opportunity of telling the world what he's going to be doing. Between the two of us, once he sets foot on this island he does not leave."

"I will make certain he stays until the work is complete and operational."

Li allowed himself a paternal smile. He patted the man on the shoulder.

"What I meant, Wang, is that he will *never* leave this island ever again. Alive or dead. When his work is finished so is he."

"I understand, Colonel. Makura will retain a great deal of sensitive information in his head once he has completed his work. Allowing him to roam free with all that knowledge would not be wise."

"Exactly. So we make certain it does not happen."

"I will make the arrangements immediately." Jun glanced at his watch. "If I leave shortly, I should be able to catch a flight to Japan later this afternoon and meet Makura tomorrow."

"Try to have him back here as soon as possible. Tell him that whatever he needs in the way of equipment will be made available. Also any staff."

Jun spent the next half hour on the telephone, making his travel arrangements and also getting a message through to Makura. It wasn't as difficult as Jun might have led the colonel to believe. He had made contact with the Japanese weeks earlier, as a backup. With urgent need for the circuit boards, and the knowledge that if their U.S. supplier let them down, they would require a reserve source, Jun had placed his operation on standby. Makura, for all his extremism, was dependable. It had been on Jun's mind to air his views on more than one occasion to the colonel, but he had stayed silent, knowing full well how angry the man could get if someone even suggested he might have made a mistake. People had died for less. Li and his mistress, Shun Wei, weren't the kind of people to defy. In that they were alike. Jun had no desire to find himself a victim of their wrath.

As the helicopter lifted off the island, taking him on the first leg of his journey to Japan, he settled back in his seat, enjoying the responsibility that had been placed on his slim shoulders. He was looking forward to seeing Hong Kong, albeit briefly. He glanced at his watch and saw that he would have at least three hours to wait before his flight from the new airport. A slow smile edged his mouth as he realized that would be ample time for him to visit his new friend. It had been almost a month since he had been in Hong Kong. He hoped that the young man hadn't forgotten him. It was one of the problems with the young. They were so very fickle.

In fact Jun's young friend hadn't forgotten him. He greeted the man as if he had never been away. Jun stayed for two hours, and after he left, the young man made a telephone call.

CHAPTER FIVE

Stony Man Farm, Virginia

"I don't know what they're for," Aaron Kurtzman admitted. "All I can say is the circuitry is pretty sophisticated, and way over my head."

He handed the board to Hal Brognola, who placed it back inside the package.

"This is going to Washington to be analyzed," he said. "From the sounds coming back from D.C., the information they found on the disks and in the bag Djin Shu left with Jenny Yeo is pretty hot. I haven't had confirmation yet, but it seems the Chinese got hold of sensitive stuff one way or another. If they start to duplicate it, they could end up with systems capable of matching ours."

"In other words they could hack into our defense systems and prevent us from defending ourselves?" Carmen Delahunt said.

"That's pretty basic, but a reasonable assessment," Kurtzman replied. "I've been doing a little quiet checking of my own, talking to people who understand these things. Most of my questions were theoretical, but I sensed they were close to the mark. It does look as if the Chinese have gained a lot of information that could, if applied correctly, put the U.S. defense network on a pretty thin edge.''

"If we've got hold of these circuit boards, doesn't that put an end to it?" Akira Tokaido asked.

"Not if they still have the original designs they stole," Kurtzman said. "I'm sure the Chinese will be canny enough to send out copies to anyone they want to help build their system. We might have stopped this consignment, but it won't have disabled the Chinese from trying again. It will set them back, but it won't stop them. They've put a lot of effort into this project. A temporary setback will be a nuisance. That's all. The Chinese are extremely patient and resourceful. Once they find what's happened over here, they will be out looking for another supplier. You can count on that."

Brognola grunted. "Aaron, that's just what I didn't want to hear."

"You can be sure the Chinese will be retreating from the U.S. now," Blancanales said. "If they realize their operations here have been compromised, they'll be pulling up stakes and getting out. And cleaning up as they go, which is why we need to find their base of operations and make sure they don't open again."

"Is that why they killed Delmont?" Barbara Price asked.

"We can't be sure exactly what went on in his office before they killed him. Some argument, maybe over money. We don't know." Lyons shrugged. "All we do know is they made sure he was dead. The shooter put a whole magazine into him, including one through the head."

"A message to everyone else they've been dealing with. Don't screw us over because we don't like it."

"Delmont was doing their dirty work," Tokaido pointed out. "He got paid in kind."

"Harsh words from one so young," Kurtzman chided. "But I suppose Akira is right. Delmont was selling out to a foreign power. He flirted with the dragon and ended up getting burned."

"All this bullshit is making me hungry," Lyons said. "I'm off to get something to eat."

"Not without me," Schwarz said. "You owe me from last time."

"Owe what?" Lyons asked. "Meals here on the Farm are free."

Schwarz pondered that for a moment. "Yeah, I know, but you got to admit I nearly had you."

Blancanales stayed behind. "Catch you guys later."

"I'd better arrange to get this stuff shipped out," Brognola said.

Kurtzman followed him in his wheelchair, determined to keep checking the background to the Chinese affair, well aware that it was far from over yet.

ROSARIO BLANCANALES had found a spare desk and was hunched over printouts. He had access to a keyboard and monitor for his own inquiries. Around him the cyberteam carried on with their own work. After a while Blancanales stood and crossed to Kurtzman.

"By the look on your face you need a question answered."

"Something's been nagging at me ever since we got hit by those Triad shooters," Blancanales said.

"The guys we took out at Jenny Yeo's hotel, the team at the safehouse and the ones at Delmont's place."

"You looking for a connection?"

"That's the easy part," Blancanales explained. "We know they were all from the same organization. What I'm looking for is their base. Most probably where they collected all the information and passed it on to Djin Shu."

"Go on."

"The SFPD had all the stuff out of the pockets of the guys at the hotel. I looked through it at the time. Nothing really stuck. Not until the safehouse. I found something in one guy's wallet that tallied with the SFPD evidence."

Blancanales placed a business card on the desk in front of Kurtzman, which bore a company name and address.

"The Water Boy Supply Company," Kurtzman read. He glanced at Blancanales. "What the hell is that?"

"I made a quick check earlier. Bottled water for offices. Factories. Hotels."

"So we have two DOAs linked by this company?"

"More than that," Blancanales said. "I had a look inside the car that brought the Chinese hit team to Delmont's place. Guess who it was registered to?"

Kurtzman began to hit the letters on his keyboard. It took him only a couple of minutes to bring up details on the company. He scrolled down the information.

"They have contracts all over," he said.

"See if any of them are for places where information has been stolen," Blancanales suggested.

Ten minutes later Kurtzman was able to hand Blancanales a printout of the information.

"Lucky strike, Pol," Kurtzman said.

Blancanales placed a final sheet of paper in front of the computer expert. It held details about Ray Dakin. A telephone number was circled. "That's Dakin's cell phone number," he explained. "Run a check on his calls and let's see if he used the Water Boy number."

By the time Lyons and Schwarz returned, Blancanales had his information laid out ready for them.

"I played a hunch based on the bottled-water company the Triad shooters had connections with. Aaron ran a check, and the company handles the bottled water contract for all the places where information was stolen from."

"I guess when you think about it, a guy delivering a bottle of water doesn't attract much attention," Schwarz said.

"That was the way I saw it," Blancanales agreed. "No need for the deliveryman to even talk to the contact. All he does is collect the empty bottle and replace it. It wouldn't be difficult to conceal a disk in the base of the cooler. The deliveryman does his collection, checks out the machine and pockets the disk. No fuss, no bother. Guy walks out with the empty bottle and drives to his next customer."

"And back at the bottling plant the information is picked up and added to the database."

"The clincher was Dakin's cell phone number. He called Water Boy a hell of a lot."

"Aaron, we need a fast flight back to Frisco," Lyons said. "Let's go, guys."

TWO HOURS LATER Brognola took a telephone call from the President.

"Hal, this is worse than we first thought. We don't know how they did it, but a lot of the information the Chinese took has to do with the Slingshot Project. You heard about that about six months back."

"I remember, Mr. President. A protective shield of missiles designed to react to incoming enemy missiles while they're still off the coast and take them out before they reach our shores. How many was it? Over a hundred missiles, strategically located in safe bunkers, all controlled via satellite tracking and a new computer network?"

"A big step up from anything we've had before. This could form the basis of our national defense shield for the next decade. A damned expensive and hard-to-beat system. Dammit, Hal, if the Chinese have gotten hold of our technology for this system, they'll blow us right out of the water from the word go. Their having the details of the way the system operates means they could press a damn button and shut us down. We're too far into the project to stop it now."

"Can't our people counter any interference? Change code systems, or whatever?"

The President sighed. "Hal, I wish it was so simple. The trouble is that the heart of the system is a new-generation computer that has the capability to do a lot of its own thinking. The thing is so complicated that to strip it down and rebuild it would cost so much it would wipe out the whole damn program. Like I already said, we're too far in to call a halt. The only thing we can do is try to locate this secret Chinese base, go in and wipe it off the face of the earth. Hal, we need your SOG teams to take out the whole thing. Zero option on this, Hal. No prisoners. Tell your men that anything they want they can have.''

''Able Team is already heading back to San Francisco. They have a location for the information-gathering center.''

''Shut it down. I'll take the flak later and face any damn questions. But not before we **have** our system back on home ground. I don't want **a** carbon copy that can mimic our control system and interfere with it. All I want now is for our system to be safe. And ours. Not anyone else's.''

''I hear you, Mr. President.''

THE AIR FORCE TRANSPORT was well into its flight to the West Coast when Lyons was summoned to the communications desk.

''Call for you, sir,'' the operator said, passing the handset to Lyons.

Slipping the headphones into position, the big ex-cop keyed the receive button.

''The word is go,'' Brognola said tersely. ''The Man is unhappy about this whole deal. You have permission for a hard strike on the target.''

''Understood,'' Lyons said. ''Over and out.''

He returned to where Blancanales and Schwarz were rigging themselves for action. They were clad in black combat fatigues, and each man wore a Kevlar bulletproof vest. Their side arms rested in high-ride holsters. Carl Lyons had chosen a Franchi SPAS-15 combat shotgun, Heckler & Koch submachine guns were the choice of both Blancanales and Schwarz. Each man had a supply of smoke and fragmentation grenades.

Blancanales unpacked and handed out compact communication gear—lightweight headsets equipped with powerful microphones. They were powered by packs that clipped to their belts. They donned the units and checked that they were working.

"Now we can sit back and enjoy the ride," Blancanales said, smiling at the set expression on Lyons's face.

THEY TOUCHED DOWN at San Francisco International, landing on a reserve runway on the far side of the airport. Washington had been in touch with the authorities at the airport, clearing the transport for a special touchdown. The moment Able Team had exited the aircraft, it taxied out and took off again. Few of the regular passengers at the airport even noticed the landing and takeoff.

An unmarked panel truck awaited Able Team. The windows of the truck were tinted so that no one could see inside. Schwarz took the wheel, and they left the airport by a service exit and took the main highway, heading toward San Francisco. The Water Boy facility was located in an industrial park in the Bay area. Lyons used his cell phone to call Jimmy Yip to let him know they were back in town. He gave Yip the location of the target and told him to have units standing by ready.

"Nobody moves until we give the word, Jimmy. I don't want any casualties on our side. Let us do the job, then you guys can move in and take over. Understood?"

"No problem."

Lyons picked up an edge to Yip's voice.

"What's wrong, Jimmy? And don't tell me 'nothing' because I hate being lied to."

"Ray Dakin is back on the street. Some hard-assed lawyer got him out on bail. Something about entrapment. Lack of real evidence. You know the score. The lawyer had all kinds of papers, so they had to let him walk."

"Next you'll be telling me he's back on the job."

"No way he'll get back on the force. If he walks in here, it'll take more than a freakin' lawyer to bail him out."

"Who paid the bail?"

"Don't know. I heard it was in cash. I bet it came from his Chinese friends."

After he had finished his call to Jimmy Yip, Lyons told Blancanales and Schwarz what he had learned. They were as astonished as he had been.

"Leave your car in a no-parking zone they give you a harder time," Blancanales fumed. "What geriatric judge let him walk? I'd like to explain a few things to him."

"Calm down," Schwarz said. "No good going into a bust with your head on fire."

"So who made you the team analyst?"

"I talked it over with myself, and we agreed I was the best choice."

"Hey!" Lyons snapped. "Cut the clowning."

"Yes, boss," the pair chorused in perfect unison.

Schwarz parked across the service road from The Water Boy Supply Company. As he switched off the engine, it began to rain, heavy drops spattering the windshield and drumming on the roof.

"I thought the sun always shone out here?" Blancanales grumbled, peering through the tinted glass.

"That's only on the righteous," Lyons told him.

"Oh. Is that why you left, boss?"

Schwarz coughed to cover a rising chuckle.

Lyons checked with Jimmy Yip via his cell phone.

"We're in position at the south end of the service road," the cop told him.

"Wait until we call you in."

"Yeah, I know," Yip said. His voice broke off, and in the background Lyons heard someone swear. Then the detective came back on the line. "You won't believe this."

"Give me a chance and tell me," Lyons snapped.

"Coming your way. Dark-blue Plymouth. It's Ray Dakin. Large as fuckin' life."

Lyons relayed the information to Blancanales and Schwarz. As they turned to check it out, the Plymouth cruised by, swinging into the yard of the bottling plant and coming to a lurching stop only feet away from the front door.

"What the hell is he doing?" Lyons asked.

"The man doesn't look too happy," Schwarz said. "In fact, he looks distinctly pissed about something."

"Great," Lyons grumbled. "Now he's waving a damn gun around."

Ray Dakin was walking toward the front entrance, a large pistol in his right hand. He wandered from side to side as he approached the entrance, his movements unsteady, and when he stopped he swayed slightly.

"Drunk as well," Blancanales observed.

Dakin started to yell a demand for someone to come out and face him.

"The guy is begging to be shot," Lyons said.

The main entrance door was flung open and an

arm-waving Chinese stepped outside. Dakin matched the man's shouts with yelling of his own. The Chinese seemed to dismiss him, making sharp cutting motions with his hands, and it was at that point that Dakin shot him. No threat, or warning. He simply raised the pistol and shot the man, who collapsed to the ground.

Stepping over the downed man, Dakin ran inside the building.

"Let's go!" Lyons said, and Schwarz gunned the panel truck across the service road and into the plant yard. He brought it to a squealing halt inches from Dakin's car.

"Pol, around the back. If you can't find a way in, make one," Lyons ordered as he followed Blancanales and Schwarz out of the truck. He tapped his headset. "And stay on-line."

As Blancanales sprinted around the end of the building, Lyons nodded to Schwarz. "Let's do it." With his teammate flanking him, Lyons pushed the door open and they stepped inside.

The reception area was deserted except for a person on the carpet, clutching at a bloody hole in his leg. A pistol lay on the carpet near the man's hand. Lyons snatched up the weapon and took out the clip.

"Party's this way," Schwarz said, picking up the sound of raised voices and crashing objects.

Double doors took them into the bottling plant's production area. The cavernous building was a maze of machines and conveyer belts. Overhead walkways filtered light through from the high ceiling. The operation appeared to be shut down.

A gun fired and the bullet clanged against steelwork over Lyons's head.

"Your left!" Schwarz yelled.

Lyons turned, dropping to a crouch, the SPAS shotgun coming on-line. He saw a heavyset Chinese with tattoos on his forehead leaning out from behind some racks. The man was aiming his weapon again. Lyons didn't cut him any slack. The SPAS snapped into position and the Able Team leader touched the trigger. The powerful weapon, with its autoload and awesome power, made the rafters rattle as it fired. The single charge caught the attacker in the upper chest and throat. The gunner never knew what hit him. He tumbled backward, his chest and face a shredded, bloody mess.

With his H&K tracking ahead, Schwarz moved into the plant. He picked up the sound of running feet and heard the ringing sound of someone on the walkway above him. He glanced up and spotted a dark-clad figure turning in his direction, handgun angling down. Schwarz fired off a short burst that drove the man back. The delay allowed the Able Team warrior to move forward, still checking the way ahead as well as keeping an eye on the walkway. The shooter came into sight again through the perforations in the metal walkway. He gripped his gun in both hands as he tried to lock on to his target's moving shape. They fired at the same time. Schwarz felt the slug hit the concrete at his feet, peppering him with fragments. He aimed the H&K toward the walkway and loosed a longer burst, catching the shooter in the upper thighs and torso. The stricken hardman crashed to the walkway.

As Schwarz reached the first intersection, he saw someone on the floor, blood pulsing from chest wounds.

It was Ray Dakin.

The cop had been hit a number of times. He was bleeding heavily from the mouth, the result of internal damage.

Schwarz spoke into his mike. "I located Dakin. He's badly hit."

"Do what you can for him," Lyons said, "but don't compromise yourself."

A burst of autofire was followed by the boom of Lyons's shotgun. Shouts rang out. Running feet slapped the concrete, and Schwarz was forced to abandon Dakin as he turned to face another opponent.

TWO CARS WERE parked at the rear of the plant, their engines running. There were files and boxes of computer disks scattered across the rear seats, as if someone were loading up quickly so he could move out without delay. As Blancanales moved by the cars, he saw an open door. He could also hear the shooting that was coming from inside the plant, and knew his Able Team partners had engaged the enemy.

As he stood by the open door, Blancanales heard running feet approaching. He eased up against the outer wall and had barely positioned himself when a running man burst through the door and headed for one of the cars. He had a couple of laptops tucked under one arm, gripping them with his hand. His right fist was closed around the butt of an autopistol. Reaching the car, the man tossed the computers on the rear seat.

"I don't think so," Blancanales said.

The man turned, bringing around his pistol in a vain attempt to ward off any interference. The weapon fired, the heavy slug whacking into the wall next to Blancanales. He returned fire, triggering a short burst that blew the guy off his feet, slamming him against the waiting car.

Before he moved inside the plant, Blancanales disabled both cars. He stepped through the open door, keying his mike to inform his teammates he was still around.

"About damn time," Lyons grumbled.

Blancanales grinned, moving forward through dimly lighted storage rooms. He was clearing the area when he heard a soft sound behind him. Turning, he saw the rapidly spreading burst of flame as an incendiary device ignited.

"Heads up, guys, somebody is torching the place," he reported.

Up ahead he saw a slowly moving figure, SMG raised as he stalked someone Blancanales couldn't see. He knew the prey had to be one of his teammates. Blancanales didn't hesitate. He put the guy down with a short burst, then moved in to kick the weapon away from the outstretched hand.

The plant erupted with more gunfire.

Lyons appeared ahead of Blancanales. He barely acknowledged his teammate as he concentrated on the Chinese coming at him from a dark corner. The guy was screaming, fumbling with a handgun that appeared to have jammed on him, still running at Lyons. The Able Team leader raised the SPAS shotgun and fired as the attacker abandoned the handgun and hauled out a keen-bladed knife, slashing the air in wild movements. The guy went down, still screaming, but that died as his ravaged body stopped functioning.

The shooting stopped as quickly as it had started.

Blancanales leaned against a conveyor, letting the tension ease. He found he was breathing quickly and took control, slowing his racing body and mind.

"Guys, we'd better get the hell out of here before the fire spreads," he advised his partners. "Out the front door."

SCHWARZ RETURNED to where Dakin lay. Shouldering his weapon, Schwarz crouched beside the man, checking him out. Dakin had slipped into semiconsciousness. He was still bleeding, the blood pooled around him on the floor. The Able Team commando moved the cop's handgun out of reach.

"Carl, you can call in the troops now," Schwarz said. "We need a medic for Dakin."

"He still alive?" Lyons asked sharply. "Son of a bitch is persistent."

AFTER HE HAD CALLED IN Jimmy Yip and his backup, Lyons made his way to the exit. The first SFPD cruisers were in the parking lot. Looking back, Lyons saw smoke curling into the rainy sky at the rear of the plant.

"You burning the place down, too?" Yip asked.

"Not us," Lyons said. "Looks like our friends set incendiary devices. They were getting ready to move out."

Yip called to one of the uniformed cops to bring in the fire department.

The medics Yip had brought along asked where Dakin was. Lyons directed them inside, and within a few minutes they were bringing him out on a gurney, Schwarz walking alongside. He left the gurney to join Lyons.

"Will he make it?" Yip asked.

Schwarz shook his head. "I don't think so. The medics don't give him much of a chance."

Blancanales watched as Dakin was lifted into the ambulance. "He say why?"

Schwarz stared at his partner. "He was mad because they dragged him into this mess. He had bad money troubles, and the Chinese made him an offer. Sounded good at the time, then he got caught out. Lost his job. Had the threat of prison hanging over him. The final straw was when the Chinese sent their lawyer to bail him out. I figure they didn't want him saying too much while he was in custody. Only condition was that from there on in he was on his own. They weren't going to do another thing for him."

"So he decided to get even first?"

"I guess so."

Jimmy Yip shook his head in disbelief. "His whole life screwed up in one go."

"His choice," Lyons said. "You know what I think? The Chinese wanted him out of jail so they could get to him. If he hadn't turned up here, he would have been dead in a couple of days."

"I'll take the truck around back," Blancanales said, "and grab that stuff out of those cars."

CHAPTER SIX

Hong Kong

David McCarter strolled into the lobby of the Hong Kong Hotel Nikko and made his way to the bar. He took a table by the window, where he could look out on the street while he waited for his contact to arrive. There was a copy of the *Hong Kong Times* on the table in front of him. McCarter picked it up and worked his way through the pages, glancing up when a white-jacketed waiter approached.

"May I bring you a drink, sir?"

"Coke Classic in a chilled glass, please," McCarter said, leaning back in the comfortable seat. Turning his head, he was able to stare out across the parking lot. He could see the car, where T. J. Hawkins and Gary Manning were waiting. Bright sunlight gleamed off the vehicle's roof, and McCarter realized it would soon start to get warm inside.

The waiter brought his soft drink and placed it on the table. McCarter could see the beads of condensation running down the outside of the long, curved glass. He picked it up and held it in front of his face for a moment before taking a long swallow. The chilled liquid slid easily down his throat.

"That was bloody good," he said softly, aware that his words could be heard by his partners through the microphone he was wearing under the collar of his light jacket. "Coldest Coke I've had in weeks."

A slow smile edged McCarter's lips as he imagined what his partners might be saying in response. Glancing at his watch, the leader of Phoenix Force saw that it was time for his contact to show. The Briton remained where he was, having a quiet drink. If his contact turned up, he would show himself.

McCarter had just ordered a second drink when he became aware of someone standing at his elbow. Glancing up, he recognized the face of his contact. He knew it from the ID photo the British MI5 had sent through to Stony Man at Brognola's request.

The man was tall, lean and well tanned. He wore a pale linen suit and his dark hair was short.

"Good afternoon," the man said. "Mr. Clancy?"

McCarter nodded and rose to take the man's hand. "Call me Jim. You're Neil Hallam?"

"Yes."

They sat, facing each other across the table.

"Drink?" McCarter asked.

Hallam beckoned a waiter. "Whiskey. Double. Straight."

They waited until the waiter was out of earshot.

"When did you arrive?" Hallam asked.

"Yesterday evening," McCarter answered brusquely.

Hallam grinned.

"What?" McCarter snapped.

"I'm the same. Not much for small talk."

"Bloody hell, is it that obvious?"

Hallam reached inside his jacket and pulled out a

manila envelope. He placed it on the table and slid it across to McCarter.

"We're pretty sure the Chinese are up to something. Since your people spoke to London and laid out a few things, the situation has started to get a little clearer. With what you have, tied in with our bits and pieces, we've started to make sense of what's been happening out here."

"To do with the information thefts?"

"Right. You see, we know the Chinese have this feeling of being second-rate where advanced technology is concerned. For years they've been trying to match everything the West does on the military scene. Problem is, you need more than enthusiasm. Internal problems take up so much of the time and money in China, they have to shave budgets all the time. And when it comes to keeping up on technology, that means very big money."

"So they decided to steal what they haven't got?"

Hallam nodded. "Short and sweet but on the mark. They did it in Britain and walked away with a lot of valuable information."

"Now the same trick has been pulled on Uncle Sam," McCarter said. "He is, to put it mildly, pretty well pissed off."

"I'm not surprised," Hallam replied. "I saw a dossier listing the areas where the Chinese have been very busy. Christ, they've really pulled off some heavy stuff this time."

"Which is why the Yanks have given us the job of sorting it out."

"I take it you and your team are not from the diplomatic service?"

McCarter shook his head. "Not exactly."

"I won't pry," Hallam promised. "Part of my job is to give you any assistance I can. When you decide what you want, just let me know." He tapped the envelope. "There's a card in there with my cell phone number. Day or night."

"Thanks." McCarter slid a slip of paper across the table. "You'll find two cell phone numbers on there. One is for my phone. The other belongs to the phone one of my partners carries. His name is Johnson."

Hallam took the paper. Leaning forward he tapped the envelope.

"You'll find details on people we believe are involved. You'll probably recognize Djin Shu, the Chinese they found in San Francisco. He was known to us. He was one of the special operatives. He was in Britain when we lost our goodies, but he was gone before our people realized what was happening."

"He didn't walk away from this one," McCarter said.

"Any thoughts on why he was killed?"

McCarter shrugged. "Only theories. The way it's been pieced together it's possible he was trying a double cross. Doing a little selling on his own time. It appears he'd got himself involved with a young woman. They were supposed to be going away together."

"Maybe Mr. Djin lost the faith. Found something better than the Communist manifesto."

"If he hadn't been killed, we wouldn't have found the disk. It was the material on the disk that burst the bubble."

"How was he killed?"

"The way the local cops see it, somebody snipered

him from a distance. Bloody good shot. Clean. Right through the back of the skull.''

"Weapon?"

"Galil sniper rifle.''

"Caliber?"

"It was 7.62 mm.''

Hallam's drink had arrived by this time. He took a sip.

"Why the interest?" McCarter asked.

"That type of weapon and ammo has been used on a number of killings over here. One was on a Chinese official caught with his finger in the till. Two construction workers were also murdered a couple of months ago. Same weapon. Same head shots.''

"And?"

"We picked up a rumor from one of our informants it was the work of a Triad assassin.''

"We did get a sniff of that in our briefing. You go with the theory that the Triads might be doing business with the mainland Chinese?''

"Why not? The Triads have the underworld sewed up in Hong Kong. The Chinese are no fools when it comes to making deals. The Triads can do a lot for them. Help raise cash. Provide muscle. Professionals for all kinds of work. And they have contacts abroad.''

"The U.S.?"

"Triads know how to get people in and out of the country. Provide cover for them, bases, anything they needed. They would also provide a disposal service for anyone jumping ship. No questions asked.''

McCarter sighed. "A lot of this is bloody guesswork, Neil.''

"Maybe. I'll bet my pension it isn't far off the mark."

"We did find out the Chinese have been buying computer hardware. Electronic stuff as well. High-tech computer processors. Nothing that would make a ripple when the sale went through. Our people are trying to come up with a full list of anything they've been involved in."

"What's the end product of all this?" Hallam asked.

McCarter shrugged. "One of the reasons we're here. To find out and stop it."

"Coming back to the Triads. There's info on the locals, the ones who have been seen with Chinese from the mainland."

McCarter opened the envelope and went through the contents. His interest was raised when he came across a photograph that caught his eye.

"I thought that one would interest you."

Hallam leaned forward, his finger moving from image to image as he identified the people in the photograph.

"That is Colonel Li Cheng, bad man to have as an enemy. He heads a special unit in the army. Seems to do just what he wants. It's an unusual position to be in considering Chinese ideology."

"He's no looker," McCarter observed.

"The man must have something. The woman on his arm is Shun Wei, his official mistress."

"Bloody hell! She makes him look like a midget."

"They were here in Hong Kong when we took the photograph."

"You have Li down as part of the deal?"

"He's always spoken out about China's weakness

in military technology. If he had the power, he would change all that.''

McCarter studied the photograph. It had been taken outside an expensive Hong Kong restaurant. He tapped the image of a man standing next to Li Cheng.

''He looks like a movie star, but I'm getting the feeling you're about to tell me different.''

''Xan Hung. Boss of a local Triad mob. And doesn't he look on friendly terms with Colonel Li?''

''Maybe he fancies the man's lady.''

''Not if he wants to stay attached to his head, he doesn't. The interesting thing about Xan is his connection with Triads in America. He also runs a construction company in Hong Kong.''

''Tell me now that the two murdered construction workers were on his payroll?''

Hallam nodded. ''They were.''

''Maybe they pinched a few bags of cement.''

Hallam didn't reply. He just sat back and downed his whiskey.

''Before we go our separate ways,'' Hallam said, ''I'm mentioning this just as a warning. I don't have proof yet, and I'm the only one who has this thought. But I think we have a leak within the department. Something tells me that information has been passed on from our office. Possibly to the Chinese. As a precaution, Jim, watch your back. Tell your team. Be careful who you trust.''

''Thanks for the warning,'' McCarter said. He scooped up the paperwork and slid it back into the envelope. Standing, he shook Hallam's hand.

''I'll be in touch if anything breaks,'' Hallam said.

''Okay. Neil, if you are right about a leak, take some of your own advice and be careful.''

McCarter made his way outside, crossing the parking lot to the waiting car. He slipped in beside Manning, who was behind the wheel.

"You get all that?" he asked, and Manning nodded.

"Came through great," Hawkins said. "I taped it all in case you need to listen to it again."

"We'll damn well need to if we want to make sense of it all," Manning said as he started the engine and rolled out of the lot onto the busy street. "Where to?"

"Bloody good question," McCarter said. He considered the matter for a moment then said, "Let's go check out this Xan Hung character."

THE XAN HUNG Construction Company was based near the docks. The company property actually extended as far as the water, where it owned the wharf and raw material stockyards. As they had made the journey, McCarter went over the notes included with Hallam's photographs.

On the surface Xan Hung operated a legitimate business. The construction setup included a freight trucking division and a number of seagoing vessels. They were used, according to the company, for bringing in construction materials as well as delivering them to sites off Hong Kong. Xan did regular business with the Chinese mainland.

He was involved in the construction of a vast leisure complex on the coast. With an eye for the expanding flood of tourists wanting to visit China, the government was gambling on this complex to lure them in.

"This Xan does things in a big way," Hawkins said.

Manning had brought the car to a halt at the side of the road. The road itself ran on down a shallow slope about fifty feet from the chain-link fence and gate closing off access to the site. Beyond the gate the area teemed with workers. A cargo ship was being loaded at the dock, cranes swinging pallets of goods over open holds.

A great deal of activity was going on around the ship being loaded. The longer he watched, the more McCarter was convinced something wasn't quite right. The business of loading cargo onto a ship such as the one at the dock should have been a routine affair. It didn't warrant so many people, especially when most of them appeared to be standing around watching. No, he corrected, not watching. They were guarding the ship. He became convinced when he saw one of the men pause to adjust his jacket over something. Something that made the jacket bulge.

"The buggers are armed," he said.

"Who?" Hawkins asked.

"Those blighters standing guard around that bloody ship. Take a close look, then tell me I'm wrong."

Manning and Hawkins scanned the area, moving their attention from man to man, assessing what they saw. Finally they eased back.

"Well?" McCarter demanded impatiently.

"Hate to say it, but I think you could be right," Manning admitted.

"T.J.?"

Hawkins deliberated. "Sure are a lot of people supervising," he said. "Too many for my liking. And they all have those bulging jackets. I'd say yes."

"So why does one ship need that level of security?" McCarter asked.

"Hey, I think we've been spotted," Manning said, nudging McCarter.

As the Briton raised his eyes, he saw the gate open and a dusty Jeep roll toward them. It swept up the slope and came to a hard stop feet from the front of the car. A wide-shouldered Chinese, dressed in a tan shirt, pants and jacket, climbed out and made his way to McCarter's side of the rental vehicle.

"I say, we appear to have gotten lost," McCarter said in an exaggerated English accent. He peered at the Chinese over the top of his sunglasses, smiling like an idiot.

The Chinese peered impatiently at him. His wide face was slightly pockmarked, and McCarter could feel his hot breath on his cheek.

"Private property. You not allowed here."

"And we wouldn't be, old boy, if we hadn't gotten lost. You see? You know how it is out here. All the bloody roads look the same to me."

Even Manning cringed at that one. He felt certain the security man was going to drag McCarter out of the car.

"You leave now."

McCarter was well into his charade at this point. He gave a snorting chuckle.

"I say, we haven't come to steal one of your boats. Just a mistake, chummy. We only stopped to get our bearings and turn around. We'll leave now and see if we can find our way back to the hotel."

The security man suddenly lost control and started

to yell at McCarter in indecipherable Chinese. His rage was so strong he placed his hands against the edge of the car's roof and began to rock it violently.

A number of Chinese appeared and rushed to the car, their arms waving wildly, all yelling. Luckily they were directing their anger at the guard, and three of them grabbed his arms and hauled him away from the vehicle. The Chinese was still yelling, spitting his rage. As they dragged him back to the Jeep, the man's jacket pulled open and McCarter spotted a heavy autopistol in a shoulder rig on the left side. Still shouting, the man was bundled into the Jeep while one of his companions took the wheel and spun the vehicle around, roaring back toward the gate.

A remaining Chinese, slender and wearing a wide smile, leaned in at McCarter's window. "Please forgive the outburst. We have been having some security problems lately. Everyone is a little agitated."

"Sorry we disturbed you, old chap," McCarter said. "I, er, hope your friend will be all right."

Manning eased the rental car into a tight circle and drove back to the top of the road.

"All the roads look the same?" Manning repeated. "That was bad even for you, David."

"You think so? I thought it was clever. If you want to hear something really funny, listen to this. They're taking a picture of the car. And our nice, apologetic Chinese is rabbiting on like a runaway tape recorder into his phone."

McCarter had seen all that through the rearview mirror.

"Don't tell me there's a big black Mercedes tailing us, too," Manning said.

"No, but I have a feeling they'll be doing some checking on us."

"I get the feeling those guys back there are pretty nervous about something," Hawkins said. "Some reaction to a car turning in their driveway."

"Could be they have something to hide," McCarter suggested. "I think we could all benefit from a nice stroll down by the waterfront. Let's get back to our hotel and brief the others. And I have a phone call to make to my new chum Neil Hallam."

AN URGENT CALL to Hallam, with some persuasion from McCarter, had produced a set of handguns for Phoenix Force. To McCarter's delight, the pistols had turned out to be 9 mm Browning Hi-Powers. The Briton had taken possession of the package on Hallam's arrival at their hotel. Following the man's departure, McCarter had called the others and invited them to his room where he passed out the weapons like a teacher bestowing favors on his favorite pupils.

"You don't have to gloat about it," Manning said as he examined the Browning.

"Don't I?" McCarter asked. "How long have I been trying to get you ladies to try these? This time, no argument."

Hawkins hefted the pistol. "Carries well," he said. "Heard tell it's a nice piece of hardware."

"God, can't you tell he's the new boy?" Manning said.

"Sucking up to the boss you mean?" James added. "Man, it makes you want to throw up."

Hawkins grinned. Since joining the team he had become used to his teammates' banter, and when the occasion called for it, he gave as good as he got.

McCarter unrolled the map that Hallam had brought along at his request. He spread it out across his bed so everyone could see.

"This is a surveyor's map of the dock area. The section marked in red is the Xan Hung dock site. From what Hallam was able to find out, that ship we saw being loaded leaves at three o'clock tomorrow morning, seven hours from now."

"Any idea where it's heading?" Encizo asked.

McCarter shook his head. "Nothing on that. Hallam said he would try to find out but won't give any guarantees."

"Once the ship leaves Hong Kong, it's out of our hands," Manning said.

"Maybe not," McCarter said. "I spoke to Barbara earlier and explained the situation. She's going to see what she can do about having a shadow assigned to our ship. The U.S. Navy has a submarine off Taiwan. If she can get Hal to swing it via the President, we might get lucky."

"Haven't seen any flying pigs since we got here," Calvin James murmured.

Encizo had been studying the map and the Xan Hung Construction section. He tapped a spot on the diagram.

"I'd say that would be our best way in."

He indicated an area beyond the eastern perimeter.

"It's marked as a construction site. Box there says it's some new warehouse development, and it butts right up to the Xan Hung fence line. Look." Encizo showed them the section. "From the road here right out to the water's edge. If that site is under construction, there'll be plenty of cover to get up to the Xan perimeter fence."

"What about security on the building site?" Hawkins asked. "There's bound to be somebody around."

"We deal with them if they get in our way," McCarter said. "Tie them up in their hut."

"If what we saw today is anything to go by, Xan will have his own security patrolling the dock site," James commented.

"Same goes for them," McCarter said.

"You realize how much rope that's going to take?" Manning said in such a somber tone that everyone laughed. "This is what happens when we have to start out with no hardware backup. Security would be no problem if we had tranquilizer dart guns."

"Then improvise," McCarter told him, pausing before adding, "and bring plenty of bloody rope."

Thirty minutes later Phoenix Force left the hotel and picked up its rental car. Although they wore civilian clothing, each man wore a blacksuit underneath. They were the only items they had been able to bring in their luggage on the flight from the U.S. Woolen caps were stuffed into their jacket pockets. The Browning Hi-Power pistols were in shoulder rigs under their jackets. James drove, guided by McCarter, and they took the quietest route they could in order to avoid traffic and possible delays. McCarter's knowledge of the area helped, though even he had to admit to failure a couple of times when they found access denied to a route due to recent construction.

They reached the dock area and drove slowly around the perimeter until they saw the construction site shown on Hanson's chart. James eased the car into the shadow of a bank of steel waste containers parked across from the construction site. Exiting the car, the men of Phoenix Force shed their outer clothing, donned their black caps and crossed the deserted road to gather near the wood fence that marked the roadside section of the site.

They checked out the wooden barrier, which wasn't high. With assistance from the others Hawkins scaled the fence, paused on the top then dropped out of sight. After a minute he tapped on the board to indicate the others should come over. They followed Hawkins's example. Last over was McCarter, given a pull from Manning and James as they leaned down to grab his hands.

The five crouched in the shadows, taking stock of their surrounding. The new warehouse construction was well into its second phase. The steel skeletons of the massive buildings were completed and now the outer shells of the buildings were being put into place. The site itself was an untidy sprawl of machines and raw materials. The good thing was that the clutter of construction provided ample hiding places for Phoenix Force as it moved across the site and up to the perimeter fence of the Xan Hung Construction company. On the far side of the chain-link fence the team was able to see the activity taking place dockside. The ship they had seen earlier was still tied-down. Now, though, smoke drifted from its stack as the vessel was readied for its voyage. The activity they had witnessed earlier that day had slackened off. Only a few men were loading small crates into an open hatch in the side of the ship, which led directly into one of the holds.

"Haven't we missed something?" James asked, glancing behind them over the construction site. "No security guards."

McCarter turned to lean his back against a fence post.

"You're right, Cal. Go take a look. T.J., you take the other side of the site."

James and Hawkins slipped away into the shadows. McCarter and the others scouted the immediate area. They all met up again ten minutes later, and all of them had the same thing to say—no security guards. There was a small hut, obviously provided for the security crew, but it was empty. James had checked it out. The hut had contained personal items, as well as clothing, and a radio tuned to a local station.

"What the hell is going on?" Manning asked. "Are we being set up or what?"

McCarter was asking himself the same thing. Something wasn't right. The situation was full of potential danger above and beyond the norm. He had to decide whether they went ahead with the incursion into Xan Hung's site. If they did, they might walk into a barrage of hostile gunfire. He glanced at his waiting teammates, aware that their lives were in his hands. It wasn't the first time, but normally the risks would have been viewed in advance, at least offering them a degree of security. This scenario was warning him that security had vanished. Beyond the perimeter fence lay totally unknown territory. There was too much working against them.

McCarter made his decision.

"We scrub the mission," he said. "No way we go in there until we know exactly what's going on."

They eased back from the perimeter fence, intending to leave the construction site the same way they had entered.

The sudden crackle of autofire brought them to a

dead stop, each man turning to look back. A firefight had erupted on the far side of the fence, from the Xan Hung dockyard.

Figures were running in the direction of the activity. A Jeep, flashing a mounted spotlight, screeched around the end of a building. Window light beamed from a top floor, and was followed by a sharp explosion that blew out glass from a number of windows.

"Now what?" Encizo asked, voicing the opinions of the whole team.

"This is crazy," Hawkins said. "Boss, what are we going to do?"

"Nothing until we know who's creating all that noise," McCarter replied. "Look, it might be a local police raid. Maybe a rival Triad gang. We can't just walk in and get ourselves caught in a local feud. We'll sit it out and observe until we can figure this out."

Another crackling explosion was followed by more gunfire. A ball of flame rolled skyward from the far side of the dockyard, and men began to run in that direction.

"Hey, look," Manning said, tapping McCarter's arm.

They all turned to see a number of black-clad figures racing toward the perimeter fence. The newcomers' path was bringing them almost directly to where Phoenix Force was waiting.

"I guess we'll know who they are any minute," Hawkins commented.

"Back off, guys," McCarter ordered. "If they see us, we could end up targets."

The running hardmen turned aside and headed for the fence some twenty feet from where Phoenix Force crouched. Reaching the barrier, one of the men pulled back a cut section of the chain-link, allowing the group to start slipping through.

"Why didn't we think of that?" Manning asked.

Autofire crackled in the distance, and slugs whined through the air around the escaping group. One of the black-clad hardmen stumbled, then went down on his knees. The shooter kept coming, still firing, driving more slugs into the wounded man.

"Bastard!" James snapped. He raised his Browning, two-fisted, and triggered a trio of shots at the shooter, the 9 mm slugs hammering the man in the chest. "See how *you* like it."

"Let's go," McCarter yelled, urging his teammates to help the escapees.

The men of Phoenix Force spaced themselves out and used their combined firepower to keep the pursuers at bay, their Brownings delivering a deadly hail of gunfire as they closed in on the gap in the fence to cover the escapees. The pursuing force retreated, taking a number of their wounded with them.

The group was almost through. One of them paused, turning to check the man who had been shot. He was on his knees, struggling, then lost the battle and pitched facedown on the ground. McCarter knew that the one who had paused was about to go back. His guess was right as the slim figure turned to help the downed man.

"Bloody idiot," McCarter said, and without hesitation he went to help, ducking through the gap.

He reached the downed man seconds after the slim figure had bent to pull him upright. McCarter took one look at the prone figure, reached to check for a pulse and found nothing.

"He's dead. Let's move, dammit. There's nothing you can do except get yourself shot," he yelled. "Get your arse into motion, mate!"

"You do not have to shout," a cool, firm voice advised him. "And I am not your mate."

McCarter turned to glance at the speaker and found himself staring into the face of a beautiful, young Chinese woman with a look in her eyes that could have frozen boiling water. Without another word she followed McCarter back through the fence and across the construction site. Phoenix Force had piled back into the rental car. The Chinese woman stuck her head in through the window, speaking to McCarter.

"Our van is just up the road. Follow us and don't try to get lost—*mate*."

Without another word she ran off along the darkened road. McCarter set the rental car in motion and followed her.

"Man, she has taken to you," Calvin James said, grinning.

"Cut that out," McCarter warned.

"Who the hell are these people?" Hawkins asked.

"Not fans of Xan Hung," Encizo said.

"They seem to know what they're doing," Manning observed. "That break-in was organized. They have access to explosives."

McCarter eased in behind a battered, dark panel truck that emerged from a side street. The truck accelerated swiftly and sped through the dimly lighted outskirts of the docks. It took corners recklessly, tires burning as it swayed back and forth.

"Hey, who have they got behind the wheel?" James asked. "Jackie Chan?"

"Bet he hasn't got a bloody license," McCarter said.

The high-speed drive lasted almost twenty minutes. They found themselves in a back-street area that seemed to comprise manufacturing plants. The streets got narrower and darker, the surface of the road bumpier. The panel truck came to a sudden halt. Someone jumped out and ran to high wooden gates, which were opened, and the truck drove through. McCarter followed, taking the rental car across a stone-flagged yard. The gates were closed behind them, and the occupants of the panel truck climbed out and approached the car.

The woman gave orders to her companions and they crossed the yard and entered the main house, leaving her alone except for one man, who stood just behind her. She brushed back her dark hair, facing McCarter squarely.

"Thank you for your help." With that said she turned to go into the house, then paused to look back over her shoulder. "Well? Are you going to sit there all night, or are you coming inside?"

"I've had nicer invitations," McCarter said, "but I think we'll join you."

"Don't think too hard," the woman stated and turned to go inside.

"She really likes you now," James said as they all got out of the car.

Phoenix Force followed the woman and her shadow inside. The interior was sparsely furnished, basic. Some kind of living room–kitchen. The air held a subtle mix of spice and wood smoke. The room had a low ceiling and the floor had smooth flagstones.

The woman, her shadow and two more of the

black-clad Chinese were waiting for them. She stepped forward and placed a handgun on the table. The others did the same. It seemed to be some kind of gesture. McCarter considered for a moment, then did the same with his Browning. Following his lead, the others did the same.

"Do we cut our thumbs and become blood brothers now?" McCarter asked.

"Are you always this funny?" the woman asked.

McCarter shook his head. "Most times I'm better. It's been an odd night so I'm not at my best. I like to know what's going on."

"At least we have that in common. So. What were you doing at Xan Hung's site?"

"We could have been looking for work."

"Dressed like that and with guns?"

"Some of those dockworkers are rough chaps."

Despite herself the woman smiled.

"Reluctant to give me a straight answer. I'll take a guess that you people are some kind of covert team sent to check out Xan Hung. Maybe even the ship setting out tonight."

"Ship? Oh, you mean the one moored at the dock."

"*Blue Water*. Yes."

The Chinese who shadowed the woman leaned close to her and said something. As the light caught his face, it showed the bad scarring that puckered his skin.

"Tsu Han wants to know who you represent. So do I."

"Let's say someone who has an interest in Xan's activities and his involvement with a certain Colonel

Li Cheng,'' McCarter replied, throwing in the name for a reaction.

He got one.

The woman's eyes flashed in recognition of the name. The other Chinese threw interested glances at one another.

"Now we seem to have a mutual interest in someone," McCarter said.

The woman leaned forward, placing her hands on the table. She studied McCarter's face for some time before she spoke.

"My name is Mei Anna. Welcome to Hong Kong.''

CHAPTER SEVEN

Hong Kong

They sat facing each other across the table. One of the Chinese had made coffee. It was scalding hot, strong and black.

Mei Anna was obviously the leader of the group. McCarter judged her to be around twenty-six or twenty-seven years old. With her jet-black hair and flawless skin, she had the looks of a model. The last place she looked like she would have been expected was on a night raid, wielding a gun with the natural ease of a professional.

McCarter had introduced himself to Mei as Jim Clancy, and the other Phoenix Force warriors under their cover names.

"We are known as the Pro-Democracy group," Mei began. "We have a very simple agenda, although we're considered extreme by some of the other groups. Most of them confine their activities to verbal protests. Gatherings. Nothing that will really do anything to cause concern. We decided to take an active role. To do everything we can to harass or interfere with the regime in Beijing. We'll do anything we can to stop the illegal operations of the government.

We're a small group, and I don't think any of us are naive enough to believe we're going to topple the government by ourselves. But we have to do something.''

"I'd say going up against this Colonel Li is something," McCarter said. "This isn't burning a flag or breaking windows. Li is no local administrator. He's a hard-nosed, real-life army colonel."

"We all know about Colonel Li," Mei replied. "Believe me. His reputation is well known."

"And Xan Hung?"

"Him, too. A local gangster with a very bad attitude. He runs a mob of violent bullies, and everyone who hears his name refuses to talk about him."

"And this is your *little* struggle?" James asked. "Lady, I don't want to be around when you figure you're ready for the big time."

Mei frowned and then nodded. "I think I understand you."

"It must be difficult for you," Hawkins said.

"We have friends who give us what help they can, but they have to be careful. Since the handover, things have become harder. If they were found to be aiding us, they would be arrested and imprisoned for twenty or thirty years with no guarantee of release at the end. They could be executed, simply vanish without trace. This is how things are in my country. The punishments are many. The risks are great."

"But people still help," McCarter said.

"Yes, because the desire for freedom is so strong. In the West it is taken for granted. Something you have always had."

"We've had our bad times, Anna."

"When I was in London I used to walk the streets

and think how lucky the people were. They could come and go where they wanted. When they wanted. Day or night. It was such a free place. When I returned to the mainland I saw the difference." She stared at McCarter, her eyes blazing with the injustice she felt so strongly. "Is it so much my people want, Jim? Why does the government deny us our freedom?"

"They're scared. The ideology is so ingrained they believe China will fall apart if they relax their grip. It's why they refuse to allow any opposition. New ideas can generate new thoughts, and that leads people to question the old regime. But if that regime was as stable as they want you to believe, why be scared of new ideas?"

Mei banged her mug on the table. "How long do they expect us to wait? Ten years? Fifty? A generation?"

"It happened in Europe," Encizo said. "Remember East Germany. And then the Soviet Union. Russia, the mother of world revolution. They're having their problems, but who isn't? It can happen. But who knows how soon?"

"So while we wait," Mei said defiantly, "we challenge the Dragon. A little piece at a time."

Calvin James raised his coffee mug. "Mei Anna, you are one brave lady."

She smiled. "Or foolish."

"Looks to me we're chasing the same dragon," McCarter said.

"Do we swap stories?"

"Just so we all know what we're up against," McCarter explained.

"We do," Mei assured him. "I would like to know about your involvement with Li and Xan Hung."

McCarter explained the background of the Li affair, including the start of it all with Djin Shu's murder in San Francisco.

"Wait!" Mei cried. "Wait. The woman who was involved with him. Her name, is it Jenny Yeo?"

"How did you know?"

"Because Jenny is one of us. When we found out what Li was involved with, we sent Jenny to America to see if she could locate his people there. We have information, gathered by our people on the mainland, that identifies many of the undercover operatives working for the government. This whole thing was supposed to be about exposing secret cells working in foreign countries. We stumbled on Li's operation almost by accident and realized that if we obtained more information it would help our case. We became so involved, but then events overtook us. By this time Jenny had located Djin Shu, befriended him and attempted to get him to defect. It worked too well. Djin Shu became so infatuated with Jenny that he devised his plan to sell information for money so he and Jenny could go away. Unfortunately, it all backfired on him. His defection was discovered and he was murdered." Mei paused. "I think you know the rest."

The information Mei was giving him matched exactly what Yeo had told Able Team.

"Djin Shu getting himself shot meant his stolen information fell into the hands of the police in San Francisco," McCarter explained. "When it became obvious that this was just the tip of the iceberg, our people sent us to look into it."

"His project could endanger all of us," Mei said. "Stealing technology in order to create some kind of power base only adds to the risks we already face. Beijing will tell us they are doing it for our protection, but what will the reaction be from other countries? Think of Taiwan. Or how Pakistan and India will see it. Not as a defensive measure for them. Just China showing another powerful weapon of war. Another threat in an area already on guard against its neighbors. Power like this is only going to make it harder for countries to trust one another. We don't need this. It has to be stopped."

"Right now," McCarter said, "we're trying to identify all the players."

"Li is a clever man," Mei said. "He's made a deal with Xan Hung to provide backup here and in America. Xan has the background to make deals, transport equipment, move people around. From what we have been able to find out, his construction company has been involved in working on what Li calls his project."

"Do you know where?" Manning asked.

"We do now. It took us some time, but we have found it."

Mei turned and spoke to Tsu Han. He went away, returning shortly with a map. He spread it out on the table, jabbing a blunt finger at a marked area.

"We are here," Mei explained. "There's a scattering of small islands off the coast. Some are nothing more than a rock sticking up out of the water. Others are a little larger. One or two are big enough to sustain small settlements, mostly fishing communities. This one is Li's island. Something like twenty miles long by six at its widest point. Mostly barren rock with a little grass. On the southwest section there are trees and brush. A small community of fishermen live there. By sea it's roughly three hours from here. There used to be a small cannery located on the island, but it closed down many years ago."

"We need to take a look."

"That can be arranged."

Manning placed his empty mug on the table, tapping the map.

"The ship at Xan's dock. That wouldn't be going to the island by any chance?"

Mei shook her head.

"No. Not there. When we were in the office we asked one of Xan's people the same question."

McCarter glanced at her. "Did you get an answer?"

"He talked before he died," she said coldly. "Han has a way when it comes to persuasion." She paused, eyeing McCarter closely. "Disapproval?"

"It's not my place to judge, Anna. This is your fight."

"This is a war," she replied. "Make no mistake about that. If we are caught, I know what will happen to me. So I use the same rule book as they do. If our way upsets you, the door is open and you can leave."

McCarter smiled. "No one said anything about leaving. We didn't come all this way just to tell Li he's been a bad boy and not to do it again."

"So. As I said, we know where the ship is going."

"Let me take a guess," McCarter said. "How about North Korea?"

"Yes. How did you know?"

"I've been thinking about it since we left the dock, eliminating the most unlikely possibilities and hopefully ending with the right answer. If Li is building himself a missile control center, it's going to have an offensive side to it. The technology his people stole is for that kind of use. So he'll need missiles. The North Koreans have the expertise in that area. They've been busy enough pushing the bloody things to anyone interested in buying. And like China, they want to be at the top of the list alongside their greatest ally.''

Mei considered that. "It makes sense. We had information a few weeks ago about Li making a trip to Pyongyang. And his aide, a man named Jun, was seen accompanying a delegation from North Korea only ten days ago.''

"Did your informant tell you what was on board the ship?'' James asked.

"Computers from America. Electronic equipment was all he would say.''

McCarter held out his mug for more coffee. "And she sails tonight.''

Mei glanced at her watch. "It left fifteen minutes ago. There's nothing we do about it now.''

"Don't be so negative,'' McCarter said. "Tell me about the ship. Name, anything useful to identify it.''

Mei gave him what he needed, not certain what he was up to.

"Do you have a telephone here?''

She nodded. "In the other room.''

She showed him to the telephone, leaving him alone. McCarter punched in Stony Man Farm's number and let the satellite link bounce his call through.

"I need that help we discussed earlier,'' he said when Barbara Price picked up.

"The interception?''

"That's it. The ship left Hong Kong harbor approximately a half hour ago, and we know it's heading for North Korea."

"I'll have it tracked by satellite."

"She's a medium-sized freighter, with a single smokestack at the bow. It's called *Blue Water*. That's on the stern in bright red. The name is in Chinese in white underneath."

"Don't make it too easy for us."

"Good hunting," McCarter said and cut the connection.

When he returned to the other room he found a meal on the table about to be served. There were bowls of steaming noodles, rice, vegetables, sliced pork and chicken. It had been some time since McCarter had tasted real Chinese food. He was only too well aware that many of the dishes served in restaurants away from China were less than genuine. The smells of the local Chinese fare were a rare pleasure as far as the Briton was concerned.

Mei Anna indicated a place next to her and watched as McCarter helped himself to a bowl of rice. His ease when it came to using chopsticks impressed her, and his way of eating in the traditional manner. Scooping rice from his bowl with the chopsticks and helping himself to the other delicacies from the large bowls, the Briton showed his expertise in the Chinese culinary art.

"This is good," McCarter said between mouthfuls.

The Chinese around the table nodded approval.

"Next you will be telling me you can speak Cantonese," Mei said.

"Only a little," he told her, falling into the dialect. "It's been some while since I practiced."

Mei nodded. "That is very good. You seem to have been around quite a lot, Jim."

"Here and there."

"And not on vacation. Not the way you and your friends operate."

McCarter smiled. "We try our best."

"SHALL WE TALK business?" Mei asked a little later.

"Can you help us with equipment?" McCarter riposted.

She nodded. "We have stockpiles located in a number of places. I'm sure we can find what you need."

"Good. Then the next thing is a visit to Li's island. We need to take a close look at the place."

Mei spoke rapidly to Tsu Han. McCarter tried to follow what she was saying, but his grasp of the language wasn't up to translating. The scarred Chinese glanced at Phoenix Force. He and Mei exchanged a few more words before he nodded his approval.

"Thank you, Tsu Han," McCarter said in his best Cantonese.

"We can take you there," Mei told him.

The sound of the telephone ringing caught everyone's attention. They watched as Tsu Han left the room to take the call.

"No one phones unless there is a problem. We call out but that is all."

Tsu returned quickly. He relayed the message he had received.

"Our visit to Xan Hung's establishment appears to have started a panic. His people are on the streets, questioning everyone they know who might be connected to us. I think they are trying to locate us once and for all.''

"Then we'd better get our bloody skates on and get the hell out of here," McCarter said.

They cleared the house quickly, piling into the two waiting vehicles. Mei, in her panel truck, led the way once again.

FOR THE SECOND TIME that night, Phoenix Force took a ride through the darker streets of Hong Kong. When they stopped it was in the cluttered yard of a store. Out front, on the street side, the establishment was still trading. The late hour didn't seem to make much difference. Business was business in Hong Kong.

"We can collect your supplies from here," Mei explained as she led McCarter and Tsu into the musty cavern of the storage area. A flimsy door opened onto a set of steep wooden steps, leading into the cellar. The squeaking of rats told McCarter they weren't alone.

Mei located a trapdoor that led to a second-level subcellar. Using a flashlight she had brought from the panel truck, she showed McCarter where a concealed opening led into a small, cramped room. Inside a steel cabinet, covered in moldy canvas sheets, he saw weapons and equipment. With Tsu's help McCarter filled a couple of canvas carryalls with weapons. For main weapons he selected 9 mm Uzi submachine guns. Mei gathered a number of extra ammunition clips, plus a selection of knives in sheaths. A pleased smile crossed McCarter's lips when he spotted a Cold Steel Tanto knife, which he took for Encizo. He spotted some compact signal devices and took one for each teammate, figuring they might come in handy if the team became separated. He located a receiver for the devices, capable of being tuned to the signal.

"Enough?" Mei asked.

"It's never enough," McCarter said. "Right now, though, it's better than we had five minutes ago."

"Let's go then."

They made their way back up to the store.

James was at the rear door. Hawkins and Manning were watching the front. Mei's people had been collecting some supplies from the rear of the store, loading them into the panel truck.

As McCarter placed his bags in the rental car, he stopped, slowly turning to check out the alley where they were parked. He felt distinctly uneasy. He wasn't sure what had alerted him, but he knew for a fact that something was wrong. He could almost hear his own thoughts.

Dammit, he thought. No bloody wonder! It was too quiet!

He turned casually and caught Mei's eye. The look on her face told him she was thinking the same thing. McCarter slid his hand to the holstered Browning, easing it free as he walked to where the woman stood beside the panel truck.

"I think we're going to have visitors," he said and moved on to alert James and Encizo.

"Cal, go tell the guys."

The black Phoenix Force warrior smiled and stepped casually inside the store. Once out of sight he moved quickly, threading his way down the heavily laden shelving units until he was able to step up behind Hawkins, who was lounging in the doorway.

"On your toes, guys," he whispered. "Visitors. And they aren't coming for the groceries."

His message delivered, James backed away and headed for the rear again.

A long black car appeared at the far end of the dimly lighted street. It wasn't showing any lights. As it stopped, the rear doors popped open and a number of men slipped out, moving to the sides of the street, trying to lose themselves in the shadows.

"Not going to work, boys," Hawkins murmured. "We already spotted you."

"Two on the left," Manning said, "three on the right. Coming up fast now."

"You want the little number or the big one?"

"Can you count to three?" the Canadian asked.

"Sure."

"You take them then."

A shouted command in Chinese set the two approaching teams running. The sound of their footsteps pinpointed them almost as well as their moving shadows. One started to shoot the moment he moved into the middle of the street, the hard crack of his weapon identifying it as a Kalashnikov. Slugs peppered the peeling woodwork of the storefront.

Behind the Phoenix Force pair a woman started to scream, more in rage than fear, anger at her property being damaged.

With surprise no longer an option, the street erupted in a barrage of gunshots.

Hawkins brought up his Browning and tracked the closest of the attackers. He held his aim, stroked the trigger and put the man down with a single shot. Dropping to a crouch, he repeated the procedure and stopped his second man with a 9 mm round to the thigh that flipped the target over and left him cursing and bleeding in the dirt.

Close by, Manning had already dropped his first target, putting two close shots into the chest of a broad, stocky man. As the shooter went down, the Phoenix Force commando altered his aim and tracked his second target. He fired and missed as the hardman threw himself back into the shadows.

The surviving attackers were having a shouted conversation. Reaching a decision, they moved in for the attack. One opened fire, spraying the storefront with slugs, while the second fumbled with something in his hand. Seconds later he hurled a grenade that hit the street and rolled to within inches of Hawkins's right foot.

The young Phoenix Force warrior didn't hesitate. He bent over, scooped up the grenade and hurled it back at the two Chinese. The grenade exploded in the air, almost over the enemy's heads. The shrapnel shredded their upper bodies, tossing them to the ground in bloody heaps.

"That was a bloody crazy thing to do," Manning said.

"Yeah? Not as crazy as letting it blow us up."

"I guess not," Manning admitted.

They scanned the empty street, watching for any further movement, while from the rear of the store they picked up the sound of more gunfire.

JAMES STEPPED OUT of the rear door as the attack came.

A group of armed men appeared in the alley, weapons up and firing as they heard the opening shots from the street.

Both McCarter and Mei joined Encizo, taking cover behind the panel truck, feeling the thud of bullets impacting against its steel body.

"This wasn't in the travel brochure," McCarter commented.

"See Naples and die," Encizo whispered as he crouched beside his team leader. "This is the Asian version."

"Not today, Rafe," McCarter said.

Mei turned to see that her people were under cover, Tsu suddenly appearing at her side.

A Chinese, wielding a stubby Ingram MAC-10, scrambled over the hood of the rental car, searching for targets. The moment his feet touched the ground, Tsu erupted from the shadows. The scarred Chinese moved with deceptive swiftness, his hands flashing as he delivered savage blows to the shocked attacker. The SMG was sent flying from the man's hands. Before he could react the Chinese was sent reeling by a series of crippling blows that reduced him to a bleeding wreck. Tsu, stepping in close, delivered a final blow to the man's throat. The jab drove in with savage force, snapping the man's head back. He fell to the ground, his body loose, blood bubbling from his slack mouth.

By this time the attack had reached its peak. The alley echoed to the exchange of gunfire as the attackers chose to keep advancing despite the accurate shooting from Phoenix Force and the Pro-Democracy group.

The firefight was fast and furious, with each side dedicated to gaining the upper hand. The outcome was certain. The Chinese seemed to be locked into a mass-charge philosophy, determined to win by simply

expending a greater number of people and overwhelming the enemy. Phoenix Force, through years
of combat experience, had learned the sense of accurate, though slower, shooting. They ignored the tre-
mendous outpouring of fire from the Chinese, prefer-
ring instead to lock on and take down their targets
with steady shooting.

As the Chinese started to become aware of their
casualties, they decided to back off. Phoenix Force
increased its fire, and in the confines of the alley, the
handguns they were using took their toll with fright-
ening regularity. Stumbling over the bodies of their
fallen comrades and ignoring the cries for help, the
enemy retreated down the alley, loosing erratic bursts
to cover their withdrawal.

Snapping a fresh clip into his Browning, McCarter
glanced over his shoulder, catching Encizo's eye.

"Go get the others," he said. "It's time we
moved."

He sprinted to the rental and grabbed the canvas
bags of equipment, then returned to where Mei knelt.

"Time to go."

She nodded. Calling her people together, she got
them to climb into the panel truck.

McCarter and James stayed in position, watching
in case any of the Chinese attackers came back. The
Phoenix Force leader heard a car engine burst into
life, tires burning against the surface of the road.

"They might be back," he said. "Let's not leave
them anything to find."

Tsu climbed behind the wheel of the panel truck
with Mei next to him. She invited McCarter to join
her. The rest of Phoenix Force climbed into the rental
car. Tsu set off, driving slowly until he was out of

the narrow streets. He stayed on the quieter roads as he headed for their new destination near the waterfront.

"Anna, how long have you been doing this?" McCarter asked.

"Four years now," she said. "I took over when my father and brother died. The security police attacked our house one night. They set fire to it and prevented those inside from leaving. I was away at the time. When I came home I was told there had been an accident. Later Han found me and told me the truth. He had been wounded during the attack, shot in the face, but he managed to escape. We went away and hid for months until Han was better. By then I had been contacted by the group. They asked me to take over. I did and here we are."

"And now?"

"Now? As I said before, we do what we can to disrupt the regime. To expose their lies and their secrets."

"Tough life."

"If you are a woman? Was that your next line?" McCarter grinned. "Now who is being touchy?"

"I've heard it before."

"I meant a tough life for anyone. How do you survive? Moving from place to place. No home or security. No family."

"I have all the family I need, Jim. The people around me and all of China is my family."

The earnest tone in her voice was all McCarter had to hear. Mei Anna had chosen her role in life, and she would pursue it until she won her battle, or died for it.

"What do you really know about this island? Are we on the right track, or just wasting our time?"

"You can judge for yourselves soon. It's why we're taking a boat ride, Clancy. I'm going to show you Colonel Li's island fortress."

They reached the waterfront after a half-hour ride. Tsu pulled up at the edge of the water. A number of moored vessels rocked on the night tide, wood creaking and furled sails gently flapping in the soft breeze.

Mei's team opened the tailgate and began to empty the gear from the truck. With Phoenix Force's help the work was completed in a short time. The supplies were carried to a rickety wooden jetty that ran alongside one of the moored vessels.

It was a Chinese junk, the workhorse of the Orient. The junk was all things to all people. To many it was a permanent home. The vessels crowded the Hong Kong harbor, creating a floating community of hundreds. At the other end of the scale it was a cargo ship, carrying all kinds of goods around the coastlines, legal or otherwise. An anonymous, plodding vessel, it was as much a part of the scenery as the Chinese themselves.

"Are we going powerboat sailing?" Hawkins asked as he examined the clumsy lines of the vessel.

"Wait and see," Mei said as she passed.

McCarter beckoned James and Manning to join him.

"I need you to stay behind and monitor things here," he said. He handed over the receiver for the signal devices he had picked up in the cellar. "I hope we won't have to use these bloody things, but if we get into a fix we might need to let you know."

James nodded. He took the piece of equipment and

stowed it in the car. McCarter handed a small business card to James.

"This is Hallam's number. You can use it to contact him if need be."

"You watch yourselves out there," Manning said.

"Don't worry, we will."

With the cargo on board and the truck hidden away nearby, the junk was eased away from the jetty, sails spread to catch the warm night breeze. The awkward configuration of the vessel belied its performance, and within minutes it was plowing steadily through the dark waters as Tsu Han steered it away from the shore.

"We should be there well before dawn," Mei informed McCarter as he joined her under the open canopy that served as a cabin.

McCarter stared down at her slim form, impressed by her calm authority. He sat on one of the low wooden stools favored by the Chinese and crossed his long legs with some difficulty. Watching him struggle, Mei suddenly laughed, and for a moment the mask slipped. The tough fighter was replaced by a beautiful young woman who would have looked at home on the front cover of any New York fashion magazine. Just as quickly the laughter faded, and Mei reached up to brush a stray strand of black hair away from her face.

"What about you, Jim?" she asked. "Who are you really?"

"Bit of a problem there," McCarter said in his best colonial voice. "*Official Secrets Act* and all that."

"You make jokes all the time, but you are not fools. Any of you. I watched you fight, and I was watching professionals."

"Takes one to know one."

She shook her head in frustration, then poked a slim finger at McCarter and allowed herself to smile.

Encizo joined them, squatting on his heels.

"Just what have you got hidden in the stern, Mei Anna?" he asked.

She gave him a classic stare, her face set. "I don't know what you mean."

"I smell gasoline," the Cuban announced. "Of course, we could be delivering a cargo of fuel to Colonel Li, but I have my doubts."

"It's nothing," Mei said. "Just a little insurance."

She took them to the stern of the junk and moved aside some coiled rope and sacking. In the deck something square was barely discernible. She lifted it and, in the dim light McCarter and Encizo were able to make out the shape of a powerful inboard motor.

"We haven't needed to use it yet," Mei said, closing the hatch and glancing at McCarter. "I have a feeling we may need it this time around."

As they moved back along the swaying deck, McCarter said, "Do you have any other surprises we don't know about?"

"If I told you, they wouldn't be surprises any longer."

The junk continued on its leisurely way. The gentle sway of the ungainly craft, coupled with the balmy temperature, made the voyage almost pleasurable. It was only when images of what lay ahead filled the thoughts of the men of Phoenix Force that the brief idyll was broken. The seasoned warriors, who seemed to spend most of their waking hours on missions such as this one, took any opportunity to relax. They all knew that these times were fleeting, mere scraps of

calm in among the furious, often bloody stretches of
combat. It had become almost a reflex action to take
their moments of peace whenever they presented
themselves. When the action erupted, the next break
might be a long time coming.

Mei and her people seemed to have a similar out-
look. The Chinese team, apart from those handling
the junk, sat around the deck in quiet contemplation.
They spoke infrequently. Most of the time they
checked their equipment and weapons, or gazed out
over the sea swell, deep in some inner calm.

An hour into the voyage Mei passed out mugs of
hot tea to Phoenix Force. The steaming liquid, served
black, had a fragrant, herbal scent to it.

McCarter sipped his and found it soothing. He was
unable to identify just exactly what was in it and perhaps, he thought on reflection, it was better not to
know. Nor would he have offended Mei by asking.
When he had finished it, the woman came around
with a metal pot and refilled his mug.

"Is it to your liking?"

McCarter nodded. "It's good, Anna."

"You will not find this in any of your supermarkets
in London."

"That I can believe."

"Has it changed? London?"

"That's the second time you've mentioned London. When were you there?"

"Eight years ago." She smiled as she recalled a
memory. "A lifetime ago. I remember walking on
Hampstead Heath in the rain in the early morning. A
girlfriend and I had been to a party. We went home
to her flat and had bacon and eggs for breakfast. All
very English."

"It's all still there," McCarter told her. "Maybe you can do it again one day, Mei Anna."

She stared at the deck under her feet, shaking her dark head.

"That was another time in another world, Jim. This is my world now. In another eight years I will still be fighting my war." She looked up suddenly. "Perhaps I will be dead by then, a forgotten itch Mother China will have rid herself of."

"Never forgotten, Mei Anna," McCarter said.

If he could have seen her face clearly in that moment, McCarter would have noticed a blush of color on her cheeks. She pushed to her feet, making some excuse about refilling the teapot, and hurried away.

IN THE PALE GLOW of predawn, the junk hove to, some three miles off the southern tip of Li's island, concealed in the shadows of a smaller island, which thrust up out of the water like a broken tooth. Thin coils of mist clung to the barren rock that formed the promontory of Li's island. A few birds swooped over the white-capped waves that rolled in toward the shingle beach, seeking unwary fish brought in by the rush of water. Some rose with a wriggling catch, only to be pursued by their less lucky companions.

"There it is," Mei Anna said.

She stood beside McCarter and the others, pointing out various landmarks along the jagged outline of the island.

"The base is around the eastern side. Even up close it is impossible to see. There are only a few communication antennas in sight. The rest is below the surface."

"Sounds like our Colonel Li has thought of everything,'' Encizo said. ''If he's going to so much trouble, he isn't playing games.''

''Li doesn't play games,'' Mei replied. ''This is no toy. If he gets his way, there will be a working base here in a few weeks.''

''Not if we have anything to do with it,'' McCarter said. ''Anna, how close in can you bring us?''

''Once we break away from here and start to move in closer, the radar will pick us up. Li is very serious when it comes to visitors.''

''I thought I heard you say you'd been on the island?'' Encizo said.

''Yes. It's not easy but it is possible. Once you are on the island, you must stay hidden from Li's roving patrols. The harder part is getting a look inside the base itself.''

''Maybe you'd better show us how it's done,'' McCarter suggested.

Mei led them back to the covered section. Once again they squatted on the wooden deck, and the woman produced a waterproof map folder and opened it. She showed them the charts and traced a finger along the island's southeast area.

''There used to be a fishery plant just about here. It closed about twenty years ago. The buildings were destroyed and cleared away. Here is where the plant used to dispose of all the remains after the fish were gutted and cleaned. An outflow pipe runs from the plant, under the water. It stretches out around thirty feet from the shore. It's possible to negotiate the pipe and get into a subbasement of the base Li is creating.''

''You got in that way?'' Hawkins asked.

"Of course," Mei said. "It was only to take a look."

"I'm impressed," Hawkins told her.

"Better stay that way," McCarter told him. "We might have to make that swim ourselves."

"I love it when you come up with these ideas."

McCarter turned to Mei. "How has Li missed this pipe? If he's so security-minded, he wouldn't overlook something like that."

"The pipe is not visible above ground. There are no longer any existing plans of the old fishery. You see, the pipe runs in a line with the perimeter of the underground caverns he's using. The island fishermen told us about the pipe. They also told us there was a break in it, which allows access to the lower levels of the caverns, away from where Li's construction takes place. The fishermen had discovered the access long before the colonel became fully established."

Tsu Han shouted a warning, breaking into the conversation. He ran to Mei and spoke to her rapidly in Chinese. Pushing to her feet, she called out instructions.

"What's going on?" McCarter asked.

She turned, pointing across the misty water. The dark outline of a Chinese patrol boat was curving in their direction. Even in the dim light, McCarter made out the shapes of uniformed figures racing to battle stations. Two heavy machine guns were mounted on the craft, and the crew was already moving to man them.

"Great!" McCarter snapped. "That's all we need."

Mei had already ordered the hatch removed from the engine compartment. One of the Chinese jumped into it. It wasn't long before the throaty rumble of the powerful engines burst into life. The junk surged forward, propelled by the churning screws beneath her stern. With Tsu at the controls, the clumsy boat picked up speed, drawing away from the patrol boat.

"This isn't going to work," Hawkins muttered as he stood at the side of the junk, hanging on to a rope, and watched the patrol boat increase its own power. "I don't care what they have under the hood. We won't outrun that damn thing."

As he saw the speed the patrol boat was putting behind it, McCarter was inclined to believe Hawkins. When Mei joined him he pointed this out to her, and grim-faced, she nodded her acceptance of the fact.

"They have improved the efficiency of their boats since we were out here last."

She turned and yelled something to her crew. The orders galvanized them into action and, dragging open one of the crates on deck, two of the Chinese moved to the junk's stern, LAW rockets in their arms.

"What next?" McCarter asked. "A bloody torpedo?"

Mei smiled. "We're in a war, Clancy, and we have to be ready for anything."

The heavy thump of the machine guns mounted on the pursuing patrol boat filled the air. The first volleys fell short, but the Chinese gunners quickly adjusted their aim and the next burst sent slugs pounding into the junk's wooden sides, tearing slivers of wood out of the hull, just above the waterline.

"Be quick about it," McCarter yelled. "If they really get our range, they'll blow this tub into sawdust."

Mei urged her crew to retaliate. The two with the

rockets positioned themselves at the stern, steadying themselves as they took aim. The first to fire watched his rocket leap across the space between the two craft and miss the patrol boat by inches. He threw down the empty casing, muttering in disgust.

More machine-gun fire sounded. Bullets whacked into the junk, tearing at the solid wood structure, filling the air with splinters. Some of the slugs found a more vulnerable target, and one of Mei's team was flung in a bloody heap on the deck, jerking and wriggling for a time before the massive damage done to his body shut him down forever.

Bullets continued to thud into the structure of the junk, tearing at the wood and rendering jagged holes.

Mei's second rocket man went down on one knee, bracing himself as he took aim. Before he could trigger the LAW a burst of machine-gun fire caught him in the side. He sprawled across the deck, blood coursing from his open wounds. The LAW slid across the deck. Hawkins hurried forward, picked up the LAW and stepped up to the firing position. Swinging the tube over his shoulder, the Phoenix Force commando steadied himself against the roll of the deck, aimed and fired almost in a single motion. The rocket leaped from the tube, skimming the waves as it flew into the path of the patrol boat and turned it into a rolling, boiling ball of flame and smoke. The destruction went on for some time as the patrol boat's fuel exploded, followed by its ammunition supply, filling the air with crackling and loud thumps. As the debris pattered back to the surface of the water, smoke billowed up from the blackened hulk of the patrol boat. Burning fuel lay on the surface of the oily water, still aflame long after the vessel had turned on its side, slowly easing below the surface.

"Remind me never to upset T.J.," Encizo commented.

"Some shot," McCarter said as Hawkins joined them.

Mei touched the young man on the shoulder. "If you ever want to leave these people, you can join us."

"I'll keep it in mind," Hawkins said, grinning.

"Is life always this interesting?" Encizo asked, pausing in his efforts to throw shattered debris over the side.

"This is the first time we have actually clashed with Li's security force," Mei said. "Lucky for us they don't have the most sophisticated equipment."

"If those machine guns had got our range, *sophisticated* wouldn't have mattered," Hawkins observed.

"Can we discuss this later?" McCarter suggested. "I'll feel safer when we leave that bloody island behind us."

Mei had already joined Tsu at the helm. After a minute she called McCarter to her side.

"I was wrong," she said. "Looks like we took some serious hits. The engine is running ragged. Han thinks we might have some power problems. We'll go as far as we can while we still have power."

McCarter nodded. "Break out the weapons. Get everyone armed and ready just in case. Anna, we need to jettison anything we don't really need to lighten the load."

"I'll see to it."

McCarter gathered his team around him. "We might have trouble getting back. The power plant has been hit. Don't know how long she'll keep running. Anna is going to have her people dump excess baggage to keep the weight down. I want everyone armed and ready in case Li sends out any more of his patrol boats."

"Looks like you'll get your action, T.J.," Encizo said.

"Hell, I didn't want it this way, guys. I prefer dry land under my feet in a firefight."

"No choice this time," McCarter said. "All right, guys, let's go."

They helped Mei and her team to jettison whatever they could. As they worked, McCarter straightened and glanced back at Tsu. The Chinese nodded briefly as he caught the Briton's concerned gaze. He had picked up the faltering tone of the junk's motor. Beside McCarter, Hawkins paused, too.

"Sounds like she's dying on us, boss."

"What is it?" Mei queried.

"The motor," McCarter said.

"Hey, you want me to go take a look?" Hawkins asked. "I might be able to coax a few more miles out of her."

"Give it a try," McCarter said.

Hawkins made his way below while the rest of the team carried on with their dumping.

Around the junk the waves started to rise, whitecaps of foam cresting the dark swell. The deck began to rise and fall with noticeable force, accompanied by a steady rolling motion.

Rafael Encizo, hanging on to a taut rope, stared up at the dawn sky and saw the heavy black clouds coming in.

"That's all we need," he muttered. The others had

seen it by then. Mei's Chinese crew exchanged knowing glances, and she approached Phoenix Force.

"It looks as if we are going to get a storm. There's nothing we can do. This time of year, it happens regularly."

"We get caught out here, there'll be more water in the damn boat than outside it," Encizo said. "How steady are these things?"

"Pretty steady," Mei replied. "But it will depend on the force of the storm."

Encizo chuckled. "With an answer like that you should be in politics."

Mei spread her hands. "What can I say?"

McCarter made his way to where Hawkins was laboring over the ragged-sounding motor.

"Any joy?"

Hawkins shook his head. He wiped his hands on a rag, leaning back against the bulkhead.

"She's shot, boss. This motor isn't taking us much farther. She's ready to call it a day."

"Bloody great. Well, let's hope this damn thing can get us back to dry land. Any dry land."

"You believe in miracles, Jim?" Mei asked, coming up behind McCarter as he climbed back on deck.

"Not since Father Christmas refused to turn me into Superman."

"Looks like you might be disappointed a second time, then. This is going to be a big storm."

"How can you tell?"

"Jim, I'm Chinese. We know these things," she said with a wry smile on her face.

Mei turned and began to yell orders to her crew. When she had finished, she faced McCarter.

"I told my people to get their equipment together.

Anything they want to keep they'll have to carry. Now come with me."

McCarter followed her along the rolling deck, his clothing quickly soaked by the water that was sloshing over the sides of the junk. As they neared the bow, a heavy wave crashed over the side and washed the deck with water. Mei faltered, almost losing her balance, and she might have fallen if McCarter's strong arm hadn't grabbed her around the waist. He hung on to a rope with his other hand, waiting until the motion of the vessel settled a little.

"You can let go now, Jim," Mei said, turning to glance up at him. Strands of her black hair were clinging to her wet cheek. Despite the urgency of their situation she made no immediate attempt to free herself from his grasp. "Tell me something. Do you always pick up women this way?"

"Only the special ones," McCarter told her.

When they reached the bow Mei showed him the upturned rowboat held to the deck by ropes.

"If we have to leave that's our lifeboat. I'm afraid we don't run to lifejackets or anything fancy like that."

The implication was clear in her tone. McCarter nodded. When he returned to Hawkins and Encizo he told them about the rowboat.

"Hey, Rafael," Hawkins said, "go take a look at the name painted on the back of this thing. How much do you bet it says *Titanic* in Chinese?"

"You could be right," Encizo said. "I figure that's our iceberg coming up fast."

They all turned to see another patrol boat, this one larger and faster than the previous one. It was bearing down on them in a hurry, its sleek bow cutting through the rough sea with ease.

"That looks a few years younger than the other one," Hawkins observed.

McCarter braced himself against the movement of the boat as he fumbled in his pockets, hoping that the cell phone he'd been carrying since they arrived was still there. He felt a wash of relief as his fingers closed over the cool plastic. He took out the phone and keyed in the speed-dial number that would connect him to the one Calvin James was carrying. He hoped James was carrying it. The connection seemed to take forever, McCarter struggling to maintain his balance while he listened to the ringing tone. Then James came on, his voice faint and breaking up slightly.

"Cal?"

"David? Is that you?"

"Listen. We've run into some opposition out here. Patrol boats. And there's a bloody bad storm. It's pretty rough."

"Okay. I got that. Wha—"

The signal cut out. The phone buzzed in McCarter's hand, then it went dead. McCarter knew he had used his one chance. He checked the readout on the cell phone. The signal indicator was at zero. If nothing else, McCarter thought, he had at least made contact.

Heavy waves began to break over the side of the junk, washing over the deck. McCarter was hit by one surge, the force knocking him backward. He reached out to grab something to support himself and the cell phone spilled from his fingers. It hit the deck and was carried out of sight by the next wave. The

Phoenix Force leader didn't give it a second thought. He was concerned with staying alive.

Even over the rising sound of the storm they all heard the solid hammer of machine-gun fire. The first volley cut through the water only feet away, but the gunner adjusted his aim for the second burst, and heavy-caliber slugs began to whack into the junk, tearing an ugly line of holes along the side. A second gun opened up, the trajectory of this one laying the fire into the deck area.

"Heads down!" McCarter yelled.

Someone screamed in agony. One of the Chinese crashed to the deck, blood gouting from his wounds. Mei started to go to him, but McCarter lunged forward and dragged her to the deck a split second before a further volley of machine-gun fire raked the air where she had been standing. The slugs cut into one of the masts, showering them with splinters. Another burst marched a line of slugs along the hull of the boat, the impact vibrating through the deck.

"Let me go, Jim!" Mei yelled, struggling to break free. "We have to fight them."

"With what? Anna, we don't have the firepower."

"We can't just—"

Her words were lost in a sudden explosion from the bow of the junk. A section of the deck lifted, blowing apart in a splintering crash. The air filled with flying debris.

"They must have something heavier than machine guns," Hawkins yelled above the din.

"Probably a cannon," McCarter said.

A second explosion ripped open more of the junk's bow. Below them the deck pitched and they slid to the rail.

"Time to get out of here," McCarter said.

He caught Mei's hand, and they stumbled across the angled deck, hanging on to whatever they could.

Tsu was already cutting the ropes holding the rowboat down. With Hawkins's help, McCarter bent to the task of rolling the boat over and preparing to drop it into the water.

"Where's Rafael?" McCarter asked anxiously.

"Last I saw he was sorting his equipment," Hawkins said. He straightened. "He was over there."

Despite the crashing waves breaching the junk's sides, they were able to see Encizo's backpack. He had secured it to a deck ring. The pack was open, contents starting to spill out. But Encizo was nowhere to be seen.

"You don't think—" Hawkins was unable to complete the sentence, as the Chinese patrol boat swept alongside and opened up with a broadside from its machine guns.

There was no more time for debate. The junk was going down, water creeping along the deck from the stern. All hands grabbed the rowboat, lifting it clear of the deck and dropping it over the side of the junk away from the patrol boat. As it hit the water, Tsu braced himself to hang on to the rope secured to the bow. He made a sweeping gesture with one hand, indicating that everyone should get in.

"Go!" McCarter yelled. "Now!"

Following on his words the skies opened and the storm hit them with ferocious intensity. The world vanished in the torrential downpour. Wind drove the rain across the deck of the stricken junk, fierce enough to almost pick them up and hurl them into the sea. It was difficult to see farther than a few feet.

There was nothing left for any of them to do but try to stay alive. Even the threat of the circling patrol boat was diminished in the storm as Phoenix Force and the Pro-Democracy group abandoned the junk and took to the rowboat.

CHAPTER EIGHT

Hong Kong

"Do you think we'll have to pay for it?" Manning asked casually.

James stopped and turned. "What?"

"Will we have to pay for the hole you're wearing in the carpet?"

"Gary, you are a funny man."

"Cal, I'm as worried as you are. I reckon it's time to do something."

"Amen to that, brother."

James picked up the telephone and punched the number for an outside line. He entered the Stony Man sequence and waited as the security procedure kicked in, bouncing the call off satellites and through numerous cutouts until he was connected with the Farm in Virginia. The number put him straight through to Hal Brognola's internal telephone, but it was Barbara Price who picked up.

"We need an assist," James explained. "There's a hell of a storm out here, and the last message from the guys said they were having a rough time. The opposition had picked up on their trip so they were catching it from both sides. We're sitting here on our butts because there isn't a damn thing we can do.''

"We were anticipating some kind of hindrance, so we sent Jack and *Dragon Slayer* out to join you. Right now he's waiting in Taiwan. By his estimate he can be in Hong Kong in three hours. He'll call via a cell phone once he's in the area. He has cargo on board I think you'll be happy to see. I'm canceling the rule on protocol. You guys need backup, and he's bringing it.''

"Best news I've heard all day.''

"You guys okay?''

"We've had worse trips abroad,'' James said. "Problem here is knowing who to trust. Right at this point, that isn't many.''

"Take it easy, guys.''

James put down the phone.

"Jack's on his way, coming in from Taiwan. Should be with us in three hours.''

"He got any presents with him?''

"I think so.'' James grinned.

"About damn time,'' Manning said.

James hadn't been expecting a call so soon. When he answered though, it wasn't Grimaldi.

"This is Hallam for Mr. Clancy.''

"He's not available. I'm Mr. Johnson. What can I do for you?''

"I need to see you, where I met Mr. Clancy last time. I can be there in twenty minutes. It's important.''

"Who was it?'' Manning asked.

"The British contact David met when we arrived. He wants a meet right now. Same place. Seemed to think it was important.''

"I'll drop you. Keep an eye out while you're in there."

James handed him the cell phone. "In case Jack calls."

THE STREETS WERE AWASH. The storm out at sea had also reached inland. The rain kept a large percentage of the people off the streets, so Manning had no problem reaching the hotel. He parked in the same spot Phoenix Force had used last time.

"Keep the engines running. If things start to hit the fan, I'm out of there," James said.

"Right," Manning said. "Hey, don't worry about David and the others. It'll take more than a rough sea and the Chinese navy to deal with them."

James nodded. He wasn't entirely convinced.

In truth, neither was Manning. He watched James sprint across the lot and vanish inside the hotel. Left to his thoughts, Manning couldn't stop himself wondering about McCarter, Hawkins and Encizo. They were out there somewhere, facing the might of the weather and the threat posed by Li's patrol boats. Phoenix Force had faced difficult challenges before and had always come through due to the tenacious spirit that was part of them all. McCarter, Hawkins and Encizo weren't the kind of men to be cowed by a rainstorm, or the presence of enemy patrol boats.

His thoughts also dwelt on Mei Anna and her people. They were putting their lives on the line every day. Defiantly challenging the great beast that was China was no small thing. Despite the enormity of the task, they were, like all fighters for freedom, optimistic and utterly devoted to their cause. Looking at it pragmatically, Manning found he was unable to envisage their efforts really causing any long-term damage. China was so vast, its human resource so limitless that the clandestine struggle of a small band such as Mei's would be like a bee sting to the hide of an elephant.

Even so, the war would go on. If not Mei's group then another, each in no small part aggravating the Dragon.

James made his way across the lobby of the hotel. He decided the best thing to do was to check at the desk. The clerk nodded when James asked if there was a Mr. Hallam waiting for him.

"That's the gentlemen, sir," the clerk said, indicating the man seated just inside the bar entrance.

James made his way to the table and introduced himself.

"Sit, Mr. Johnson," Hallam said. "Can I order you anything?"

"Thanks, no. Sorry to be blunt, Mr. Hallam, but I'm in a hurry. Things are happening we need to stay on top of."

"One of my contacts called me. He had a visit from a certain Mr. Jun, who is Colonel Li's adviser. He's not a military man, but he ranks high in Li's organization. He also has, luckily, a rather loose tongue. While he was enjoying the company of my contact, he let it slip he was making a trip to Japan to meet a Mr. Kobashi Makura and bring him back here to Hong Kong. Jun told his friend this because he wanted the young man to arrange some entertainment for Makura."

"What does Makura specialize in?" James asked.

"Anything and everything allied to computers. Makura is a genius when it comes to creating computer hardware. Give him the schematics, and he'll build you a motherboard. He used to be employed by one of the Japanese giants. Unfortunately, Makura is his own worst enemy. His ideas were too radical for the commercial world, and they parted company on less-than-friendly terms. Since then he's used his skills to help radical groups, terrorist organizations. He's become an outlaw, ready and willing to help if the price is right.''

''And now Jun is bringing him here? Because Li needs him?''

Hallam shrugged. ''The pieces do fit. I'll have to let you work out the reasons why, because I don't know.''

''Well, thanks for that anyhow,'' James said.

''I'll walk out with you. Car's in the lot.''

As they stepped out into the rain, Hallam paused to turn up his coat collar.

''If you need anything else, call me,'' Hallam said. ''And good luck.''

''Way things are going we may need tha—''

Neil Hallam's head burst apart like a ripe melon. The bullet entered just above his left eye and cored through, exiting the back of his skull in a dark fountain. Hallam took a faltering step to the side, twisting as he went down, blood spilling over his jacket and shirt, spreading across the steps before the rain washed it away.

James heard the crack of the shot and drew his Browning as he ran down the hotel steps and across the parking lot. Manning had seen the incident, and he gunned the rental car across the wet surface, rocking to a halt beside James.

The second shot scored a burn mark across the

paintwork of the car's hood. The next one, fired a little too hastily, shattered the side window of a parked car. More shots rang out, tearing chunks from the road and gouging a hole in the car's roof, but Manning drove in a zigzag course, preventing the hidden shooter from settling his sights long enough for a killing shot.

James reached for the door handle and wrenched it open. He fell inside, across the passenger's seat, yelling for Manning to keep going. Dragging his legs inside, the Phoenix Force commando slammed the door shut.

The car's tires slithered on the rain slick surface of the lot as Manning burned up the distance to the exit. Hauling on the wheel, the big Canadian guided the vehicle onto the street and floored the accelerator. Luckily the street was still quiet from the downpour, so Manning didn't come face-to-face with any traffic. The lack of traffic left them exposed, and the Phoenix Force duo heard the crack of the sniper rifle twice more before they sped out of range.

Manning took the first corner he saw, then the next, bringing them around in a circle until they were behind the building directly opposite the hotel. He brought the car to a stop, cut the engine and switched off the lights. He took out his Browning, pushed open his door and stepped out. On the far side of the car James did the same, and they eased back into the shadows of the building's wall and waited.

No more than a couple of minutes went by before a fire-exit door eased open and a lean, black-haired man slipped out. He was clad in black from head to foot, the collar of his expensive leather jacket turned up against the rain. He paused to close the door, turn-

ing to check the street before he stepped away from
the building and started to cross the street. In his left
hand he carried a long, narrow case bound in black
leather.

"Is he our man or what?" James asked.

In the far distance the sound of a police siren
reached them. The black-clad figure paused, listening,
then hurried on. His objective appeared to be a dark
Toyota sports car parked a little way along the street.

"Hold it!" Manning called. "Police."

The man paused for a fraction of a second, then
continued. Even in the dim light James could see his
right hand work its way under his leather jacket. Subdued light gleamed on the matte-black finish of a pistol the sniper pulled from his clothing.

"Stop now!" Manning commanded.

The man whirled in the direction of Manning's
voice. His reflexes were fast. The barrel of the pistol
tracked in and he fired. The bullet scored the brick-
work directly behind Manning's former position. The
big Canadian had stepped aside the moment he'd uttered the challenge, dropping to a crouch, as well.
Now he brought his Browning into play, gripping the
weapon in both hands and triggering two fast shots.
The sniper danced sideways, dropping the leather-
bound case as he felt the impact of the 9 mm slugs.
They drilled through his body, breaking two ribs as
they went. He clamped a hand over the entry wounds,
as if the very act would control the pain. Injured but
not out of the game, he aimed his gun in Manning's
general direction. He hadn't accounted for Calvin
James, who had moved a good ten feet to the side.
James brought up his own Browning, snap-aimed and
fired three times. The slugs punched through the

sniper's chest and laid him flat-out on the road. By the time the Phoenix Force duo reached him, the sniper was dead.

Manning checked the leather case. Inside, resting on black velvet, was the sniper rifle, a 7.62 mm Galil. Next to the rifle lay a telescopic sight.

"Let's get out of here before the cops arrive," James suggested.

The squeal of tires attracted their attention. As the two men turned, they saw a gleaming dark Mercedes coming at them from the far end of the street.

"Great," Manning said. "He brought backup."

They sprinted for their car, the big Canadian starting the engine and dropping the gear into first. He floored the gas, taking the vehicle away from the curb in a fishtailing surge. Ignoring the street signs, Manning executed a wide sweep, cornering wildly. In the passenger's seat James looked over his shoulder and saw that the Mercedes was still in pursuit.

Taking control of the situation, Manning went for every side street he could find, pushing the car to the limit and risking severe damage to the vehicle, himself and James as he kept up his speed through the narrow gaps.

"What?" Manning asked sharply.

"I didn't say a word," James said. "Just ease off."

"What about our pals back there? They going to ease off?"

"Hey, I didn't say it was a perfect solution."

The conversation was abandoned as Manning wrenched the wheel to one side, narrowly avoiding a handcart standing at the side of the street. He missed the cart but ran the opposite side of the car into the stone wall. Sparks flew, trailing behind them like a fiery banner. The side mirror was ripped off during the contact. James hung on as the car bounced heavily from side to side.

"Yeah, I know," Manning said. "Take it easy."

The road ahead started to climb as they emerged from the side streets. Buildings slid away in their wake, and the road they traveled presented Manning with a series of sharp left and right bends as it pushed into the hills behind the city. The streetlights became fewer, and Manning put on the headlights so he was able to anticipate the bends before he hit them. The car's engine howled under the strain, and the tires screamed as they were twisted back and forth by the car's motion. Someone opened fire from the pursuit car. The thump of bullets hitting the vehicle's bodywork wasn't a sound the Phoenix Force commandos had wanted to hear. The rear window imploded, showering them with glass. A further burst thudded into the car's body.

"Did we piss somebody off or what?" James asked.

He wound down his window and leaned out, aiming the Hi-Power at the dark shape of the pursuing Mercedes. Fighting the slap of the rain against his face, James triggered a pair of shots. The second round knocked out a headlight. The driver refused to fall back. Instead, he stepped on the gas and rammed into the rear of the rental. The lighter car went into a rear-end slide and Manning lost control for brief, heart-thumping seconds. The car slid across the wet road, sideswiping the adjacent low wall. Fighting the wheel, the big Canadian brought the vehicle back under control.

"Coming again!" James warned.

Even though they were braced for impact, the Phoenix Force commandos were shaken by the solid impact. James almost lost his grip on the Browning as he was rammed against the open window frame. The rental car hit the wall a second time. The right front tire burst, the wheel rim blazing a stream of sparks as it shredded away the rubber and came in contact with the road's surface. Manning hung grimly on to the wheel, feeling the heavy pull to the side. He put all his skill into keeping the car on the road, while still negotiating the sharp bends. Despite his efforts the car began to slide in toward the sloping bank on the inner curve of the road. The forward momentum took the vehicle partway up the bank until the soft, rain-soaked earth acted as a drag and brought the vehicle to a sudden, jolting stop.

James had already freed his door. As the damaged car came to a halt, he kicked the door wide and exited in a long dive. He landed on his left shoulder, executing a roll and coming up in a firing stance, the Browning held in a two-handed combat grip.

The Mercedes slithered to a halt. Doors were flung open and a pair of dark-clad figures wielding stubby SMGs stepped out.

James had his target set before the would-be shooter could sight in his weapon. The Browning cracked twice, a pair of 9 mm slugs coring into the shooter's chest and knocking him into the open car door. He struggled to stay upright, but the bullets quickly drained away his resistance, and he went down without a sound, spread-eagled on his back, face turned up to the falling rain.

Emerging from his side of the car, Manning leaned

across the roof and traded shots with the driver of the Mercedes.

The Chinese shooter, leather coat glistening with rain, mouthed angry words that were lost in the fire-fight as his SMG expended its load, the stream of slugs chewing ragged holes in the rental car. The shooter failed to adjust his aim in time, and Manning's second pair of slugs pounded his upper chest. He stumbled away from the protection of the big, solid Mercedes. Manning fired again as the man became fully exposed, driving the flailing figure into the soft mud of the sloping bank.

Moving in, James and Manning checked out the downed men.

"Gary, this is the guy we saw in the photos David got from Hallam. The Triad boss, Xan Hung."

Manning stepped away from the dead driver and joined James. He checked out the body.

"That's him."

"Liked to do his own dirty work," James said.

"Yeah? Well, tonight was the last time," Manning answered.

He went to check out the rental car, and determined that it was out of commission.

"We'll have to use the Mercedes," he said.

Once behind the wheel, Manning turned the Mercedes and drove back to the city and their hotel. He parked the vehicle in a far corner of the lot, away from any illumination. He didn't want anyone spotting the shattered headlight.

Back in Manning's room, they put through a call to Stony Man Farm and reported the shooting incident.

Brognola listened in silence until the update was complete.

"Sounds like you met up with our mystery shooter," he said, referring to the sniper.

"He just had his license revoked," James commented.

"Xan Hung turning up makes another connection. This is getting to be a family affair."

"This kind of family I can do without."

"Heard anything from the others?"

"No."

"Damn. It's up to you guys now."

"You could try a satellite scan of the area."

"We will."

"Anything come back on our rogue ship yet?"

"Should be any time now."

"Contact you later."

MANNING AND JAMES had completed packing when the cell phone rang. James answered and heard Jack Grimaldi's voice.

"Forty minutes and counting," he reported. "You got a map down there?"

"Yeah," James said.

"Check these coordinates. Okay?"

Grimaldi rattled off the location of his LZ.

"Confirmed."

"That's where I'll be. Don't be late, guys. This is a once-only pickup. Over and out."

"On our way," James responded.

THE HELICOPTER touched down ten minutes ahead of schedule. Jack Grimaldi cut the power and lights, then secured the cabin.

He settled down to wait, angling back the body-form pilot seat to allow him to stretch. He could hear the rain bouncing off the canopy, but inside the compartment, isolated and temperature-controlled, Grimaldi was protected from the outside world.

It was a pity, he thought, that life couldn't be like that. Controlled and secure from the twisted evil that still lurked in many regions of the world. When he considered the thought he realized he was being naive. Being shut away from evil didn't eliminate it. Isolationism was a one-sided condition. Every man, woman and child was part of the global family. What affected one section often spilled over and tainted another. Closing eyes and ears to the suffering on the other side of the planet was just allowing the savages to win by proxy. Facing up to it was the only way the world would ever defeat evil. Ignoring the horror, turning the cheek and pretending it wasn't really happening only helped strengthen the hold savages had on civilization. There had to be a confrontation with evil, an ongoing battle that never stopped. There were times when that battle might seem hopeless, that the bad guys would never be defeated. It was in those moments that true courage shone through and the battle continued. In the end it would make a difference. Jack Grimaldi had been witness to that a long time ago. It was why he was there this day, and why he would stay the course. He owed it to one man, a lone warrior who had made a difference, and was still making that difference.

Grimaldi spotted a light gently winking in the semidarkness of the compartment. He sat up and keyed in a code. Moments later Barbara Price's voice was coming through as if she were in the seat next to him.

"We caught an update for that storm. Looks like it could be around for some while yet. The satellite scan doesn't look too promising."

"Soon as the guys get here we'll take a sweep over the area. Maybe I can pick up something from one of the signal devices."

"We'll keep checking via the satellites. See if we can locate anything. It's a long shot. The bad weather isn't going to make it easy."

"Okay. We'll come back if we get anything. Jack, take it easy out there. That goes for all of you."

"Thanks. Over and out."

Leaning forward to switch off, Grimaldi caught a flicker of light coming in from the direction of the road. He watched as the flicker became a single beam. Grimaldi frowned. He didn't expect Phoenix Force to turn up on one motorcycle. He eased his Beretta from his shoulder rig and took off the safety. He picked up his cell phone and speed-dialed the number he wanted.

"If I don't get the answer I'm expecting, watch your ass out there," he said when the call was accepted.

Gary Manning's voice came through loud and clear. "Tough talk, pal, but can you back it up?"

Grimaldi laughed. "You had me worried when I could only see one headlight."

"We had to change cars and this one had a light shot out."

"I wonder who did that?"

Grimaldi hit the spotlight button and the combat helicopter's underslung lights threw dazzling illumination across the dark ground. The black Mercedes came to a stop in the center of the beams. The doors opened and Manning and James stepped out, pulling their collars around them as they ran for the helicopter. The access door hissed open as they reached *Dragon Slayer*, and the Phoenix Force pair climbed inside. The door closed behind them with a solid thump, shutting out the rain and wind. Manning and James dropped onto the long side seats, struggling out of the coats.

"I just had a weather check from Barb," Grimaldi said. "Isn't looking too good. The storm's set to hang in for a while yet. Stony Man is going to try to pick up something from the satellites, but no guarantees. We'll overfly the area and see if any of the guys activated a homing signal."

"Okay," James said. "Go when you're ready, Jack."

Grimaldi began his takeoff checks. "Clothing and weapons are in the compartments," he said. "I wasn't sure what you guys might need, so I brought pretty well everything I could get my hands on."

When James opened the equipment lockers he realized Grimaldi hadn't been joking. There was enough weaponry to start a small war. The clothing compartment had been similarly filled.

"Jack, you opening a store, or what?" Manning asked as he selected his gear.

"I know you hotshots. You've got a reputation for going through gear like Imelda Marcos went through shoes. So I upped the inventory a little."

"A little?" James remarked. "We could equip a small country with this stuff. Not that I'm complaining, Jack."

"You forgot who the bad guys are this time around? Only China. I think you might find you're still a couple of rounds short."

"If that happens, we'll bring you in to charm them into surrendering."

Grimaldi took *Dragon Slayer* into the stormy sky with a big smile on his face. He pumped up the speed, sending the sleek black combat chopper hurtling out over the water, his busy fingers activating the search facility. Within *Dragon Slayer*'s electronic heart the scanners and probes began their silent hunt for any signal put out by the missing Phoenix Force. If any of the signal devices had been activated, the seek-and-find capability of the helicopter would recognize them.

James, now clad in black combat gear, dropped into the seat next to Grimaldi's and asked for a map. The pilot handed him one covering the area between Hong Kong, the mainland and Li's island.

"From what we knew about the junk's trip, she was heading in this direction. The idea was to make a run past the island so our guys could size it up. Last thing we heard from them was they'd run into opposition and were in the middle of the storm. Then we lost all contact. Heard nothing since."

"So they could be anywhere within a hell of an area," Grimaldi pointed out.

"Yeah." James sighed. "And it's even bigger when you're trying to find something."

"There are a couple of other possibilities," Manning said. "Maybe the storm hit the junk so hard it sank. Or maybe they were captured by Li's security force."

"He always so optimistic?" Grimaldi asked.

"Something that happens with the onset of old age," James said.

"Ouch!" Grimaldi said.

From the weapons locker Manning passed out a pair of 9 mm Beretta 92-Fs. He followed with Heckler & Koch MP-5 subguns. Both he and James went through weapons-check procedures, loading and adding extra magazines for both weapons to their combat harness. There was a H&K G-3 sniper rifle stowed in the locker, which carried a 20-round magazine of 7.62 mm bullets and was fitted with a Zeiss telescopic sight. Manning took the rifle and placed it beside his backpack. Each man selected a knife and slid it into a belt sheath. Grenades followed, plus an assortment of smaller items each man chose specifically. Thinking ahead to what they might find when they located their teammates, James made sure he had a well-stocked medical kit in his backpack.

"Transceivers are in there, too," Grimaldi informed them. "I set them to my frequency. And there are some homing devices, as well, in case you guys get lost too."

"Everyone is a comedian today," Manning said as he located the transceivers.

Grimaldi busied himself with his tracking sensors, keying buttons that fed information to *Dragon Slayer*'s onboard computer system. He scanned the monitor screens on the control module, searching for anything that might indicate a sourced signal, shaking his head in disappointment when nothing showed. Leaving the sensors to do their work he checked his weapons, making sure all circuits were active. Chain gun. Rocket pods. He checked and double-checked, maintaining the link between the firing control and his helmet, which allowed him to aim and lock on to a target simply by looking at it. The curved console in front of him glowed with subdued light, readouts flickering as they scrolled across the screens. The helicopter was fully operational and ready for anything that might show up.

Behind Grimaldi, James and Manning went about their preparations in silence, concentrating their efforts into making certain that all their equipment was functioning correctly, that nothing was left to chance. Once they exited the chopper, dropping into unknown territory where anything could happen without warning, there would be no time for fixing something that had malfunctioned. In combat situations time wasn't a luxury. Things happened in the blink of an eye, and the enemy wouldn't stand back and wait while a jammed gun was cleared. The capability to respond instantly determined life or death.

The helicopter yawed suddenly as a powerful gust of wind slammed into it. Grimaldi corrected the drift and put the machine back on course. He was barely able to see beyond the canopy in front of him. Rain drove at them, smashing against the clear screen with a ferocity that was startling to see. Grimaldi's instinct and skill as a pilot, coupled with *Dragon Slayer*'s state-of-the-art electronics, kept the craft on a level, safe course.

"We should be close to the last point of reference in a few minutes," Grimaldi said over his shoulder. He watched his monitors. Still nothing.

"We keep looking until we find something," James said.

"We will," Grimaldi assured him.

Dragon Slayer flew on, into the darkness. They

were over the sea now, with little around them. Li's island lay to the west, the direction the storm was pushing. The sensors instructed the chopper to alter course and move in that direction, and Grimaldi noticed the autoresponse.

"Hey, we might have something here. The lady is changing direction."

James and Manning peered over his shoulder, watching the myriad banks of information scrolling down the monitors. They felt the slight roll as *Dragon Slayer* corrected course and settled into steady flight once more.

"Damned if she hasn't found something," Grimaldi said.

On screen a faint, steady blip appeared. Grimaldi touched a small keypad, increasing the on-screen image.

"Shit!" Grimaldi muttered.

"What?" Manning asked.

"We picked up a signal all right," Grimaldi said. He jabbed a finger at the monitor. "Problem is it's coming from Li's island."

Identifying the signal was only the start. Once they had verified there was something on the island, Grimaldi turned the around and headed out to sea.

"Hey, where're we going?" James asked. "I thought—"

"Don't worry, guys, we're going back. First we need reinforcements. Now settle down and relax. There's coffee in a flask behind you. Have a cup and decide how you want to tackle this setup."

Grimaldi poured on the power, taking *Dragon Slayer* over the waves at near sea level. His course was plotted and logged in to the onboard system, so he had little to do as far as staying on course was concerned. Flying *Dragon Slayer* had always been a pleasure. Now, with the latest refinements to both power plants and the electronic control system, it was easy. The combat helicopter's responses had never been better. The silent mode meant the machine could hover with barely a sound coming from her engines, and when it came to maneuverability, the helicopter simply had no match.

In the early hours Grimaldi brought the chopper down to a gentle landing in a corner of a military airfield. Behind-the-scenes discussions between political heavyweights from the U.S. and Taiwan had resulted in the granting of concessions where *Dragon Slayer* was concerned. A U.S. military adviser oversaw the covert presence of the chopper and the people who went with it. The Taiwanese authorities, themselves concerned over the possible expansion of Chinese superiority in the immediate area, were only too glad to allow the United States the opportunity of dealing with the matter.

As *Dragon Slayer* touched down and Grimaldi broke the hatch, allowing the cool air of the night to slide inside, James and Manning roused themselves. They had used the flight time to catch up on some needed sleep. As they stepped out of the chopper, feeling the chill of the predawn, they were both still bringing themselves to full awareness.

Despite their less-than-alert condition, neither failed to recognize the dry tones of Rosario Blancanales as he came out to meet them.

"Never fails. Let this bunch out alone and they just lose one another."

"Hello, Pol," Manning said.

"How's it going?" Lyons asked, wasting little time on greetings. "You locate any of the guys?"

"We did find a signal trace from one of the devices we'd picked up in Hong Kong. The only thing we know definitely is that it was on Li's island."

Grimaldi appeared, carrying a rolled-up chart. He had shut down *Dragon Slayer,* locking the access hatches when he had climbed out.

"Let's get inside and sort this out," he said.

A small hut had been allocated to the Stony Man teams. Once inside they were able to relax a little. Grimaldi spread the chart across a table and indicated points on the map.

"Hong Kong here. Li's island here. Our information is that the colonel is building his project on this island. Right so far?"

James nodded. "We don't know where the guys are. Or even how many survived abandoning the junk."

"What about the signal device that's working?" Schwarz asked.

"It's working, sure," James said. "But under what circumstances? For all we know it could be on a corpse. Maybe washed up on a beach."

"Okay," Lyons said. "The choice is simple. We go in. Twofold operation: to terminate Li's so-called project and to search for any survivors."

The discussions went on for the next half hour, during which the Stony Man teams were able to help themselves to coffee and food that had been provided by the U.S. liaison.

The plan of action finally decided upon was for Grimaldi to take them in the following evening under cover of darkness, then land *Dragon Slayer* in some secluded spot to be on hand when the call came for evacuation. There was also the added bonus of the combat chopper's powerful arsenal of weapons.

The teams took turns to get some rest as the daylight pushed away the shadows. Grimaldi spent most of the morning checking *Dragon Slayer* from stem to stern. He had the fuel tanks filled to the brim and made repeated checks on his communication equipment and computer setup.

Both SOG teams made sure all their own weaponry was fully functional. They equipped themselves with extra ammunition, grenades and explosives. The men carried small backpacks into which were packed the items they needed to take with them.

"What's the weather forecast?" Schwarz asked in the afternoon.

"By the time we go in, the storm should have blown itself out," Grimaldi said. "No guarantees, of course. Cloud formation is looking a little heavy. If it moves in our direction, we could get some more tricky weather."

"We can't be sure of the strength of Li's security on the island," James said. "We do know he has his own special troops out there, so we can't expect to just walk in and take over."

"From what we've learned about him, Li is no pushover. He's tough, and determined to complete this project," Manning said. "The way I read it, he's ambitious. This setup could do him a lot of good with the top brass in Beijing. If he pulls it off, he's going to be a favored man."

"We can't have that," Blancanales said. "No way."

CHAPTER NINE

At first Rafael Encizo couldn't remember a thing. He woke up to find himself draped across a wet, slime-covered slab of rock half submerged by the sea. Each time a wave came barreling in over the rock, catching Encizo in its grip, it threatened to drag him back into the deep water. Some inner survival instinct made him cling tightly, resisting the pull, and inch by pain-ful inch the Cuban fighter worked his way across the surface of the greasy rock until he was able to roll into a natural cleft, wedging himself in tight. He made that shallow crevice his bolt-hole, somewhere he could rest until he had regained some strength and a lot of his memories of the recent past.

As for his immediate situation, Encizo knew a few material things. He was cold. He was wet. His body ached from head to foot, and he had sustained a gash across his forehead that stung from contact with the seawater. He was still clad in his black combat suit. When he made a cursory check, he found that all he had with him was his Cold Steel Tanto knife, still secure in the sheath fixed to his belt. As he collected his thoughts and returned to the last few, hectic minutes on board the floundering junk, the little Cu-ban remembered that he had been in the process of getting his gear together. McCarter had ordered the preparation in case the unexpected happened. He wanted everyone to be ready. And that had been why Encizo had been checking his gear.

He remembered a sudden surge in the water, lashing wind and torrents of water smashing down on the boat, tossing it about as if it were nothing but a leaf in the wind. There had been no time for any organized evacuation of the junk. No one was that prepared. Above the roar of the waves and the battering wind Encizo had heard one last yell from McCarter, and then a great invisible hand took the vessel, lifting it.

Encizo was caught by the raging torrents of water. He felt himself picked up and dragged over the side. He felt buried in water as he was twisted and turned, plunged headfirst into the raging sea. He had gone under, barely snatching a breath of air before the salty chill of the sea grabbed at him and dragged him down. He struggled against it, knowing that if he didn't find his way to the surface he would drown.

He couldn't recall how long he was under. All he dimly recalled was suddenly being able to breathe again, sucking cold air into his starved, aching lungs. In those frantic moments he had twisted back and forth, searching for any signs of his teammates. He hadn't been able to see any of them. He was unable to see any farther than the next wavetop. He had been swept along by the moving body of water, dragged this way and that, unable to do a thing. He was a victim of the swirling currents. The biting cold of the water had eventually forced him to swim, if only to keep his blood circulating.

The power of the storm had increased, both wind

and rain adding to Encizo's difficulties. He was unable to chart his position. The heavy swell of the waves took him in different directions each time he tried to maintain a solitary course. In the end he had to go with the currents, hoping that he would see something, anything that might offer a way out.

His hopes had sunk as the driving storm refused to ease. Encizo might have given up and allowed himself to simply go under and end his torment, but he had a stubborn streak within him that refused to allow him to quit. He had endured and survived too many bitter experiences, both before and during his stint with Phoenix Force, and each time he had come out alive. As far as Rafael Encizo was concerned, this was no different. The circumstances might change with each situation, but the determination to stay alive was the same. He had too much to live for. Too many things he had to do in his life, so every day—every moment—was precious to him. To surrender to what some might term the inevitable never crossed his mind. It wasn't within him to lay down and say *I give in.* He would never do it.

Despite his struggles to stay conscious, Encizo had found himself starting to slip. He was ready to accept that if he did he might not awaken. But his weary body, resistance weakened by the increasing chill of the water and the constant downpour, begged for release. As the time drifted by, Encizo had found his attempts to keep his eyes open become more difficult. A number of times he had slipped beneath the surface, battling his way back each time. Once he was too late to stop seawater from filling his throat, and he had coughed and gagged for a long time after.

Pulled by the swirling currents, his eyes stinging

from the saltwater, Encizo had almost missed the dark bulk in his path. He blinked furiously, peering through the rain and the constant rising of the waves, hoping that he had seen something and wasn't hallucinating. For a while he thought he had imagined it, but suddenly it was there again, larger this time. And closer. Encizo realized he was looking at some kind of rock formation, jutting above the water. It had to be land. Or it might turn out to be a small rock, barely large enough for him to climb onto. He didn't give a damn. Anything was preferable to spending another minute in the water.

He had struck out for the rock, using his waning strength to fight against the current, and just when he thought he wasn't going to be able to fight any longer, the movement of the current changed and he found himself being pushed swiftly in the direction of the rock. Too quickly in fact. He had tried to backpedal, but the water had him then and it thrust him at the rock with increasing speed. The little Cuban found himself being lifted and realized he was in the center of a wave formation. He saw waves ahead of him dashing against the rock and breaking into a thousand watery droplets, filling the air with spray. Then he could hear the thunder of waves breaking and realized that what he was seeing was only part of a shoreline stretching beyond on either side. At least he was bearing down on something of substantial size.

Encizo's feet had scraped against submerged rock. He had tried to get a grip to slow his approach, but it had been no use. The gathering waves lifted him, and he was helpless in the grip of the surging water. He felt himself rising, being tumbled back and forth so that he lost all sense of direction. He had no way of knowing how close the rocks were, only that the thunder of the breaking water had become so loud it drowned out any other noise. Encizo rose, was held by the onrushing wave and then hurled forward.

He caught a fleeting glimpse of the rock an instant before he landed. The wind had slammed from his aching body as Encizo bounced across the slick, wet surface. A dull, aching pain swelled across his ribs on the left side where he had struck the unyielding surface of the rock. It made him catch his breath. A second wave crashed down over him, rolling him. Encizo's head crashed against the rock and he felt himself losing consciousness. Just before he had blacked out, he felt himself slithering back down the rock face, the waves crashing around him. His fingers clawed for a grip on the slippery surface of the rock, but he had been unable to maintain it. As he drifted into the blackness he had felt cold water lapping at his feet.

After that—nothing.

MEI ANNA GLANCED across the crowded boat and caught McCarter's eye. He gave her a cheery grin that raised her spirits. There was something about the Briton's attitude that wouldn't allow anyone to become depressed. He had typical British fortitude. It wouldn't let him get in a self-pitying mood. Whatever the situation the man would always be one step ahead, keeping up people's spirits and convincing them that no matter what they would come out the other side alive and still able—as the Americans said—to kick ass.

The young American looked as if he were cast in

the same mold. He was perched at the bow of the small boat, his weapon cradled in his arms as he maintained a constant watch. He had been the only one to keep hold of his SMG. There was something comforting in his manner. Brash, yet exuding an air of solid dependability that matched that of the Briton. On the surface they were different. Underneath, Mei decided, they were the same—men who had come into their profession with both eyes open to the horrors and the evil they would face, yet convinced of ultimate victory. They knew the score and in battle they would be as hard as any enemy, giving nothing and expecting no compromise. Despite their backgrounds still being shrouded in mystery, Mei realized that these men were specialists. Once they had completed their mission, they would vanish as quickly as they had appeared, leaving little trace of their true identities behind. One thing she did know. Their enemies would know them—those who lived. The dead wouldn't care.

Hawkins threw up a hand. The rowers ceased and the small craft glided along without a sound. Easing his way through the seated men, McCarter joined Hawkins.

"You see something?"

Hawkins pointed, and when McCarter checked he was able to make out a dark formation a few hundred yards ahead.

"Looks like solid land to me, boss," Hawkins said.

McCarter moved back to where Mei sat.

"What is it?" she asked.

"Land."

"I wonder where?"

"Sorry, Anna, they haven't left any signs up for

us. But I'll bet next month's paycheck it belongs to our chum Colonel Li.''

"It could also be one of the little islands in the area,'' Mei said.

"My gut feeling says it's Li's little paradise.''

"If it is, they'll pick us up on their radar.''

"Not likely,'' Hawkins said as he came within earshot. "I doubt we're big enough to be picked up. Being this low in the water is an advantage, too.''

"I hope you are right.''

"We'll find out soon enough,'' McCarter replied.

On his instruction Mei got the Chinese to paddle them in close to the rocky shoreline. It took a good half hour, maneuvering the boat among the rocks that edged the stony beach, before they were able to jump out and drag it onto the shore. With everyone helping they slid the boat into a shallow depression and hid it as best they could with seaweed, which they gathered from the abundance littering the shore.

"We need to establish just where we are, what we're up against. And we need to get hold of some weapons,'' McCarter said. He waited until Mei had translated for her people. "If we meet any of the island's occupants, be careful. Don't trust anyone until we can be sure they are hostile to Li. Anna, I know what you told me, but until we're certain, play it down. Some might still have decided Li is on their side. Finding that out by having a knife stuck in your side is just bloody stupid.''

Mei had been ready to challenge him but decided he had a point. It wouldn't hurt to be absolutely certain.

"Do we stay together, or break up into groups?'' she asked.

McCarter glanced around the group. "If we split up, we can cover more ground. We each take a direction and go out and scout it. All meet up back here before dark."

Mei explained to her people. They discussed the suggestion, occasionally glancing at McCarter to nod.

"It is agreed. Tsu Han and I will come with you. Jim, your Chinese is not good enough to get you through this."

"Can't argue that one, boss." Hawkins said.

"I could but there isn't time," McCarter replied.

Mei gave the word and her four people split into pairs and moved out, leaving McCarter to choose the direction they would travel.

Hawkins took the point and they began their slow trek across the island, unsure what lay ahead.

DAYLIGHT WAS CLEARING the sky. Although it was still cool, the day promised to be warm. Rafael Encizo opened his eyes and lifted his head. From his position he could see the open sky above him, scrappy clouds drifting across his field of vision.

Pushing upright, he eased the stiffness from his body. He was still cold, his damp clothing clinging to his body. He checked out the area before he made any moves that might be spotted from a distance. He was aware of his vulnerability and decided that his first priority was to locate a more secure hiding place. He scanned the shoreline and spotted a stand of trees a hundred yards up from his position. Making a final spot check, Encizo cut across the rocky shore and angled sharply in the direction of the trees. He kept low, moving in quick bursts, then pausing before moving again. It was impossible to be absolutely certain he wasn't being watched, so all he could do was to keep moving and try to reach his objective.

Encizo made it to the trees and moved to the far side of the stand, crouching in the shadows provided by the low branches, checking out the terrain ahead of him. Off to his right he could see what looked like the remains of a village—tumbledown wooden huts with their roofs partially caved in, and scattered remnants of furniture and implements. Grass and weeds had grown up around the base of the buildings. The place looked as if it had been deserted for some time.

He remained where he was for several minutes, checking out the immediate area. Nothing moved within his field of vision apart from tall grass swaying in a faint breeze. The Phoenix Force commando took his time, wanting to be sure the village *was* deserted before he moved in. When he did break from the trees he held his combat knife in his hand.

There was a faint smell of decay in the air. As Encizo reached the first hut, he passed a pile of rotting vegetation. Flies buzzed around the mound. Peering in through the open doorway, he spotted an untidy mess. Scattered furniture and broken clay pots lay on the dirt floor. He found the same state of chaos in all the other buildings. He got the impression the villagers had been forced to leave quickly and hadn't even been allowed time to gather their belongings.

His checks completed, Encizo paused beside the village well. He peered into the dark shaft and caught a glimpse of water at the bottom. A rope was attached to the crosspiece of wood at the head of the well. Taking the rope in both hands, he hauled on it and eventually was presented with a wooden pail filled with clear, cold water. Encizo tasted it carefully. It was fresh and clean. He drank only a little, aware of the folly of overindulging on an empty stomach, then splashed more on his face. The cold water stung the gash on his head, but he ignored that and made sure the wound was rinsed clean.

He sat with his back to the well, resting briefly, and his thoughts turned to his teammates, McCarter and Hawkins. What had happened to them? Had they ended up in the water, along with Mei Anna and her crew? And if so, how had they fared? They had at least been in the process of launching the rowboat. With luck they might have made it, and even then could be out on the water. Maybe they had made land—this island, or one of the others in the area. Encizo also admitted to the possibility they had been picked up by one of Li's patrol boats. There were, he realized, a number of combinations that could be applied to the fate of his partners.

He accepted, too, the possibility that they might not have made it. As much as he wanted to deny the fact, death came into the frame. Losing his friends was a fact Encizo lived with every day they were on a mission, and up to then fate had been kind to Phoenix Force. Nevertheless, he had to acknowledge that the time could come when one or more of them might not return from some battle zone. None of them were immortal. They could die just as easily as the next man, and death showed no distinction between the good or the evil.

Encizo cleared his mind of morbid thoughts. It was far too early to dismiss his teammates. He had no intention of writing them off as dead. Not until he had absolute proof. So until that happened he had them down as still alive, maybe somewhere close by, and that would stay with him while he carried on with the mission.

He made another tour of the village. On the far side from where he had come ashore he found tire tracks. Squatting, he examined the impressions and concluded that they were fairly recent. He saw where a light vehicle had stopped and the passengers had stepped out, moving around for a time. The footprints, like the tire marks, were recent. And so was the cigarette butt he found. Although it was damp, the paper surrounding the tobacco was still intact. Encizo broke the butt open and rubbed the tobacco between his fingers, sniffing the result. The tobacco still retained its odor. Reasonably fresh.

Deserted or not, the village had been visited recently. Within the past day or so. He cast about the area and found other tire tracks, those definitely old ones. The visits were regular.

Part of a patrol? A regular, military patrol?

Encizo allowed himself a smile as the implication sank home. It looked like his ordeal in the water had resulted in his being cast ashore on the very island he and Phoenix Force had been observing before the storm.

He studied the tire tracks, which cut toward the west. Heading back to their base? The only way he was going to find out was by following them. Encizo decided to do just that.

Why not?

He had nothing else to do at the moment, and he *was* still on mission time.

IT WAS AS IF THERE HAD BEEN no storm at all. The sky held a few scraps of white cloud. Otherwise it was blue. The sun had returned with a vengeance, casting its heat over the island. Steam rose from damp foliage.

They had stayed close to the shoreline, following the undulating terrain, with Mei Anna and Tsu Han directing them without hesitation. They seemed to know the island intimately.

"If we keep on this course," Mei informed them, "we will come to where that outflow pipe lies."

"Not much use to us without underwater gear," Hawkins pointed out.

"At this time the tide is out. The level of water in the pipe drops. It will stay that way until the tide begins to turn in the afternoon."

"Sounds easy when you say it like that," McCarter said.

"I didn't promise you it would be easy."

Tsu held up a warning hand, then gestured for them to find cover. Pulling back, they eased into a hollow close to a thorny run of bushes.

As they settled, the sound of chattering voices reached them. Then they saw a small group of men, dressed in civilian clothing, coming over the crest of a slope. If they had kept going, they would have met them head-on.

"It's all right," Mei said. "I know them. They are fishermen from the village along the coast."

"So?" Hawkins asked.

"So they could get us clean clothing. Maybe food."

"Yeah? And maybe run and tell Li we're on his turf."

"These people don't like Li. He came and took over their island. The only reason they are still here is because he makes them stay. If anyone passes the island, they think the fishermen are the only ones here.''

McCarter had been listening to Mei. He considered her words, deciding that she seemed to know what she was doing. Her past record had been good, so why not now?

"Go and talk to them. See what they think."

Mei stood and walked into view, calling to the fishermen. When they recognized her they gathered around her as if they had just met a long-lost relative.

"Let's see how they react when we show our white faces," Hawkins commented.

McCarter eased the Browning Hi-Power from under his belt.

"Give it a chance, chum. Give it a chance."

As Mei talked to the group, the fishermen began to look in the direction of the bushes. McCarter realized that she had brought them into the conversation, and before long the fishermen edged toward them.

"Come out," Mei called. "They want to see you."

McCarter stood. Next was Hawkins, then Tsu.

The fishermen clustered around the group, talking excitedly among themselves. One spoke directly to Mei.

"They want to know if it is true you have come to destroy Li."

"That's calling a spade a spade," Hawkins muttered so only McCarter could hear.

"I can make something up," Mei said, "or tell the truth to them."

"What the hell," McCarter said. "They've seen us

now. Can't go around shooting every civilian who sees us.''

Mei smiled at that. ''Jim, the hard man,'' she mocked him.

''Tell them what you bloody well like,'' McCarter said.

It took her no more than a couple of minutes to explain their presence to the fishermen. They nodded in understanding, turning to glance at McCarter and Hawkins from time to time.

''David, what's going on?'' Hawkins asked. ''We should be on the move. Not shooting the breeze with the locals.''

''They say they can help,'' Mei told McCarter.

''How?''

''In one of their fishing boats. They could sail close to the outlet pipe and get you directly over it. It would save you a lot of time, Jim. If you try on your own, you'll have to swim out from shore. You said yourself you have no underwater gear so you'd have to stay on the surface all the time. More likely to be spotted that way. And you would lose time.''

McCarter glanced at the fishermen.

''Tell me why.''

''Because they have little love for Li. Since he moved here, he's destroyed their way of life. Decimated the fish population by polluting the waters around the island. He has used them for slave labor building his project. A number of their friends died during that construction. Jim, they're fishermen, not fools. They understand what Li is doing. They know it isn't going to benefit the real people of China. It's just another game being played by the powermongers: raising a fist to the world so they can say China is strong, ready to defy you all. And while they're doing that the masses are suffering, being deprived their chances because the Beijing authorities still have the real power within China.''

''Pity you can't stand up and say that to their faces,'' Hawkins said.

''Unlike your country, we are denied even that right. In China you don't speak out against the authorities. Not if you want to stay free. Even one voice raised against them makes them run scared. So they come at night and arrest you. Send you hundreds of miles from your home and friends. Put you in some nameless prison and let you waste your years away in solitary confinement. They are frightened, gray old men desperate to hold on to power because they dare not let the real people gain control.''

''Destroying Li and his project isn't going to change things,'' McCarter pointed out.

''We understand that. But it will at least delay their selfish plans. Take away Li's electronic devices, and the shift in power won't happen. His scheme to alter the balance will crumble. The colonel will also lose face, and Beijing will distance itself from him because they deny his project exists.''

''She doesn't need us, boss. She's got it all worked out.''

McCarter shook his head. ''We all need one another on this one. Let's get to it, Anna. Now, did I hear you say these blokes might be able to find us some food?''

THE TIRE TRACKS LED Encizo to a dead end.

Or so it appeared until he took time to check out the immediate area. He had been traveling for more than an hour when the trail he was following petered out at a jagged rock mass. Encizo slumped to the ground, massaging his aching side, and scanned the area to see if the tire tracks had turned off. They hadn't. He checked the trail's end again, shaking his head when he saw the reason.

The rock face was nothing more than a camouflaged entrance. Taking a closer look, Encizo made out the edges of the net concealing the opening that had allowed vehicles to penetrate the interior.

He sat back, hidden by tangled grass, and contemplated his next move. This was the reason Phoenix Force had made the trip from Hong Kong. The mission objective. Encizo's problem was his lack of backup. He was on his own, and at this point he had no way of knowing the strength of the opposition. His lack of weapons and equipment was also a drawback, but not a reason for defeat. Rafael Encizo was nothing if not creative. He would, if necessary, find some way to advance the mission.

He picked up the sound of voices. They were coming from off to his right, and getting closer. Encizo scanned the vicinity. A group of six men appeared, four of them were in the uniform of the Chinese military. The other two wore civilian clothing.

Encizo's hand dropped to his sheathed combat knife in a purely reflex motion. He eased back, following the course the men took as they made their way past the concealed entrance, pausing to discuss some point. One of the uniformed men crouched and pointed at the ground. A second man spoke into a com unit he was carrying. After a short pause Encizo saw a dark-colored rod emerge from the ground and extend to a height of about ten feet. It had to be some kind of communication aerial, he thought, part of the underground complex. The group gathered around it, still conversing. After another communication via the hand unit, the aerial withdrew. The group nodded and smiled to one another, turning and retreating the way they had come.

The Phoenix Force commando circled them, keeping the group in sight as they walked around the outcropping. At a specific point they paused, and one of the uniformed men pulled open a door set into the rock, camouflaged to blend in. In single file the group stepped inside, and the door was closed behind them. From his observation point Encizo smiled to himself. It had been nice of them to show him the way in.

The faintly audible crunch of boots on gravel just behind him warned Encizo he was no longer alone. He glanced to one side without moving and saw the shadow on the ground. The extended outline of a rifle barrel and bayonet told him his visitor was armed, and the metallic click of a safety being released suggested the visitor's intentions were less than hospitable.

Encizo remained in position hoping to convey that he was still unaware of his visitor. It gave him brief, but useful seconds in which to ease his right hand across his body and grip the handle of the combat knife. A sharp command in Chinese clearly indicated that the armed man wanted Encizo to stand. This he did, twisting his body to cover his hand on the knife. Coming upright, Encizo turned his head to position his would-be captor. He saw a lone soldier, clad in the baggy, ill-fitting tunic and pants that were standard in the Chinese military. The man was about Encizo's height, which made the Cuban's next move less of a problem. Continuing his turn, he slid the knife free of the sheath. Increasing the speed of his turn, Encizo reached out with his left hand to knock the muzzle of the rifle aside, then swept up his right hand in a deadly curving arc. The blade sliced across the soldier's throat, deep and wide. He made a single gurgling sound before he let go of his rifle and clutched at his throat. Blood spurted between his fingers as he tried to stem the flow. He stepped back, his eyes flicking back and forth as if he were desperately seeking help. But there was none. He had thrown his dice in the game of life and death, and he had lost.

Encizo had already snatched up the discarded rifle. It was a version of the Soviet AK-47 that the Chinese had designated Type 56. It had a folding bayonet fixed to the underside of the barrel. Nothing very sophisticated, but it would do the job it had been made for.

After checking to insure the rifle was fully loaded, Encizo folded the bayonet, clicking it into the locked position, and hung the weapon from his shoulder by the strap. He crossed to where the Chinese soldier lay. The man was dead, the dusty ground around his head dark with blood. Grabbing the man's tunic, the Phoenix Force commando dragged him out of sight behind the nearest outcropping. He went through the man's belt pouches and located two full magazines for the rifle and stuffed them into one of his big zip pockets.

Killing one of the enemy had committed Encizo. There was no turning back now. Sooner or later the man was going to be missed and his body would be found. That would raise the alarm, and in that event,

Encizo was going to have the full might of Colonel Li's island force on his tail. With that ahead of him the most useful thing Encizo could do, against the odds or not, would be to go for the mission objective—the total eradication of the project. He had no idea how he was going to achieve that yet, but it was to be his sole purpose. As long as he was able, the Cuban had to make an attempt at carrying through Phoenix Force's mission.

CHAPTER TEN

Stony Man Farm, Virginia

"According to the satellite scans, the storm has moved on. The area we're interested in is clear for the moment," Barbara Price said. She stood by one of the big wall monitors in the War Room, tracing the section with her finger. "Aaron has run an update, and it shows that the weather is going to remain unsteady. Some heavy cloud formations are in the vicinity, which could bring in more bad weather. That's out of our hands, unfortunately."

"Let's hope it stays clear for the present," Yakov Katzenelenbogen said.

"Okay," Price continued. "Able has joined up with Cal and Gary. The first solid report we got was that Jack had picked up a signal from one of the devices David had obtained from the Chinese group. According to his report, the signal was coming from Li's island."

"That could be interpreted in two ways," Katz said. "One of the guys is on the island, but we don't know what his status is—free and clear or in the hands of Colonel Li's people."

"There's a third possibility," Price said. "That the signal device washed ashore on its own."

None of them wanted to accept that, but it was an option they couldn't ignore. Losing any members of Phoenix Force would be a devastating blow to the entire SOG organization. They all knew it could happen. At any time. Once the teams were in the field they lost the protection of Stony Man. The Farm became nothing more than a distant voice, heard over communication setups. It could advise and guide them, provide all kinds of information and contacts. But there was no protection from an enemy bullet, or a sudden turn of events that might leave them exposed and entirely alone. No matter how good the computers or the other electronic equipment, none of it could shield them from the harsh realities of a combat zone. Or the whim of Nature when she decided to brew a storm out of the blue.

"I prefer the first two options," Katz said.

The Israeli, ex-commander of Phoenix Force, knew his people well. They had been a family, working, playing and fighting through countless missions. Each man knew the others as well as himself. And they trusted one another implicitly. If there was one thing Katz did know, and held on to, it was that Phoenix Force was capable of extraordinary achievements. They had a survival instinct that would have been the envy of Nature's best. And despite the current lack of information about McCarter and his team, Katz refused to let go. His people were still alive. They had to be.

He knew they weren't indestructible—the difference between life and death was only a sliver away.

The brief moment of reflection over, they got down to business.

"We've received confirmation from the Navy. Their sub will be intercepting that cargo ship very soon." Brognola cleared his throat. "The President has given the go-ahead for the ship to be stopped and searched."

"Sensitive stuff," Price said. "Let's hope they find what they're looking for."

"I've been looking at the initial reports coming in from the team checking out the bottling plant. With Able Team arriving when they did, the fires were put out before they could do a great deal of damage," Katz said.

"What have they found?" Brognola asked.

"Makes interesting reading. The Chinese took the place over twelve months ago. They let the existing people run it, with their people in select positions. From what we've found, the plant was a clearing-house for stolen information. A great deal was picked up by the employees who collected the empty bottles and left fresh ones. The information on disks was placed inside a specially constructed cavity in the tube holding the empty plastic cups. All the collector had to do was slip the disk out while he refilled the tube. Disks are thin enough to be concealed easily, and who would think to check the guy coming in to change the water bottle? A regular visitor who comes maybe twice a week in some instances. Very few people even give him a second glance."

"Damn well worked in this case," Brognola said.

"Too well," Price added. "Katz, did the team find anything else?"

"It appears that one of the offices had been set up

as a secure area. The place had a number of computers, all linked and capable of handling the kind of information being brought in. A great deal of the stored data had been deleted, but sometimes even deleted material can be rescued. Although it appears to have been fully wiped, the computer sometimes stores it in a remote area within its own memory banks. Using the right kind of technology, it's possible to reach in and pull it out."

"What about the stuff the guys found in the getaway cars?"

"Quite a find. Lists of names, locations, bank accounts. The Chinese were pulling out of San Francisco, but they weren't abandoning their data pool. I figure they were intending to move on and set up shop again somewhere else. The stored data will pinpoint people working for them, companies they've infiltrated. It will point the finger at a significant number of people who are going to be extremely embarrassed when all this comes out."

"Are we talking Americans here?" Price asked.

Katz nodded. "Ray Dakin and Alexander Delmont weren't the only ones. You'll hear of a number of arrests over the next few weeks."

"I hope they lock them up for life," Price said.

"I do like someone with an impartial viewpoint," Katz stated wryly.

"In this case I don't feel very impartial. Not when it comes to people selling out their country."

"No arguments from me," Katz said.

"To summarize," Brognola said. "We seem to have contained the situation at home, but the scenario in the field is unclear at present."

"Simply put," Price agreed, "but accurate. We

have, gentlemen, time to sit back and see what happens. At this moment it's all we can do.''

The Island

THE FISHERMAN LED THEM back to their settlement by a circuitous route that avoided the armed patrols Colonel Li maintained. Although outwardly peaceful, the island was run like a military base, with checks made on the fishermen in case they resorted to anything liable to upset the regime.

As he listened to the fishermen talking to Mei, partially through her translation and partially through his knowledge of basic Cantonese, McCarter evolved a picture of life on Li's island. He also began to see what kind of a man the colonel was.

In the Briton's own vernacular Colonel Li was a paranoid nutcase. The man was obsessed with his island and what he was creating. His vision of a high-tech electronic power base had completely taken him over. He thought of nothing else. His devotion to the project had become all-consuming. His underground facility had become the reason for the island's existence. His special force team, which looked after security, was feared for its savagery and its harsh attitude toward the islanders. Although the settlement had been maintained and the people retained, it was merely for show, to dissuade anyone, foreign or Chinese, from the notion that anything untoward was taking place. In reality it was a naive pantomime. Mei Anna and her Pro-Democracy group had found out about the island and its secrets. They had made two low-key visits to the island, checking out the construction in its early stages, and during their second trip Mei had made contact with the fishermen, promising them that she would be back with the intention of destroying Li's facility. That had been some months earlier, and though the fishermen hadn't given up hope, they had begun to wonder when she would return.

Now she had, bringing with her two foreigners, an Englishman and an American. Mei had explained that McCarter and Hawkins were part of a team sent to find out what Li was up to. They were also under instructions to destroy anything they found.

As they squatted on the hard-packed dirt floor of one of the huts, eating bowls of rice and steamed fish, sharing jars of home-brewed rice wine, McCarter extracted scraps of information from the fishermen. The fact that he could speak their language, albeit slowly and not always correctly, fascinated and delighted the fishermen. They were a hardy lot, lean and wiry, their faces burned brown from exposure to the sun and the salt-laden wind. They spent their lives hunting the sea for fish and seldom went far from the island. It was the place of their ancestors, once a holy island where Chinese monks had maintained a temple. Those days had gone, swept away during the tide of communism when religious freedom fell under the heel of the Marxist credo. Many of the monks had died, refusing to abandon their faith, while others had fled into exile. Even now the fishermen and their families hoped for a return to the old days when China had a soul of her own, not an ideology forced upon its people and kept in power through repression and terror.

One of the fishermen showed McCarter the ruins of what had been the island's temple. The structure was derelict now, overgrown and a long way from its former glory. The old man had spoken of the time when the island had been a good place to live. Now, he said, it was only his faith that kept him there.

"Perhaps one day it will change," McCarter said.

The old man had scratched at his thin white beard with a bony hand. "Only if I live into my second century."

"Hopefully that rather than Colonel Li completing his first."

The old man found that amusing. He was still chuckling when McCarter, hearing a soft sound behind him, turned to find Mei Anna listening, a smile on her lips.

"Quite the charmer, Jim," she said. "You've made that old man happy."

"From what I've heard, all these people deserve to be happy."

"And you'd like to give them happiness?"

McCarter shrugged, a little embarrassed.

"Don't go all coy on me now." She leaned forward and catching him off guard, kissed him soundly.

"Next you'll be telling me you've never done that before."

"Not likely," he replied.

The old man touched Mei's arm and spoke to her quietly. McCarter didn't catch whatever he said. It made her burst into laughter, and also made her blush hotly. She glanced at McCarter, her eyes bright with mischief.

"So what did he say?" McCarter demanded.

Mei shook her head. "I dare not repeat it."

McCarter looked at the old man, who was standing with a wide, toothless grin on his face.

The old man gestured to McCarter and led him up

the dusty slope to the temple. They walked the ground where hundreds had most probably trodden over the decades. There, though only a short distance from the settlement, the atmosphere held an air of calm. Even McCarter, no religious man, felt at peace. The old man walked up the worn steps, staring into the temple. McCarter could hear the soft chanting as the old man repeated his mantra, drawing himself into a state of inner concentration. With this simple sound the old man allowed himself to be drawn into the enveloping peace of mind he took from his devotions.

"Here, as in most of China," Mei explained, "the islanders follow Mahayana Buddhism, developed over the years into its present form."

"Do you follow it?" McCarter asked.

Mei's smile held a trace of regret. "Not as much as I used to. Perhaps I have become a nonbeliever."

"Maybe you just need to find the path again."

"Yes, I know. When all this is over. Was that what you were going to say?"

"Anna, I'm the last one to give opinions on other people's lives. Not with my track record."

Their brief reverie was disturbed when Hawkins appeared at their side.

"Hate to bother you folks," he said, "but we have company on the way."

"Let's move," McCarter snapped. He grabbed Mei's arm and pushed her toward the settlement. "I'll tell the old man."

There was no need. Already on his feet the old man gestured sharply for them to go ahead. As they retraced their steps, they could hear him chiding them like a shepherd chasing his flock.

When they reached the islanders' clearing, Tsu Han was waiting, his face anxious.

"Tell them we're leaving," McCarter said to Mei. "If they're questioned and they can't talk their way out, they can say we threatened them with guns."

Mei related his words and the fishermen nodded, then ushered them to the far end of the settlement. Tsu took the lead, taking them away from the straggle of huts and the bamboo frames supporting the nets. They slipped quickly and silently into the bushes that fringed the area beyond.

Glancing back over his shoulder, McCarter saw a cloud of dust as vehicles entered the settlement. Someone started to yell through a megaphone, the commands strident, and even Mei paused as she picked up the message.

"What?" McCarter asked.

"They are asking if they have seen any foreigners. White devils."

"Hell, I thought they only said things like that in Charlie Chan movies," Hawkins said.

"In propaganda they still resort to crude descriptions. Remember that many people in China are still peasants. They lack the sophistication of western people, mainly because they are denied international contact through the media. The Beijing regime finds that keeping information at a basic level satisfies the mass of the population in isolated rural areas."

"Crude or not," McCarter said, "I don't want to be responsible for any harm coming to those people."

"If it happens, there isn't a thing we can do, Jim," Mei said. "Your priority is to get to Li's base and destroy it. Isn't that why you are here?"

ENCIZO'S PROBLEM started and ended with the Chinese soldier he had killed.

At first he felt he needed to maintain a close watch over the entrance to Li's base, but he also had the dead soldier concealed not far away. However he played it, Encizo realized that he couldn't stay where he was in case the dead man's companions came looking for him and stumbled across his killer. If he distanced himself from the body, he was going to lose his vantage point.

It came down to a simple choice. Did he compromise himself for the sake of maintaining an easy oversight of the entrance, or did he move away and conceal himself until nightfall? Encizo weighed the odds and decided that if he was going to breach the entrance it would be better to do it at night, and so his present objective was to hide himself and take his chances on the discovery of the dead soldier.

He wriggled back into the undergrowth, keeping low and never once taking his eyes off the terrain. He knew that sooner or later the missing man would prompt a search. Once the soldier was found to be dead, then that search would widen. Before that happened, Encizo needed to find himself a good place to hide.

His slow speed meant it took him some time to distance himself from the entrance. Encizo had it fixed in his mind, so finding it again wouldn't be difficult. He knew the location, and that was half the battle. Even the most carefully camouflaged object was easily discernible to a person who had spotted it before. Blending in with the surroundings brought its own problems. Though the concealment worked from a distance, due to undulations in the terrain and the camouflage itself, there were angles and shadows, distortions and textures that were more apparent in close proximity. He would be able to find the spot again with no trouble.

In the end Encizo settled for a deep overhang of rock where he was able to wriggle his body into the fissure beneath. Once he was installed, he found he could see the defined track that was obviously used by Li's forces as they traveled the island. He pulled himself farther in, making sure that the metal of his weapon wasn't catching the light. A reflection from the barrel would give away his position within seconds.

Encizo bedded himself down as comfortably as he could, searching out pebbles that would cause discomfort as he lay prone until dark. He thought he had eliminated them all, but found there was still something digging into his hip. It took him a while before he realized that it was no pebble but something in the pocket of his blacksuit. Encizo unzipped the pocket and reached inside, pulling out the forgotten black, rectangular signal device McCarter had handed out. Only now did he recall slipping the compact device in his pocket as he had bent over his pack on the shifting, waterlogged deck of the floundering junk. He stared at the object and saw the tiny, red winking light embedded in the top edge of the transmitter. He had activated the thing before slipping it into his pocket, closing the zip seconds before the yawing deck and a massive wave had pitched him into the sea.

Encizo wondered whether the signal had been picked up by James and Manning on their receiver. If so, had they acted on it? And had they picked up any signals from the others? He could only speculate. He had no way of knowing where they were, or even whether any of them were still alive. If they were, the same thought might have occurred to them concerning *his* whereabouts.

He dropped the device back in his pocket and closed the zipper. Pulling his weapon close to his body, he closed his eyes and tried to catch up on a little rest. One way or another he was going to have a busy night.

HAWKINS SPOTTED the tank tracks. They weren't new, probably a couple of days old. He called McCarter over and pointed them out.

"Bloody great. Now we've got a Chinese tank squad roaming about the place."

"Hardly that," Mei said. "There are a couple of lightweight tanks based on the island. They're old models. Not very fast."

"Is this Li paranoid, or what?" Hawkins asked. "Is he expecting a full-scale attack from Taiwan?"

"Li is very strong on the defense of his project," Mei said. "He'll do anything to keep it from being compromised."

Tsu Han attracted their attention.

"I see them, too," Hawkins said.

A quarter mile away, three uniformed soldiers and an officer were climbing out of a jeep. The officer spoke to them and the group began to advance across the rocky terrain.

"If they keep in this direction they'll spot us sooner or later," McCarter said. He glanced around the immediate area, seeking some handy place where they could hide. There was little choice. The rocky section they were crossing had little to offer in the way of real cover.

"Right now we really do need to cover our asses," Hawkins said.

"Tell me about it," McCarter replied.

With the force at the settlement behind them and this new group ahead, there were few places they could go. McCarter saw that the minute they emerged from their present position, the lay of the land would leave them fully exposed.

He took out his Browning, checking that it was ready for use. The others did the same.

"You good at bluffing?" McCarter asked Mei.

"What have you got in mind, Jim?"

"How would those blokes down there react if you walked Hawkins and me in at gunpoint. We'll have our hands on our heads like we were captured. How close could we get before they realized you and Tsu weren't from the island?"

"I don't know," Mei replied, "and I'm not sure I want to find out. You realize what you are suggesting is insane?"

"It won't be long before those guys from the settlement move this way," Hawkins pointed out. "Then we'll be stuck between a rock and a hard place. That means—"

"I know what it means," Mei said. "I saw *The Magnificent Seven* on TV. Jim, are you saying you will walk up to those soldiers unarmed and risk being shot on sight?"

"I don't believe Colonel Li wants us dead yet. If he's as suspicious as you imply, he'll want to know who sent us, why we're here and what we know." McCarter grinned at her. "Wouldn't you?"

"I'm *not* Colonel Li, Jim."

"It's a gamble. So is getting out of bloody bed every day. Oh, and by the way, I'm not that suicidal. We'll have our pistols stuck in the back pockets of our suits."

"Let's do it," Hawkins said. "At least it gives us a fighting chance before those others walk up behind us."

Mei relayed the conversation to Tsu Han. The scarred man eyed McCarter, then nodded. There was no need for any translation.

THE OFFICER IN CHARGE of the patrol watched the four figures heading down the slope in his direction. The group he was watching comprised two white men, hands on their heads, walking ahead of two Chinese, who held guns on the prisoners. He smiled to himself when he realized that these had to be part of the group the colonel had been raving about. Li's anger had been a fearsome thing to witness. Not a man in the security force dared make a sound or a move while Li was having his wild moments. The man became unreasonable, his rage terrifying in its intensity.

The moment he had heard about the destruction of one of the patrol boats, he had ordered out a second one, despite the storm that had dropped to cover the area. The second boat had gone out and had managed to destroy the junk. Li's people hadn't been so lucky with the crew of the vessel. They had managed to escape in a small rowboat, vanishing into the storm, leaving the patrol boat crew to look to their own survival. The patrol boat had barely reached the island intact. The storm had severely damaged it, but Colonel Li hadn't concerned himself with that. His only worry was that the crew of the junk had escaped. From that moment the island was on full alert in case any of the junk's crew had made it to shore alive. If they had, Li was convinced they were coming to destroy the project. His priority was protecting his brainchild, his control center, which would be even better than the American original on which it was based. The project was Li's opportunity to show the Beijing bosses his skill at creating a superweapon that would rival the Americans'. The colonel saw it as his ladder for stepping up in the hierarchy. He had his eye on loftier things within the government itself, and he was an old hand at playing the game. He had worked his way into the good books of several influential members, who in turn, had brokered his deal for the project. They had given him their patronage. If all went according to plan, the colonel would most likely find himself a place on one of the influential government panels. A man with a voice. It was Li's goal.

So when things started to go wrong, Li vented his rage on those around him. His anger only increased as he received reports that other matters weren't working to plan. But he refused to slow down. He simply changed his plans, looking elsewhere for his backup, pursued those he thought responsible, and even when that didn't work out as he had expected, still carried on, pushing everyone that much harder.

The whole of his island security force was under threat. It was up to them to scour the island and make sure that the interlopers, if they had survived and had actually reached the island, were to be located and taken prisoner. They weren't to be killed. If they were captured, he wanted to interrogate them personally.

The officer stepped forward, drawing his pistol as he neared the group. He ordered his squad to move forward, ready to take charge of the two foreigners. He eyed them as he moved closer. They were tall men, clad in some kind of one-piece suit made from a black material. Combat clothing, he decided, just like that worn by the two Chinese who had them—

Something sounded alarms inside his head.

Just like the clothing worn by the Chinese.

But that couldn't be so. He had assumed the Chinese to be from the fishing settlement, but then they would have been wearing the same type of handwoven, basic clothing as all the other fishermen. Not black combat suits. And not on a woman. The "prisoners" weren't captives.

McCarter became aware of the man's suspicions in the same instant the officer realized his mistake. He saw it in the man's changing expression, which moved quickly from one of triumph to one of surprise mingled with anger.

The man had seen through their deception, but it had lasted long enough to give them their fighting chance.

The officer raised his pistol, aiming the muzzle at McCarter.

"Now!" the Briton yelled, dropping to a crouch to give Mei a clear shot as he went for the Browning tucked into the rear pocket of his blacksuit.

At McCarter's side Hawkins executed the same move.

Mei, directly behind McCarter, fired the opening shot. She already had her weapon up, and she triggered it with dead accuracy, drilling a single bullet directly between the eyes of the startled officer. He keeled over, his finger jerking the trigger of his own weapon, discharging a bullet into the empty sky.

McCarter, Hawkins and Tsu chose their targets and fired. The crackle of shots filled the air as the firefight blossomed briefly, then faded. Only one of the Chinese got off a shot, a single trigger-pull that put a bullet between McCarter and Hawkins. The soldier had no opportunity to fire a second time. He was already dying, his heart pierced by twin shots from the Phoenix Force leader's Browning.

"Let's move," McCarter snapped. "Bring their weapons and ammo."

He ran to the jeep, although that was no true description of the vehicle. It was an extremely basic affair—little more than four wheels and an engine, with a light body. It made the original U.S. jeep look like a Cadillac. McCarter got behind the wheel as the others piled in behind him, carrying the scavenged weapons and ammunition. He got the engine started and worked the gearshift to get the vehicle moving. It lurched forward as he fought the loose clutch.

"Head in that direction," Mei said. "Highest point on the island. It should give us a good look at the area."

McCarter stepped on the gas, finding the jeep surprisingly fast. Despite its ugly appearance, the vehicle had plenty of power under its flat hood. The steering was heavy, pulling to the left, and he had to hang on to the wheel with both hands to keep it on a straight course.

In the back of the jeep, Hawkins and Tsu were checking over and loading the weapons they had confiscated. There were three Chinese rifles and the pistol the officer had been carrying, which was an adapted version of the German Mauser designated the Type 80. Although it had been around for a long time, it was still an accurate, dependable weapon.

"Not exactly state-of-the-art," Hawkins said, "but better than nothing."

"Don't be a snob," McCarter told him. "As long as they fire when we need them, they'll do fine."

"They will fire," Mei said.

"How can you be so sure?" Hawkins asked.

She turned to look at him. "Because they were made in China."

"She's got you there, mate," McCarter said.

Chinese Mainland

"THIS IS GETTING out of hand," Shun Wei had yelled when the news reached them. The rage in her voice was reflected in her eyes, which glittered with fury. "What are you going to do?"

Li regarded her over the rim of his wineglass.

"I could pay for the funeral," he said quietly.

Shun Wei stared at him as if she couldn't believe what she had heard. His serenity on receiving the news of Xan Hung's death in Hong Kong had surprised her greatly. She had been expecting him to lose control. Instead, he had stared at the telephone receiver in his hand before replacing it in its cradle.

"You realize that one of our most important contacts is dead?"

"Wei, I am not an imbecile, nor am I going to pretend that the death of Hung has caused me any pain. I used him for what he could provide when to build the project, and for his expertise in transporting people and information. With the death of Djin Shu a lot of things have changed, like our need for Xan Hung. To be truthful, I was finding his association tiresome. He was, after all, nothing more than a common gangster."

"You knew that when you took him on."

"I know. That was *why* I asked for his help. His connections and expertise were useful then, but we outgrew him. And the actions of his people in Hong Kong have done little to enhance his credibility. He was becoming superfluous to requirements. Getting himself killed has saved me the trouble."

"Do you feel the same about Kwai?"

"He was useful and would have remained so. His ability to assassinate efficiently would have kept him employed for a long time. However, he must have allowed himself to become a little slipshod. If not, he would still be alive. Killing that British agent, Hallam, should have been easy work for him. Why he walked into opposition we will never know."

"Too much has gone wrong in a short time," Shun said. "You must be careful, Cheng. The project has to be completed and these interlopers must be destroyed."

Li sipped his wine, only half listening to her tirade.

"Cheng?"

He glanced at her and smiled. "Of course, my dear," he said. "It will all be taken care of."

"Perhaps you should be getting back to the island. Do you trust those idiots out there to handle something like this without your guidance?"

"The helicopter is already on its way."

Shun slumped into a chair, still angry. Li knew

what was upsetting her. She had visions of him failing, of something going wrong and the project being destroyed. If that happened, his opportunity for promotion would be compromised, and if that happened Shun Wei would be a very unhappy woman. Although Li wanted the glory a successful conclusion would bring, Shun Wei wanted it more. She saw it as a once-only opportunity, a golden chance to become known and accepted. Her disappointment if things went wrong would not be a pleasant thing to see.

Stony Man Farm, Virginia

"MESSAGE FROM the Navy sub," Akira Tokaido said. "They have the ship in sight and they're closing fast."

"Where are they exactly?" Carmen Delahunt asked.

He studied the readout, then crossed to one of the wall maps, checking the position and tapping the map with his finger.

"Just about here," he said.

"Are they going to board her?"

Barbara Price put down her coffee mug.

"The President has sanctioned an all-scenario operation. In other words if they have to, the Marine contingent on the sub can take that action. It depends on the reaction of the ship."

"Take a look, people," Kurtzman said.

He transferred the image from his monitor to all the others in the room. Everyone was able to see the satellite image of the *Blue Water*. Kurtzman manipulated his image and the satellite scan moved in closer. The ship could be seen moving slowly across the surface of the sea. White trails were left behind as the ship cleaved the water.

"What if the ship calls for help?" Tokaido asked. "I mean, won't the Chinese send in one of their subs? Or fighter jets?"

"It will be interesting to see how they react," Price said. "If our assumptions are correct, they should ignore any contact. If we go for the ship, the Chinese will know we're on to their game. Deniability is the most likely option. If they show their hand, it indicates they know what's on board that ship, and that could lead to the truth coming out—that they have been stealing U.S. technology and are intending to use it in a provocative manner. They would have to do a lot of explaining, and one way or another, their neighbors aren't going to be happy."

"And just lately the Chinese have been doing their best to show cooperation with the U.S.," Delahunt commented. "Allowing trade deals to be completed, opening up the barriers, making nice on one hand, playing dirty behind our backs."

"Political maneuvering," Price said.

Tokaido shook his head in frustration.

"Politics is something I'll never understand. I mean, we all know what's going on. So do the Chinese. But we all pretend it isn't happening. Man, it could drive you crazy. I think I'll stick to my music."

He pulled on his headphones and went back to his computer.

"Hey, look," Huntington Wethers said.

They all turned to check the monitors and were in time to see the sleek dark outline of the Navy sub as it broke the surface and came alongside the *Blue Water*.

"Fingers crossed," Price said. "This is where it could all turn nasty."

CHAPTER ELEVEN

The Island

They drove to a point where they could look back on the settlement. McCarter had a bad feeling about the place, and his intuition proved correct. With the jeep parked in the shadow of a high outcropping, they bellied down on an overlooking ridge and saw that the place was in ruins. The huts had been wrecked and their contents had been scattered around the area.

What incensed McCarter even more was that bodies strewed the wrecked huts. He felt his anger rising, tinged with regret because he felt partly responsible for what had happened. His unwelcome presence on Li's island had generated the hunt that had brought the security force to the settlement and the violence that had followed.

The Briton drew back from the ridge, silent as he stared out across the barren hillside. His feelings were mixed. His need to lash out grew with every passing moment.

"Jim, don't blame yourself."

Mei was by his side, reaching out to touch his arm. He glanced at her, his face still showing the anger he felt.

"I'll bet they refused to tell them anything. That's why they were attacked. You know it and I know it."

"It was their choice, Jim. It was something they could do because they chose to. Not because Beijing said it was the way they had to think and act. It was a free choice, a decision they made regardless of the consequences. It's why we're here. You and I. To try to stop Li and all the others who want to keep China under their thumb."

"Anna, you could talk the birds out of the trees," McCarter said.

"It's a lousy job, Jim, but someone has to do it."

Tsu spoke briefly to Mei.

"He is going to work his way down to the settlement and take a look," she explained.

McCarter crossed to where Hawkins squatted, his rifle resting between his knees.

"I don't like the look in your eyes, David."

McCarter explained that Tsu was going to take a closer look at the destroyed village.

"Want me to go with him?"

McCarter smiled at Hawkins's intuition.

"Take care, mate," he said.

The pair vanished from sight, leaving McCarter and Mei to keep watch from the ridge and to provide covering fire.

"Alone at last," she said after some time.

McCarter glanced at her, then reached up to rub his unshaven jaw.

"And me not looking my best."

"But if we were walking along the Embankment, with the Thames shining under a full moon?"

"Looking for a side-street café for an egg-and-bacon breakfast?"

"And they say Englishmen are not romantic."

From below they heard a shout. Hawkins was standing in the open, waving for them to join him.

McCarter and Mei made their way down and entered the settlement. Up close the devastation was even worse. The casualties were all around them, bodies lying in the awkward postures of death, flies already gathering to hover over them.

"What bloody need was there?" McCarter stormed. "These poor buggers were no threat."

"But they knew we were here," Mei said. "Li's men would have wanted to know how many. What we were going to do. Where we were."

"Their own people." McCarter walked among the dead, surveying the brutalized corpses. Most of them had been beaten and run through with bayonets as they lay helpless on the ground. He stood over the body of the old man, remembering the mischief in his eyes and the reverence when he had walked to the ruins of the temple.

"The regime has no time for anyone who stands against it," Mei said. "Look what they did to the innocent protesters in Tiananmen Square. They sent armed troops and tanks out to disperse a crowd of civilians. Jim, they were their own people, too."

"Let's get out of here," McCarter said. "I'm finished playing games with this bloody Colonel Li. It's time we got on with what we came for."

He looked around for Tsu and joined him.

"Tsu, we need a boat to get us to that outflow pipe."

The man nodded, then beckoned for them to follow him. They fell in line, making their way to the shore.

THE FISHING BOAT WAS narrow, with nothing inside except bare boards, which provided seating. The oars were crude, handmade, the wood worn smooth by long usage. Under Tsu's command they sailed the boat from the shore and followed the ragged coastline to where the abandoned processing plant once stood. They kept as close to the shore as possible, rowing against the drag of the current, and fighting the swell of the waves. The rugged shoreline along that section of the island was dotted with coarse grass and shrub, even gnarled and skinny trees, which helped to conceal their passing, except from anyone actually standing on the shore's edge.

"I'm banking on Li's security force looking for us inland," McCarter said. "We've already made our presence known and once they find that dead patrol and their missing vehicle, it should keep them busy for a time."

THEY REACHED the position a couple of hours after leaving the settlement. A ragged straggle of black rock ran out from the shore, reaching close to twenty feet. Waves were crashing against the rocks constantly. They pulled the rowboat as close as they could to the inner side of the rocks where they formed a curve that hooked toward the shore. Although the water rose and fell, the waves lost a great deal of their power.

"The mouth of the pipe is directly below us," Mei explained. "About eight feet down. Once inside we have to swim for around fifteen feet before the pipe starts to rise."

She pointed to where the shore began to rise up a sloping bank.

"Is that where the plant was?" McCarter asked.

"Yes. The pipe is actually buried under that bank. The other end was concreted over when the plant was demolished."

McCarter glanced at Hawkins. The younger man had been listening carefully.

"We don't have much else going for us," he said. "What the hell, let's give her a try. One thing, Anna. What about your people? When they get back to our rendezvous, we won't be there."

"I thought about that. Right now time is not on our side. I wish I could let them know what we're doing. But I can't, so they will have to make their own decisions."

"If we get inside and start making noise," McCarter said, "they'll know where we are."

The three rifles were slung over their backs. Only Tsu carried a single weapon—his handgun. Once they secured their weapons, they eased themselves into the water, hanging on to the side of the rowboat.

"I will go first," Mei said. "Tsu Han will be last. He knows the way, too, so if either of you stray, he can guide you. Stay close and don't hesitate. Keep moving once you are in the pipe. You can't get lost. There is only one way to go."

They spent some time breathing deeply, saturating their lungs with air to give themselves the maximum time once they were submerged. At Mei's signal they all drew in their final breaths and followed her under.

McCarter could see the woman's black-clad form ahead of him. She was a strong swimmer and there was no hesitation in her course. She angled down the rock face, following it until she made a sharp dip, turning to the left. As the Phoenix Force leader followed in her wake, he saw the crusted outline of the concrete block that housed the pipe section.

Mei twisted her body and vanished from sight. McCarter kept moving forward and saw the dark opening she had swum into. He kicked hard, propelling himself into the wide mouth of the pipe. Within a few feet the daylight faded and the interior blacked out. He swam on, feeling the rough curves of the pipe brush his hands. He bumped against the roof of the pipe more than once and even heard the rifle scrape against the metal.

McCarter seemed to have been swimming for an eternity. His eyes stung and the air in his lungs was starting to bubble from his lips. In the silence he could hear the increased beating of his heart. He pushed himself harder, kicking out with his feet and forcing the water aside with his hands. His head banged against the top of the pipe again. As the pounding in his head increased and the burning sensation in his chest grew to almost unbearable proportions, McCarter decided that this would be a terrible place to die.

The bottom of the pipe scraped his thighs. For a moment McCarter imagined he was drowning and his water-laden body had sunk to the bottom of the pipe. He banged against it again, this time with his upper body. He reached out with both hands and traced the outline of the pipe, then realized what was happening. The pipe had started to rise. He tilted back his head and saw a faint circle of light.

It was either the surface of the water or he had died and gone to heaven.

When he broke free into the open he cleared his lungs with a gasp. Treading water, he twisted and came face-to-face with Mei. At that precise moment nothing had ever looked so good to him, even though her black hair was plastered to her head and her cheeks were smeared with dirt from the pipe.

"Easy, wasn't it?" she said.

"Don't bloody well ask."

McCarter checked out their situation. The wide pipe rose above them at an angle, and there was faint light coming from somewhere above. Barely enough to see by, but better than the complete blackness of the swim.

"There must be a way the light gets in above," Mei said.

Hawkins burst into view, rising like some wild creature of the deep. He spit out a mouthful of water and pushed to the side of the pipe where he clung as if he didn't trust it to stay intact. Shaking his hair out of his eyes, he glared at McCarter.

"Hell, Jim, don't ever ask me to do something like that again, or else I'll shoot you myself."

"I already decided that."

Tsu surfaced moments later. They helped one another out of the water and onto the sloping, corrugated surface of the inclined pipe.

"We have somewhere around forty feet to climb," Mei said. "Not too hard because of the incline and the corrugations."

"The sooner we do it, the better I'll feel," Hawkins replied.

They commenced their climb, moving at a steady pace. Despite the corrugations in the metal, the climb was risky. The surface of the pipe was damp, covered in places by a coating of slime. The angle of the pipe meant they were putting a heavy strain on their leg and back muscles, so they were forced to take a break a number of times. At the three-quarter mark they were all sweating. The stale air within the pipe did little to ease their discomfort.

"I can think of more pleasant ways to spend a day," McCarter muttered.

"Shoveling out a hog wallow has the edge on this," Hawkins agreed.

They moved on, their pace slowing even though they had rested.

Without warning Tsu lost his grip and began to slide down the pipe. Hawkins threw out a hand and caught hold of the man's arm, stopping his downward plunge. The Phoenix Force commando felt the hard jerk as Tsu's weight threatened to pull him off balance, as well. Almost at the point of falling, Hawkins felt his own body being supported by McCarter and Mei. The four of them maintained their holds on one another until they had regained their balance.

"Hell of a time for a group hug," Hawkins commented. "But thanks, guys."

Tsu said something to Mei and she passed the message to Hawkins.

"Tsu Han owes you his life," Mei said. "He won't forget it."

Hawkins nodded to the man. "Tell him any time."

As they neared the end of the climb, the pipe angled away from them and they had to climb over the lip it created. On the comparatively flat surface they sat back and regained their breath.

"The breach is just along here," Mei told them. "It won't take long to break through."

Her words were thrown back in her face when they

reached the breach. The pipe was partially blocked by a heavy fall of earth and stones.

"Damn! This must have happened during the construction. The breach is directly behind that fall."

"Looks like we're about to do some digging, folks," Hawkins said. "As far as I'm concerned the only way out of here is through that breach. No way I'm going back down that pipe and through the water again."

They laid their weapons aside and started to move the earth and stones, pushing the debris behind them. Tsu and Hawkins rolled hefty chunks of stone aside. Mei dug at the earth with her hands, ignoring the broken nails and scraped skin. Beside her McCarter's admiration grew for the slim woman as she labored without pause. They worked for almost an hour before McCarter called a halt and they all slumped back against the pipe. They were covered in dirt, faces gleaming with sweat, and they ached from head to foot.

They allowed themselves a fifteen-minute rest before they returned to their task. They were making headway. The blockage was getting substantially smaller now, and after another half hour they had removed enough of the debris to have exposed the break in the pipe and the access to Li's underground facility.

McCarter pushed his head and shoulders into the gap and checked it out. What he saw didn't please him.

"The section overhead looks very shaky. It must be where the rock fall originated. We need to get through fast and hope we can get right inside the facility. Taking away all the debris has removed any support holding up the rest.''

''It could come down again?'' Mei asked.

''Yes.''

''Through the breach you'll see a narrow gap between rock faces. It runs for about three feet, then there is a space where you have to push yourself upright. The rock looks solid, but about four feet up you can pull yourself onto a wide ledge. That ledge is inside the facility.''

McCarter took off all his weaponry and handed it to Hawkins.

''When I'm through, slide this stuff to me. Might as well pass me yours. I'll go on, and as soon as I'm clear you come through.''

The Briton stretched out and eased himself into the gap, aware of a steady trickle of dirt from above his head. He could feel it pattering onto his clothing as he wriggled his way through the narrow opening. He was forced to move on his stomach, clawing at the sides of the gap with his hands to aid his passage. It was confining in the narrow gap, with the solid rock faces pressing against him. He could understand how some people panicked when they found themselves in restricted places. He closed his mind to such things and moved on, inch by inch, until he was able to push himself to his knees as the rock opened up.

''Okay,'' he called to Hawkins, who pushed the bundle of weapons through. McCarter had to lean back into the space he'd just crawled through until he could catch hold of the weapons and slide them to him. He eased on the shoulder rig and adjusted the hang of the holstered Browning.

McCarter reached up and found the ledge. He

hauled himself onto it and crawled along so there was room for the others to join him. While they made the trip through the gap, the Phoenix Force leader went ahead to check out their position.

Mei's information turned out to be correct. When he reached the extreme end of the ledge, McCarter found himself looking down on one of the natural caves below Li's facility.

"THERE SHE IS," Grimaldi said.

Calvin James leaned forward and followed Grimaldi's pointing finger. He saw the dark shape ahead and slightly to the left. In the dying light of day the island wasn't showing much detail.

"Gear up, guys," James called over his shoulder.

Grimaldi leaned forward to check his instruments and the computer readouts spread across *Dragon Slayer's* console. His gaze was drawn to the pulsing red light that showed him the signal device was still functioning. The pilot keyed his board and fed the signal into the computer. It digested the input and displayed a location on the map of the island.

"Our signal is still showing," Grimaldi reported. "Not moving at present, but it's on-line."

Blancanales worked his way forward and dropped into the seat beside Grimaldi. He studied the signal location and matched it to his own chart. With the pilot's help he worked out the coordinates.

"If he's down there, we'll find him."

Grimaldi turned his attention back to guiding the helicopter toward the island. He switched to silent mode, the mufflers coming into action to reduce the sound of the combat chopper's powerful engines. He ran a series of checks, cutting back the power as the sleek machine began its descent. Grimaldi wanted to reach sea level, bringing *Dragon Slayer* in at low level to avoid any radar scans. He knew there was no guarantee he would avoid the island's electronic eyes, but there was no other way to do it.

In the rear the combat teams were finalizing equipment and weapons checks. In addition to the standard weaponry they had specialty items. Manning had his sniper rifle. On his back he carried a pack containing explosive devices rigged with detonators controlled by small timing units. His combat harness was heavy with grenades, fragmentation and thermal. Schwarz had been assigned communications duty. He wore a portable tracking unit, which they hoped would enable them to locate the carrier of the signal device. Each man wore a light, powerful radio, which was linked to *Dragon Slayer* and the rest of the team. Night-vision goggles were being worn for the landing.

Up front, Grimaldi made his final checks, scanning the landing coordinates the onboard computer had generated. He eased the controls and sent the chopper into a low dive, skimming the waves as he flew the aircraft toward the island. Turning, he followed the ragged coastline, sweeping around the tip of the island and throttling back to bring *Dragon Slayer* inland, hopping the low hills and vegetation that covered the terrain below him. His sensors and electronic readouts showed no interference from external scans.

Grimaldi ran a final weapons check, activating the chain-gun array and missile pods. He switched to the slaved helmet, which allowed him control over aiming by moving his head, tracking visually and locking on to target. Once the missile was fired, its own internal guidance system took over.

"Two minutes to LZ," the pilot called over his shoulder. "Activate those tracking devices, guys. I don't need any more lost sheep to round up."

"Don't you worry about us, Jack," Blancanales said. "If we get lost, you'll hear us yelling."

"I'll go find a place to sit and wait. When I see the fires I'll come running."

Grimaldi swooped in over the chosen LZ and dropped the helicopter to within a couple of feet of the ground. He tapped the button that broke the seal on the hatch, and it slid open.

The Stony Man team was gone in seconds, dropping to the ground and heading for cover. The moment they were out of the chopper, Grimaldi hit the power and took the aircraft up and away. He closed the door, shutting out the darkness, and boosted the chopper up and over the low ridge that showed ahead. His course took him across the island and into a run parallel with the shoreline. Turning, Grimaldi took it down until the extended landing gear touched the ground. He maneuvered *Dragon Slayer* into position and cut the power. With the chopper silent then, Grimaldi turned his attention to his readouts.

There were the steady signals coming from the tracking devices worn by Phoenix and Able, and on another small monitor he was able to pick up the signal that was still coming from the lone device James and Manning had picked up earlier.

Grimaldi wondered just who it was carrying the device.

WITH THE ONSET OF DARKNESS Rafael Encizo emerged from his fissure and prepared to move on the facility. During the daylight hours he had rested, watching the surrounding terrain, and had only seen movement in the late afternoon. A medium-sized truck, with a flatbed body, had rolled along the rough track he could see from his hideaway. There had been a squad of four sitting on the flatbed. Smoking and exchanging light banter, rifles slung casually over their shoulders, they looked as if they were out for a break. Encizo had watched the truck bounce along, then vanish over a slight hump in the track. The sound of its passing drifted away. He had relaxed his grip on the rifle, pushed himself back into the fissure and prepared to wait again.

With the sunset he roused himself, checking the rifle before he worked his way from the fissure. He took a few minutes to stand erect and work the stiffness out of his joints. It was then he realized how long he had gone without food or water. Encizo wasn't concerned about the lack of food. He did need water, though, and made a point of checking out the ground as he moved off. He found a small stream a little time later and knelt to moisten his lips, swishing out his mouth. He couldn't be sure how pure the water was, so he didn't swallow any. Though dehydration was a concern, he accepted the fact that he was going to have to wait until he found a safe supply.

The deepening gloom made it easier for him. He was able to blend with the lengthening shadows, staying off ridges where he might be silhouetted against the skyline, and made steady time retracing his steps to the facility.

Encizo reached the spot he had observed from before full dark. He made a thorough check of the area.

He had already identified the camouflaged opening and the entrance door. Now he crouched in the shadows and made his plans.

He was aware that once he entered the facility his main problem was going to be getting out again. The Phoenix Force commando had no illusions about what he did. Every combat situation brought with it the clear chance of sudden death, or being wounded so badly that he might become helpless. He knew those things and accepted them, which was why he always considered what he was doing and whether the risks balanced with the possible result that could be achieved. In this case Encizo had little to deliberate over. The facility Li was creating would, once put into operation, jeopardize the security of the United States. If Li got his calculations right and the computer systems worked the way they were intended, then the American defense procedures could be accessed and neutralized. Not only that, but the missile systems being produced by the North Koreans would also add weight to the threat. Li's facility would cast a shadow over the whole area, putting everyone on their guard as they viewed the Chinese capability as a direct confrontational stance. It wouldn't matter if China claimed the capability was merely defensive. That was an excuse used in the past by many nations, which would then simply turn around and show that their words had been nothing but lies to assuage their neighbors' fears.

Encizo planned to hit the facility hard, create the maximum damage possible, then get out before doors closed in his face. It was a high risk, one he was prepared to take, but he didn't intend to let it become a suicide mission.

GRIMALDI SAW the lone signal move. He watched it as the wearer headed cross-country, taking a cautious approach—stopping often, but always moving forward with deliberate intent. The carrier knew where he was going. There was a definite end to this trail.

He opened his radio link and spoke to James. "Mystery man is on the move, way to the south of you. But I have a feeling he's going to hit the spot."

"I read you," James replied.

Grimaldi sat back in his padded seat and watched both sets of signals. In his capacity as backup for the teams, he often had to sit and watch, an isolated observer seeing scenarios come together, knowing that they could end in death and destruction. He felt removed from reality as he waited out the missions in comparative safety, away from the fire zones, locked away inside his protective casing, surrounded by electronic sensors and cameras that told him what was going on outside without putting him at risk. Grimaldi would rather have been out there with the guys, sharing the danger. He was no coward, often becoming involved in combat situations himself; but as the Stony Man pilot, his job was to be there in case the teams needed to be extracted, or had to call in the firepower he could unleash from whatever he was flying. If the teams needed his help, he had to be able to respond quickly, so his enforced isolation was as necessary to the mission as the weapons the Stony Man warriors carried.

HE HAD DECIDED on his strategy. Being solo, his options were limited to the amount of damage he could inflict in a short time. Encizo didn't fool himself. A strike against the facility was most certainly going to be a walk on the wild side. With no backup and scant intelligence, his attack was going to be fast and furious.

Crouching in the darkness, concealed by tangled vegetation, Encizo checked his rifle for the last time. He also made certain that the extra magazines and his combat knife were accessible.

He circled around, keeping the access door in sight at all times. Angling closer, he saw a lone guard lolling against the rock face, catching a quick smoke. Coming up behind the man, Encizo slung the rifle, muzzle down. Every few steps he paused to check the area. Encizo couldn't afford unexpected attackers. He wanted a quick, silent kill, to take out the guard and infiltrate the facility without causing any noise or commotion.

The guard finished his illicit smoke. He dropped the butt on the ground at his feet, leaning slightly forward prior to crushing it underfoot. He was at the point of placing the toe of his boot on the butt when his world changed forever.

Encizo snaked his left hand around to cover the man's mouth. As he clamped his hand tight, his right brought the combat knife up and across the guard's throat. The man stiffened as the blade cut deep, opening a severe gash that immediately gushed warm blood. As initial shock became pain, the guard began to spasm. He made an attempt to fight against the onrush of lethargy brought about by extreme blood loss, but weakness restricted his ability to resist, and with each passing moment Encizo felt the man struggle less. He held the guard upright, pulled tightly against his own body and didn't relax until the man's futile resistance ceased completely.

As the guard's deadweight dragged against his arms, Encizo dragged the body into the deeper shadows away from the door. He lay the body on the ground and rolled it tight up against the base of the rock formation. Returning to the door, the Phoenix Force commando retrieved the guard's rifle from where it had been left leaning against the rock face. Checking the weapon, he found it loaded, with a double magazine in place, the second taped to the first for quick reversal.

Now that he was committed, Encizo kept up his momentum. He turned, opened the door and slipped through.

A quick scan of the interior revealed a featureless area hewed out of the solid rock. It was no more than ten feet square with a low ceiling. Electric lights encased in thick glass hung from the walls by metal hooks, a power-supply cable snaking across the rock and disappearing down the wall of the steep stone steps that plainly led to the lower levels. A thick rope was attached to one wall, hung from metal rings embedded in the rock.

Encizo checked that the rifle's safety was off as he started down the steps, keeping to the right-hand side after noticing that the steps curved to the left after ten feet. Staying on the right allowed him a wider view around the curve as he approached it. He was acutely aware of his position. Now that he was partway down the flight he was open to discovery from both above and below, but, as Encizo wryly admitted to himself, it was seldom that any incursion into enemy-occupied territory was without risk. Moving into such areas left blank spots where the unexpected could—and often did—happen.

The steps dropped farther than Encizo had expected. When he finally spotted the foot of the steps he paused, straining his ears to pick up any sounds, and was greeted with an eerie silence, which put him on alert. He waited. It was only after a time that he did pick up the faintest pulse of sound, and it took him a few seconds to work out what he was listening to—the steady rhythm coming from a distant generator. It was slight, and as Encizo tuned in to it, he realized it was as much a recurring vibration, transmitted through the solid rock, as it was an audible sound.

He reached bottom and paused on the final step, peering out beyond the walls on either side to see what lay before him.

Ahead was a blank wall, to left and right a narrow access tunnel. As with the steps, there were more sealed light units fixed to the wall, exposed cables drooping between them.

Encizo made his decision quickly. Time wasn't on his side. His next move was forced on him by the sound of approaching soldiers. There was no mistaking the rattle of equipment and harness, the snapped commands, even though they were in Chinese. The noise came from Encizo's right, so he turned left, moving quickly along the tunnel and hoping for a way out.

It came faster than he had expected. An opening revealed a branch tunnel. Encizo took it, immediately noticing that the floor angled down. Every step took him deeper underground.

The slope leveled out as Encizo emerged in a long, wide area that held the generators he had been hearing since entering the facility. There were two of them, large and diesel-powered. One was silent, on standby in case the working unit malfunctioned. Twin, stainless-steel ducting pipes took the exhaust fumes away from the plant by channeling them up through the rock ceiling, no doubt to be dispersed in the outside atmosphere.

As the Phoenix Force commando moved into the generator room, he saw the main control panel, mounted on the wall between the two units. A pair of men in work-stained uniforms manned the controls. He was moving up behind them when one of the technicians turned to speak to his partner and came face-to-face with Encizo.

For a split second the two stood totally immobile. Then Encizo reacted. He used the rifle as a club, hammering a savage blow to the side of the technician's skull. The blow spun the man, blood spraying from the gash in his head, his attempt to draw his side arm forgotten as he dropped to his knees. Encizo followed through with a second blow to the back of the man's skull. The force pitched the man forward, slamming facedown on the stone floor.

Encizo turned toward the second technician as the man reached for the pistol still in its holster where it rested on a ledge. He drove the butt of the rifle into the base of the man's spine, drawing a shrill cry. Despite his injury, the man kicked back with his left foot, catching Encizo just above the knee. The Cuban stepped back, swinging the rifle again as the technician lunged at him. Encizo sidestepped and, as the Chinese pulled himself to a stop, lashing out with a stiffened hand, the Cuban made an unexpected drive with the rifle butt, catching his adversary in the face.

The man stumbled back, pawing at his bloody crushed nose.

The technician gave a shrill cry and launched himself at Encizo, who dropped to one knee and rammed the butt of the rifle up between the man's thighs. The butt caught the man in the testicles, crushing them. The Chinese fell to the floor, doubled over in agony, clutching himself. Encizo stood over the man and delivered a final blow with the rifle butt, ending the technician's suffering.

Encizo made a quick tour of the generator room, checking out the design of the place. The most obvious plan would be to disable the generators and cut all the power to the facility. He considered that but rejected it. If he plunged the place into total darkness, he would be as helpless as the Chinese. He needed light and power to help him locate the control center. That was his main objective—to find and destroy the facility's capability to duplicate America's systems. He was going to need the generator output until he was ready to exit the facility.

The commando armed himself with the weapons from the two technicians. He used the belt and holster he found on the ledge, strapping it around his waist and tucking the second pistol behind the belt. He recalled seeing a diagram taped to the control box and went back to check. The words were in Chinese script and he couldn't understand them, but Encizo saw that he was looking at a schematic of the facility. The details probably referred to the electrical distribution, but there was an actual side view of the facility. He managed to pinpoint the entrance he had used, then traced his way along and down until he found the generator room, where he was now. According to the diagram, there were two levels above him and one below. Encizo took his time, finally finding the control room, which lay one level above him.

He pulled the diagram off the wall and folded it before pushing it into one of his pockets. Leaving the generator room, Encizo scouted until he found the stone steps that would take him down a level.

THE STONY MAN TEAM lay prone on a dark slope, checking the terrain below them. The night-vision goggles bathed the scene in shimmering green.

Gary Manning lay close to Calvin James. He nudged his teammate.

"If there is anyone down there, they don't seem to be moving around much."

"You said it."

James eased back from the slope and rolled into a shallow depression he had found only minutes earlier. Manning crawled to join him.

"What do you think?"

James lifted his goggles and rubbed his face. "Doesn't seem to be much activity anywhere."

"I suppose with an underground base there wouldn't be much to see on top."

Lyons's voice broke through on their headsets. "Heads up. Vehicle coming in from the south."

They waited and after a short time they heard it. Soon they were able to pick out the glare of headlights from a flatbed truck. They watched the vehicle as it passed below their vantage point. It continued for another few hundred yards, then stopped. Soldiers in the flatbed climbed down and began to check out the area.

"Keep them in sight, guys," Blancanales said.

"When they move we could follow and see where they go."

The armed soldiers had spread out in a line as they searched the area. The truck began to move, staying a couple hundred yards ahead.

"That's good, guys," James whispered into his mike. "Keep moving and take the brothers home."

"Son of a bitch," they heard Lyons mutter through their headsets.

The cursing ceased and they picked up the sound of hard breathing, followed by a short scuffle. Someone grunted in surprised pain. There was more muttering from Lyons.

"Carl? Carl, you okay?" Schwarz asked.

"Yeah. I'm fine now," Lyons assured them.

"What the hell was all that?" Manning demanded.

"They must have some scouting behind us. This Chinese mother stepped on me."

"You see any more?"

"Not right now. But don't bank on this being easy."

"Two coming in from my left," Schwarz reported. "Damn, they're all over the—"

The rattle of autofire split the calm night air, the shots coming from Able Team's area.

James turned to check the soldiers ahead of him and saw they had about-faced and were heading back toward his position.

"Here they come, guys," he said.

A bright flare suddenly exploded overhead, illuminating the area. In the stark bright light James saw that the few soldiers from the truck had been joined by others. They were racing toward the Stony Man positions, firing their weapons and yelling wildly.

The battle for Li's island had begun.

CHAPTER TWELVE

Gary Manning and Calvin James were both protected by the cover of the depression they had picked out earlier, so they had the advantage for the first round. It had only been intended to provide initial concealment while they observed, but now it was going to have to serve as a defensive position.

With the Chinese security force moving up the angled slope, the Phoenix Force commandos had the upper hand. They were shooting down on the attackers, and that gave them full firing angles.

Manning unlimbered his G-3 sniper rifle. He was up and ready in seconds, bringing the weapon to his shoulder and starting to lay down accurate, deadly fire. His first two shots put down both targets. He fired methodically, taking time to pick and secure his targets. Whether or not the Chinese knew the kind of weapon he had in his hands, it didn't seem to make any difference. They just kept coming, leaving their fallen comrades where they dropped. They used the classic Chinese attack scenario, throwing in a large number of ground troops to overwhelm a position by sheer weight of numbers. In this instance that tactic didn't gain them a great deal.

James joined Manning, laying down a volley of

selective shots with his H&K. He concentrated on the soldiers who had gained the most distance, leaving the longer-range work to Manning's sniper rifle. Short, scything bursts from the subgun cut into the groups who were racing up the slope and dropped a number of them. James plucked a grenade from his harness, pulled the pin and lobbed the bomb at the attackers. The blast took out three of the soldiers.

ABLE TEAM EXCHANGED shots with the squad that had appeared from the shadows behind them. The earth around the three Americans shook from the impact of slugs from the Chinese assault rifles. They returned fire with equal ferocity, pumping shot after shot at the enemy.

Overhead more flares burst and filled the night with glaring light. Schwarz caught a glimpse of a shadowy, squat figure lunging at him. Light played along the blade of the fixed bayonet on the end of the rifle as it was thrust at him. He twisted his body aside, and as the soldier stumbled past, Schwarz kicked him hard in the side. The man went down on his knees, the tip of the bayonet sinking into the earth. Before he could recover, Schwarz rammed the muzzle of the H&K into the base of his spine and triggered a burst.

The Able Team commando returned to his original position, firing on everyone he saw moving in his direction. He felt the trigger click on an empty chamber and ejected the magazine, reversing it and snapping in the fresh one he had taped to the first.

CARL LYONS HAD HIS BACK against the gnarled trunk of a tree. He used it as a prop to hold himself erect while he went about the business of combat, wielding his flaming H&K subgun like some cleansing sword. The muzzle arced left and right as the Able Team leader put out short, accurate bursts. He drove back the squad of security troops who were racing in his direction, firing on the run. The weapons bobbed up and down in the hands of their screaming owners, but the shots they expended were off target.

Lyons remained as calm as only he could be under fire, firing on his attackers and gaining a higher body count because of his steady shots. He neither acknowledged nor counted how many he took down. His sole purpose was to drive the enemy back and allow Able Team the chance to regroup and select a better firing position.

When his weapon locked empty, the big ex-cop dropped to one knee ejected the magazine and rammed home a fresh one. He used the brief moment to free a grenade, take out the pin and lob the bomb at his attackers. The blast reduced their number considerably, and the Chinese fell back.

Lyons repeated the maneuver. Under cover of the explosion he backed away from his tree and joined Schwarz and Blancanales. They moved quickly downslope to where Manning and James were holed up in the depression they had spotted earlier.

The five formed a tight circle, enabling them to cover all directions. As the light from the Chinese flares began to fade, they saw the attacking force dropping back, a ragged few left from the main force that had initiated the assault.

"Where the hell did they all come from?" Blancanales asked. "It was like a floodgate opened and there they were."

"It's what China has most of," James said. "People. The largest land army in the world. We send out a platoon, and they send out a couple of thousand.''

''That was a comforting observation,'' Blancanales said. ''Thanks, Cal.''

''They might think about it before they do it again,'' Manning pointed out. ''This is an island. I don't expect they'll have that many troops here.''

''Let's hope you don't regret that last comment,'' James said.

The unexpected lull allowed the Stony Man team to reload its weapons and establish its position.

''TIME WE MOVED,'' Lyons suggested.

''The longer we stay here the better chance they have of pulling in reinforcements.''

''You could be right,'' Schwarz said.

They all picked up the sound filtering through the darkness, the unmistakable, echoing chug of a diesel engine, accompanying the rattle of metal tracks.

''A tank!''

It appeared slowly, rising over the top of a low ridge a couple hundred yards away, the front end dropping suddenly as the weight of the armored vehicle brought it down. The engine roared, gears grinding as the driver fought to gain more traction. Then the stubby outline of a lightweight tank came into full view.

Studying it through his night-vision goggles, Manning saw the short barrel of the small-caliber gun on the turret. There was also a side-mounted machine gun on a swivel arm. The tank was no heavyweight and probably only had a low top speed, but it was formidable enough under the circumstances. About to turn away Manning saw a dark mass moving behind the tank and realized now why the ground assault had stopped. The troops were using the tank as cover as they advanced on the Stony Man team.

"Troops behind the tank," Manning said. "That thing is going to start laying down covering fire any time."

The big Canadian stretched out on the ground, bringing his rifle into play. He brought the sights on-line, adjusting for distance.

"Gary, what the hell are you doing?" James asked. "There aren't any tires to shoot out."

Manning ignored him. He was concentrating on his target, letting the tank come.

He was going for the driver.

The man's head, covered by a leather helmet fitted with a headset, could just be seen through the opening in the front deck. Manning took his time, knowing that if he missed, the driver would be aware of the shot's impact and would immediately close the hatch cover.

The Phoenix Force sniper took a breath and held it, then relaxed as the tank sank into a dip. The vehicle rocked on its tracks as it clawed its way out of the hollow and hauled itself onto comparatively level ground. Manning exhaled, breathed in again and lowered the muzzle. This time he gained full target acquisition. He stroked the trigger and the rifle jumped as it cracked and sent out its deadly slug. Keeping the sights on target, he saw the driver's head snap to one side, then flip back.

The tank's engine growled, faltered, then built again as the stricken driver's foot went into a spasm that jammed it down hard on the pedal. Moments later the tank began to swivel on one track, traversing a circle. The turret-mounted machine gun began to stutter, a continuous blast of high-caliber shells that howled through the air. They struck the ground many yards away from where the Stony Man operatives lay, but they all knew that the aim of any gun could be changed.

Manning brought his rifle into play again, targeting the tank commander who was using the machine gun, and whose torso was well exposed as he moved the machine gun back and forth, seeking a target he was unable to see.

With his target acquired Manning stroked the trigger. The rifle cracked sharply and the commander jerked as he was hit. His body swayed drunkenly, pulling the machine gun to one side. It sprayed another long burst before the commander's finger slipped from the trigger.

"Grenades!" James snapped, and the whole team lobbed armed projectiles at the mass of troops clustered behind the rotating tank. The moment the bombs began to explode they pushed to their feet and broke from cover, heading down the slope, away from the advancing Chinese.

They reached the base of the slope without incident, gathering in a tight group as they hit the edge of the rough track that served as a road.

"We keep moving," James said. "Follow this track but keep to one side. Use whatever cover we can find."

"I'll take point," Lyons said and moved ahead.

The rest of them strung out in a line, weapons held ready. Manning brought up the rear.

Schwarz ran regular checks on the signal scanner, trying to pinpoint the source of the lone signal still being transmitted. At this stage it was weak, intermittent. Either the power cell was wearing down, or the device was being blocked by some structure that interfered with the signal. The only certain thing was the direction the signal was coming from.

Ahead of them, which meant they were at least moving in the right direction.

WITHIN THE NEXT thirty minutes the rain started. It was coming in off the sea, and they all felt the push of the wind behind it. It looked as if the report they had been given about a possible continuation of bad weather was coming true.

Schwarz contacted Grimaldi. "We made contact with the opposition."

"Do I stay put?"

"For now. You got a weather update?"

"Nothing you guys are going to like. Satellite data has that storm still brewing in the vicinity. Looks like you're going to get wet."

"Thanks for that."

"Any time. Hey, if things get heavy you call. Okay?"

"Okay."

Over the next few minutes the rain increased. It hit hard, slapping at faces and bodies, soaking their clothing quickly. The ground underfoot became quickly waterlogged, mud starting to drag at their feet as they pushed on.

LYONS'S VOICE CAME through the com sets.

"Hold it. Roadblock up ahead. Truck across the road. Five-man squad. Machine gun on the flatbed."

They pulled into the shadows, moving up in stages

until they were at Lyons's back. From where they crouched they could make out the roadblock and the Chinese squad. They looked a sorry sight as they clustered around the truck, uniforms soaked by the downpour.

James studied the terrain. There was no way around the roadblock. The land was fairly flat at this location, and the sparse vegetation yielded no significant cover.

"If we can't go around, we go through them," Lyons said.

"He always so aggressive?" Manning asked.

Lyons turned to stare at him. "Yeah," he admitted, "and especially when I'm pissed off and wet."

"Sounds reasonable to me," James said.

Manning checked his sniper rifle, moving to one side so he could get a clear shot at the soldier behind the machine gun.

"I'll take him out. The rest is up to you guys."

"Go for it, Gary."

The falling rain reduced visibility, so Manning took his time lining up his shot. The machine gunner was low behind his weapon. Only his head remained clear, reducing the target size and making the shot that much harder.

James had a grenade ready in his hand, the pin removed.

The machine gunner flew backward when Manning's shot struck him in the center of his forehead. The 7.62 mm round cored through and blew out the back of his head. Before his body struck the flatbed, James had thrown his grenade. It landed short but the detonation was still effective. Two of the soldiers went down, their bodies torn by the blast. The remaining pair returned fire, but they were dazed from the blast and had lost target acquisition. Before they regained their faculties, Blancanales and Schwarz opened fire, sending sharp bursts from their MP-5s, knocking the Chinese back against the side of the truck.

The team regrouped, skirting the vehicle and continuing along the muddy track. They could feel the strength of the wind increasing as they traveled, and though the storm aided their concealment it also made travel difficult. Being in unknown territory, they had to stop to assess their position regularly. The continuing incoming signal though weak, was helping. It acted like a beacon, giving them a destination, which they all hoped would be near the concealed base.

RAFAEL ENCIZO WASN'T aware of the situation aboveground. He had his own particular problems, mainly in the form of armed soldiers who began to appear from every direction. Orders were shouted, and the clatter of boots rang on the stone and concrete floors as Li's security force broke into action.

Whatever the cause, the agitation forced Encizo into a retreat. His incursion into the facility was difficult enough. He hadn't expected to be confronted by such a large number of armed troops at this early stage of his assault. He managed to draw back into a recess, easing behind a freestanding air-conditioning unit. He waited until the rush had died down and the passage was silent again.

Encizo was about to move on when something drew him back. He stood examining the air-conditioning unit, wondering why this was the first piece of sophisticated machinery he'd seen since his arrival. Nothing like this had been installed on any of the other levels, not even in the dormitories he had spotted during his climb from the generator room. The long, bare room had contained ranks of wooden bunks, but no other adornments. Just the bunks and a few basic items. Nothing to aid the comfort of the men who would have to sleep in the drab section.

Now, suddenly, in a bare passage, with little sense to it, he had found a softly humming air-conditioning unit. He became aware of the change in temperature in this section. The air was fresher, flowing, as if there were a need to control the environment. Encizo could think of only a couple of reasons, and one of them made him recall the care that Kurtzman took over the ambient temperature within the Stony Man Computer Room. The large array of electronic equipment within the room needed to be in a controlled, comfortable atmosphere. The electronics produced a considerable amount of heat, and this needed to be removed and replaced to prevent overheating and upsetting the intricate balance required to keep the computer banks and their peripherals running accurately.

Encizo examined the passage, finding more of the units on both sides, maintaining an even, dry temperature. This controlled environment was creating a stable atmosphere around *what?*

The Cuban made his way along the passage until he came to a smooth, metal door. A small window was set in the upper section and when Encizo peered through, he knew he had hit the spot.

He had found what he was looking for—the heart of Colonel Li's illicit computer center.

He checked the door, but couldn't find a handle to open it, then spotted the keypad set in the wall to one side of the door. It was of no use to him without the correct code sequence. Keying in an incorrect code might trigger alarms.

The only way he was going to get inside was to be ready if and when someone opened the door.

Encizo backed off, easing himself behind the closest of the tall air-conditioner units. He leaned against the stone wall at his back and prepared to wait.

MCCARTER LED THE WAY up the slope until they reached a level section that showed evidence of having had concrete laid over it. A door-sized opening led into a dimly lighted passage smelling of diesel. They were obviously on the lowest level of the facility, where most likely they would find storage tanks holding the fuel they could smell. The fuel would be needed to power something like a generator, which in turn would provide the power needed to bring life to Li's fortress.

"Did you ever get into the main part of the base?" McCarter asked.

"When we came last time they were still building the place. It was a mess. Construction crews supplied by Xan Hung were all over. We had to be careful."

"If the storage tanks are down here, the generators can't be far away," McCarter said.

"We need to find them," Hawkins stated. "Shut them down, and the whole place will go off-line."

"Not until we've located the actual control center," McCarter said. "That has to be put out of action, and I don't just mean we pull out the power sockets. If we disable the power supply now, we'll be stumbling around in the dark for the rest of our bloody lives."

"So let's go," Mei said. "If we're at the bottom, the only way is up."

Hawkins grinned. "She gets snappy, boss. Just like you."

"Remind me to have a word about your attitude later," McCarter said. "I don't like it. You sound too much like me."

They followed the passage to its end, reaching crudely carved steps. They climbed them quickly, McCarter in the lead, followed by Mei and Tsu, with Hawkins bringing up the rear. At the top, the Phoenix Force leader peered around the corner of the wall. The next passage led off in both directions. He made a choice and they moved quickly along until they reached a heavy steel door that swung open on balanced, lubricated bearings. They found themselves in the storage tank area. The smell of diesel fuel was even stronger. A pair of huge, steel storage tanks stood side by side, metal pipes running off and snaking along the floor and into the shadows overhead.

"Now they are what I call *big,*" Hawkins said.

"I wouldn't want to have to pay his fuel costs," McCarter agreed.

"If we set charges here," Mei said, "the whole place would go up."

"We don't have any charges," McCarter reminded her.

"Improvise."

"Later," McCarter said and led them out of the storage room and up the next flight of steps.

He had picked up the sound of the generators and they followed along the empty passages cautiously, knowing that their luck couldn't last forever. Sooner or later they were going to meet some of Li's people.

The first ones they did meet were dead. They were the technicians in the generator room Encizo had clashed with.

"These guys either fought over something pretty important," Hawkins said, "or we aren't the only visitors Li is having tonight."

McCarter stared at the dead men. They had been killed quickly and efficiently. No gunshot wounds. Someone had taken them down with minimal fuss, not wanting to make too much noise for fear of attracting undue attention.

Because he wanted to move about the facility without being discovered?

Possibly because he was looking for the same thing McCarter and his team were after.

The control room.

David McCarter hoped that person was Rafael Encizo.

He kept the thought to himself because he wanted to be right, and voicing his thoughts might raise false hopes all around.

LI WAS APOPLECTIC. His rage was threatening to become physical as he paced back and forth in his office, pausing only to peer through the glass down into the control room where the technicians still worked away at the intricate installations. He would take a breath as he stood at the window, his eyes taking in the quiet calm on the other side of the glass, then he would round on his officers, or whoever fell under his gaze, and rage at them.

He couldn't believe the reports coming in from the security force. The interlopers, whether American or Chinese, or both, had already faced his force in the opening round of hostilities. Not only had they survived, but they had managed to defeat the first squads he had sent to capture them.

News had been far from encouraging from other quarters since the discovery of a dead guard earlier in the day. The man had been dead from a cut throat for a considerable time. Which meant that someone was walking free on the island. He blamed his security force commanders, accusing them of allowing their troops to become lax, too complacent. The security force had found life on the island easy compared to their usual military duty, and rather than give their full attention to their work they had allowed lethargy and self-indulgence to creep in to undermine them. Which was why the interlopers had invaded the island.

Li had ordered his squads out to track down the invaders, and to strengthen their resolve with harsh action against anyone suspected of harboring the strangers. The choice wasn't a wide one. The island had only a small population—the fishermen who occupied the small settlement farther along the coast. Li had ordered that they be questioned. He knew how they felt about him and his facility. The project meant nothing to them. In the colonel's eyes they were worthless, and he now regretted allowing them to stay on the island and be there to paint a picture of peace and tranquility.

He was no fool. He had done a great deal to upset them, so they wouldn't carry any sympathy in their hearts as far as Colonel Li was concerned. That fact didn't worry him in the slightest. He wasn't interested in the opinion of a bunch of lowly, dirty peasants. His ideals were far above their primitive intellect. So when the suspicion was raised that the fishermen might have aided the interlopers, Li sent his security people to interrogate the men and then dispose of them in a way that would send a clear message to the invaders.

The fishermen died.

So did one of Li's squads. The unit's vehicle had also been stolen, but was found later on a hill overlooking the settlement.

Then there had been a period of quiet. Li, considering the options, felt that if there was to be some kind of attack on his force and his project, it would come at night. A night attack was favored by many military men. The darkness gave the advantage to the attacker because those on the defense would never be sure where and when hostility might come from. He decided to send out a strong squad of men, backed by one of his two tanks. The plan had been sound. His people would be out in the darkness, ready to move if and when the attack came. Although his force carried out their maneuver to the letter, the results weren't what Li anticipated.

The opposition proved to be a formidable fighting force. When challenged by the colonel's force they hit back harder than expected. Harder and faster, carrying the fight with surprising ferocity and skill. It was obvious that this force was highly experienced in the art of war.

The ignominy of being told that the attackers had even killed the driver and the commander of one of the tanks might have frightened a lesser man. But Li had vision, and he had the respect of his men and his officers. So he ordered them out into the night to meet the attackers head-on and defeat them. The project had to be protected at all costs. Lives were there to be sacrificed as far as Li was concerned, because his dream of besting America and placing China in a prominent military position was paramount.

Now he had heard that the facility itself had also been breached. That news created even more anger. He couldn't believe that his project was under threat from some group of American fanatics.

"Find them," he roared at his officers. "How have they gotten inside? What are your men doing? Find them or I will have you all executed, and believe me I *will* do it. If I have to, I will do it personally. It won't be the first time."

Li didn't need to explain himself. All his people knew his reputation, and his penchant for carrying out his threats. His reputation preceded him like a banner waved ahead of an army.

As the officers left, the colonel slumped in his chair. He glanced at Jun Wang, who had stood quietly to one side, his head slightly bowed as Li's rage had filled the room. He never interfered when Li was castigating his subordinates. It wasn't his business. Jun knew his place.

"Do you think I frightened them enough?"

"I believe some of them will have to change their trousers before they go outside," Jun said quietly.

Li stared at him, his expression taut, but after a short time he allowed a thin smile to curl his lips.

"The situation is becoming intolerable, Wang. At this crucial stage in the project, the last thing we need is armed mercenaries from America trying to destroy everything we have created."

"Perhaps it is fortunate that Makura is on the

mainland. Bringing him here could have placed him at risk.''

"You were wise to make me listen, Wang. If I did not have you to advise me, I would go out and do something stupid.''

"That's hard to believe, Colonel.''

"You think so? One of my failings is not thinking too deeply before I act. I admit that openly. But I'm a fortunate man. I have you to advise me and also Shun Wei. Her counsel is always good.''

Jun smiled in acknowledgment. He kept his own thoughts to himself. In truth he didn't like Shun Wei. As far as he was concerned, she was little more than a shrewd fortune hunter. She had latched on to Li because she saw him going far in the Chinese military and beyond. His ideas were extreme yet always workable, and none more so than the project.

At first it had seemed nothing more than an ambitious dream, a fantasy that would never see the light of day. Now, though, the people had to look to see what could be achieved through dedication and a single-minded agenda. The colonel was close to completing his project, and if he did Shun Wei would ride the crest of success with him, milking it for everything she could get from the event. Her own ambition was as intense as that of Li himself, but the colonel couldn't see that. He was so infatuated with her that he overlooked any fault, pretending it didn't exist. But Jun knew better. He had mistrusted her from the moment he met her. Without telling Li, he had the woman checked out through some of his contacts. What he had learned had made interesting reading.

Shun Wei, despite her intelligence and bearing,

was of peasant stock. Her parents, both now dead, had been servants in the house of a government minister. Shun had learned at an early age that if she stayed within her parents' status she would end up doing the same thing. Using her natural beauty and an ability to charm the male sex, she became the minister's confidante and probably his mistress. She used her new position to elevate herself, taking up his offers of education and grooming.

Within a few years she had attained the position of head of his household, ruling the place with a steel hand. But the minister, who she had seen as her way to the top, fell from grace. He descended into a great depression as his importance crumbled. His death, by his own hand, left Shun a wealthy woman. Only a week before his death he had willed everything he owned to her. From what Jun's people had gleaned, there were those who believed she had been responsible for the minister's death. There was no proof in any form, only suspicion. Shun herself had challenged the innuendo, demanding that if there was any proof it should be produced.

By this time she had already ingratiated herself with an important local party member, a middle-aged man who was dazzled by her attentions and her promises of loyalty to him. In the year she was with the man, Shun continued to build her reputation. She was fiercely loyal to her new man, working tirelessly on his behalf, and also beginning to show a stronger side to her character. She denounced those in his party who didn't toe the line, having no qualms at using extreme measures when it came to handing out punishment to wrongdoers. Jun wasn't surprised when evidence came to light that this second admirer of

Shun Wei also died in mysterious circumstances. This time it was a car crash. The only other passenger in the car was Shun herself, who emerged with nothing more than a few bruises and scratches. Her companion was found to be dead at the scene of the "accident."

Once again Shun Wei moved on, feigning her sorrow and being feted as the sympathetic survivor. When she came into the spotlight again it was on the arm of Colonel Li Cheng. Betraying his usual character, Li was in awe of this young beauty. He hung on her every word and gesture, and before long she had usurped Li's family and had become his constant companion. Now that she was ensconced in military circles, her influence increased. She had a natural grasp of power politics, knew everything about military affairs and became a favorite of many. But she stayed faithful to Li. She had seen his future, his natural leadership qualities, and as before she maintained her grip on him by using everything she could to keep him interested. She also, as she had done with her previous conquests, chose her cronies—those who would bend to her will and those she decided would get in her way. Not Li's—*hers*.

Jun saw all this through the eyes of a like-minded person. His career was based on pleasing Li in every way he could. Pandering to the man's whims and never allowing himself to get on the wrong side. Jun was a survivor, and he maintained that by anticipating what was coming and neatly sidestepping when it turned out to be dangerous. He was also very skilled at his job. He had to be. Li expected total commitment and extreme responses to everything he demanded.

Nodding at the colonel's praise of Shun Wei, the slender man said, "She is very clever, Colonel."

Li failed to see the irony in Jun's words.

A telephone on his desk rang and he snatched it up. After the message had been delivered, Li banged down the receiver.

"The interlopers who have breached the facility have clashed with one of our squads.

"Have they been stopped?" Jun asked, though by the look on the colonel's face he knew what the answer would be.

CHAPTER THIRTEEN

McCarter's group made contact suddenly and with no time to do anything but react.

They had been moving steadily along the next level, aware of distant noises, but finding themselves unable to pinpoint the source. The interconnecting passages and the steps that joined them made the facility like a large echo chamber. It played with sound, magnifying and distorting it, so it was impossible to identify where anything actually came from.

David McCarter, in the lead, had stepped onto a landing, where two levels were connected by a set of stone steps that led up to one level and down to the next. As he rounded the end of the passage, he encountered a group of Li's security troops on their way down the steps.

Both parties stared for a fraction of a second, then McCarter dropped to one knee and swung his rifle into firing position.

"Watch out!" he yelled over his shoulder.

The soldiers opened fire, slugs crackling into the stone sides of the passage and filling the air with dust and chips. McCarter felt something sting the side of his face as he loosed a tight burst. His slugs caught one gunner in the midsection, flipping the man over the edge of the landing. The wounded man crashed down the stone steps, dislodging two of his companions.

A gun barrel cleaved the air above McCarter's head as Hawkins joined the fray, pumping single shots at the soldiers.

Hawkins felt something hard punch into his side, and he was pulled back by the impact. He grunted in pain, clamping a hand over his wound, and felt warm blood seeping through his fingers. Then someone caught hold of his clothing and pulled him back behind cover. As Hawkins sagged against the wall, held there by Tsu Han, he saw Mei take his place by McCarter's side. She didn't waste any time as she returned the fire of the Chinese troops.

The clatter of autofire petered out moments later as the soldiers still on their feet dropped down the steps out of sight, leaving four of their number dead on the landing.

Mei darted from cover and began to collect all the magazines she could lay her hands on. She retrieved one of the assault rifles dropped by a soldier and handed it to Tsu Han. He propped it against the wall, then returned to ministering to Hawkins's gashed side. He tore strips from the Phoenix Force commando's undershirt and made a pad, then used a longer strip to fasten it in place.

"You okay?" McCarter asked.

"I'll be fine," Hawkins replied, pushing to his feet.

"Now they know we're here," McCarter said. "I figure we'll have one chance to go for the control center, or whatever Li calls it."

"Let's go," Hawkins said.

ENCIZO HAD PICKED UP the distant crackle of gunfire. He remained in position, hoping that the shooting might bring someone out of the control center. It didn't. Whoever was in there seemed determined to stay put for the moment.

He wondered who had been involved in the shooting.

McCarter? Hawkins? Mei Anna and her people?

He was guessing, but he held the hope that he might be right. That his Phoenix Force teammates had survived the shipwreck as he had, and like himself were making their attempt on Li's base. There was even the possibility that James and Manning were mounting a strike. Encizo didn't spend too much time on supposition. It wouldn't ease his particular situation until he came face-to-face with whoever it was. Until then he was on his own.

The clicking of tumblers told him the sealed door was opening. Encizo spotted movement on the other side of the glass. He checked his weapon, then slid around the cabinet, ready to move the moment the door opened enough for him to enter. The final click told him the door had been unlocked. It swung open with a soft electric hum, and a lab-coated Chinese stepped through. The man was consulting a clipboard of paperwork, so he failed to see Encizo until it was too late.

The Cuban hit the guy head-on, slamming him against the steel frame of the door. The man slumped unconscious to the floor, his limp form wedged against the door, holding it open. Encizo stepped over him, the assault rifle held out in front of him, his finger near the trigger.

The control center spread out before him. It was a

long, curving room with banks of monitors, hard-drive towers and an array of electronic equipment that Encizo was at a loss to understand. On the long wall facing him across the center was a multiscreen array of large monitors. Very few of the screens were active. Those that were, showed scrolling text, flickering and changing as the technicians in lab coats checked and adjusted, moving from section to section as they worked to bring the center to life. Lengths of cable snaked across the floor. Equipment stood with the backs off. Li's center existed, but it was still far from being completed.

Encizo took all this in during the first seconds of his entry into the center. The technicians, intent on their work, didn't even notice his presence until one of them, crossing the floor, happened to glance up.

The Chinese took a long look at the unshaven, filthy Cuban wielding an assault rifle, and let out a yell of alarm. The center erupted with raised voices and the clatter of footsteps as the technicians all began to gather on the far side of the room. In the process one of them had pressed a button. A loud alarm began to whoop.

One of the lab-coated technicians produced a handgun from beside his workstation. He raised it and fired at the intruder.

The bullet caught Encizo in the left upper arm, tearing into soft flesh and knocking him off balance. A wave of nausea flooded through the Cuban as the numbing impact of the bullet hit his nervous system. He pulled himself upright as the shooter, a strange smile on his face strode forward, lifting the heavy pistol again.

Encizo triggered the assault rifle. His blast caught

the technician in the torso, ripping his organs apart as it blew him off his feet. The man crashed to the floor, bloody and dying, his screams of pain filling the room and adding further panic.

Trying to ignore the pulse of pain in his arm, Encizo braced himself against the wall and tucked the stock of the rifle under his right arm. He triggered a long burst, sweeping the muzzle across the banks of monitors and equipment in front of him. Glass and plastic exploded, electric sparks arcing through the air as the slugs chewed into the heart of Li's electronic machine. The moment the magazine was empty, Encizo fumbled a second into place and began to fire again, this time at the wall screens opposite.

He was halfway through his magazine when he heard the thump of feet and knew his entry into the complex center had been discovered. He swung around, bringing the muzzle of the assault rifle to bear on the door just as the first of the newcomers showed.

"GET THEM BACK! Get them to the command center," Li roared as he saw what was happening through the bulletproof glass of his office.

Jun Wang grabbed one of the phones and began to shout orders.

The alarm's siren made speech difficult. Its volume was ear-shattering. Someone had set the noise level too high, and though Jun had someone on the other end of the line he couldn't make himself heard above the noise. In frustration he threw down the phone and picked up one of the autoweapons racked on the wall of Li's office. He ran out, snapping the magazine into place and cocking the weapon.

He reached the level below and turned along the

brightly lighted passage that led to the door on the opposite side of the command center to the intruder. Jun was met by the stream of technicians as they erupted from the door and spilled out into the passage. He ordered them out of the way and forced himself through the crowd. He could still hear the crackle of gunfire inside the center and hoped he reached the interior before too much damage was done.

Jun shoved aside a technician, ignoring the man's protest as he slammed into the wall. Then he was through the door and into the center. His anger welled as he saw the destruction the intruder had already done. The facility administrator thought of the time and expense, the organization that he had engineered, and a wild rage coiled and exploded inside him. He stared at the intruder, seeing him across the room, and he focused all his anger on that lone figure. It had been a long time since Jun had practiced using the Type 56 assault rifle and he had forgotten just how powerful the weapon was. The kickback caught him unaware and the muzzle rose, sending a stream of slugs into the wall well above the target's head.

Jun swore, gripping the weapon tightly, and drew down for a second burst.

Before he pulled the trigger, he saw figures entering the center through the door close to the intruder. Jun started to smile. The security troops had arrived after all. Then his smile turned to dismay when he saw that the newcomers were not Chinese troops, but more intruders.

With a growing feeling of doom spreading through him, Jun turned his weapon on them. Again he failed to fire a second burst.

One of the newcomers, to one side of a tall foreigner, brought his own assault rifle to bear with astonishing speed. Jun saw the lance of flame from the muzzle and felt the slam of the bullets as they tore into his body. He felt himself punched back against the wall. His head struck the barrier with incredible force, and pain burst into a haze of blurred light. He slithered to the floor, torn and bloody, the assault rifle dropping from his hands. The last things he saw were spidery trails of blood spreading out across the shiny floor of the command center.

"TOOK YOUR TIME," Encizo said as McCarter joined him.

"Nice to see you, too," the Briton replied.

Hawkins, who had fired on the slender Chinese on the far side of the room, leaned across and grinned at the Cuban.

"Hell, boss, he's too mean to drown."

Mei caught McCarter's arm. "Up there behind the glass," she said, pointing. "Colonel Li."

They could see the uniformed figure staring down at them.

"I guess he's a little pissed at us right now," Hawkins ventured.

Mei raced forward, firing a full magazine at the wide glass. The bullets did little more than star the glass.

"Save your ammunition," McCarter said. "It's bulletproof glass."

"Well, these aren't," Mei said, snapping in a fresh magazine. She cocked the rifle and began to fire into the computers and monitors.

"You okay to watch the door?" McCarter asked Encizo.

The Cuban nodded. The Briton sprinted across the center and slammed the far door shut, making sure that the internal locks were secured.

"Let's make sure this place is disabled," he said. "We don't have explosive charges, but we can still do plenty of damage with what we do have."

Hawkins appeared at McCarter's side, holding a folded sheet of electronic diagrams. He didn't say anything; he simply handed the sheet to the Phoenix Force leader. When he opened the sheet he found himself looking at a photocopy of a document with English text. Across the top of the sheet were two words: Project Slingshot.

At that precise moment they didn't mean that much to McCarter. All he needed to know was in the words printed in the bottom right corner of the sheet: Department of Defense—United States of America.

McCarter handed the sheet back to Hawkins.

"Keep that safe. We need it to go back home."

THE TREK THROUGH the storm took its toll. The ground underfoot had turned into nothing less than a mud bath. The Stony Man team disregarded the discomfort and pushed on, following the track. It was becoming harder to follow in the constant downpour.

Since the roadblock, they hadn't seen or heard anything from the security troops. None of them let the fact make them complacent. The Chinese force was out there, maybe on their trail, or even racing by another route to cut them off. All they could do was keep moving, heading for the source of the signal. They had nothing else to go on.

Time became irrelevant. The team slogged on through the torrential downpour, fighting the drag of the wind, the pull of the mud on their boots and the weight of soaked clothing and equipment. No one could choose the time or place for engagement. When it happened those involved accepted whatever the weather threw at them. It didn't make life easier. On the other hand, it also hampered the opposition.

They took a break, sheltering as best they could in the lee of a sprawl of rocks. The rain still found them, but they had some protection from the wind.

Schwarz contacted Grimaldi. The pilot wanted to pick them up, but despite his protests, he was asked to stand by.

"We need you as backup," Schwarz said. "Right now you're better out of the frame."

"I feel bad sitting here all comfortable while you guys are out there in this weather."

"Jack, it sucks out here. Nobody wants to be in it. If we get caught up in some hard fighting and need to get out, that's when we'll yell. As long as we have you waiting it's an advantage."

"You don't lie too well, pal."

Schwarz laughed. "Best I can do tonight."

"You still on that signal?"

"Kind of. We had to divert to lose our Chinese friends, so we ended up adding a few miles. But we're getting there. You got *us* on your TV?"

"Good and strong, guys. I won't lose you."

"Okay, talk later. Over and out."

THE FIRST SHELL landed twenty yards to their right. It exploded with a hard crash, blowing rocks and dirt into the air.

"Mortar," Blancanales said.

"We should have known they wouldn't up and quit," James said.

"Yeah?" Lyons said. "That makes two of us then."

They heard the second shell coming. It landed closer this time.

"Let's move," Manning suggested.

They moved off in line, skirting the edge of the track, pushing through tangled brush until they were well clear of the mortars, which were still dropping. Crouching in scant cover, they took time to assess their current position.

Off to their right they could hear the sound of waves crashing against the shore.

"How did they pick us up?" Blancanales asked. "Okay, I know they're smart, but pinpointing us in this weather and the dark?"

"I don't think they did it that way," James said.

"So how did they?" Manning asked.

"I think we're close to the base. If Colonel Li is as security conscious as we've learned, maybe he has the place ringed by defense teams. Could be all we actually did was trip some outer security alarm. Maybe a wire. Or an infrared scanner. They're just reacting to an unseen threat."

"Could be," Schwarz agreed. "We can still get killed."

"Part of the deal," Lyons said. "If they have detectors out where we were, they could have them all around us."

"Right now is the best chance we have," James said. "Heavy weather. Strong wind. Gives us some natural cover."

"You want to keep heading in?"

"Sitting out here isn't doing any good," Manning pointed out.

"We going to do the gung-ho bit?" Blancanales asked.

"Might get us out of the rain," Manning said.

"How many grenades we got left?" Lyons asked, and when a count had been taken he added, "Should provide us with some diversions."

Schwarz had been checking his signal detector again. He did some mental calculation.

"Listen up," he said. "I'm picking up a stronger pulse from that signal now. And it's moving again. I'm pretty certain we are close."

"We are going to look like prize dicks if that thing is stuck to the sole of some Chinese boot," Blancanales said.

The howl of an incoming mortar made them duck. It landed yards away, showering them with wet mud.

"Jeez, this is getting close," James said.

Two more shells landed within the following two minutes, and the Stony Man team made the unanimous decision to move out.

They each primed grenades and broke from cover after the next salvo dropped. As they ran forward, they lobbed the grenades in different directions, and as the projectiles detonated, they were rewarded by the sound of screams of pain coming from their left where two of the grenades had landed.

Although the torrential rain reduced visibility, they were all able to see a patch of light ahead of them. What they also saw was the squat outline of a light tank, silhouetted against the light. It was crawling forward, seeming to come out of nowhere, and seconds after it appeared the misty light faded behind it.

Down in the mud, watching closely through his night goggles, Gary Manning made out the shapes of Chinese soldiers moving back and forth, seemingly adjusting something across a wide rock face. A grin crossed the Canadian's face as he studied the area.

"Son of a bitch," Manning said.

He reached across and tapped Lyons's shoulder. "Straight ahead. Twenty yards. Rock face. There's a camouflage cover over it. That damn tank just rolled out, then they dropped the cover back."

"You sure?" Lyons queried.

"Carl, I don't really have time for making up stories right now."

"I take that as a yes. Okay, let's go for it." Lyons relayed the message to the others through his mike. "Let's hope we don't hit solid rock."

They rose as one and dug in their heels as they broke for the rock face.

Five yards in they ran into a machine-gun post, the gunner and loader were frantic in their haste to bring the weapon around. The chatter of the assault rifles filled the night, and the Stony Man team moved on, leaving the two Chinese slumped over their weapon.

As they closed in on their objective they heard the sound of voices. Someone was shouting orders. In the background came the clatter of the tank as it began a slow turn in their direction. A powerful spotlight came on, hand operated by someone in the turret. It cut a harsh swath through the shadows, rain streaking across the bright-white beam.

"Down, guys," Manning said. He was already on his stomach, bringing the G-3 into play.

Dark shapes moved out from behind the tank, weapons up as they raced toward the Stony Man team's position. Muzzle-flashes winked as the Chinese troops began to fire.

Returning fire, the team aimed at the figures behind the muzzle-flashes, scoring a number of hits before the Chinese realized their mistake and backed off.

The G-3 cracked once, and the spotlight blew with a crackle and a coil of smoke. The tank rolled on a couple more yards, then jerked to a halt. The engine roared, gears clashing, then it began to reverse.

James and Blancanales threw a pair of fragmentation grenades at the squat shape. Shrapnel burned the air around the tank, and a man screamed in pain.

"Let's go," James yelled.

They were moving again, heading in the direction Manning had indicated.

The shape of the rock face became more defined as they shortened the gap. The hostility increased. Gunfire crisscrossed the darkness. The Stony Man team dropped to the sodden earth and returned fire, picking their targets with care, not firing until they were sure of a hit. They used their rapidly depleting supply of grenades, the vicious blasts taking a deadly toll. Up on their feet again, pushing forward, they fired on the run.

Blancanales gave a grunt of pain and went down on his knees. Lyons was at his side before the man could slip farther to the ground. The Able Team leader hauled his partner upright and hooked an arm around his waist. Manning moved in close to protect them as Lyons struggled on, supporting Blancanales.

Firing at anything that moved, the Stony Man team closed on the rock face, able to see now that a heavy camouflage curtain hung over a wide opening. Driving back the Chinese who had emerged from the rain, the Stony Man commandos breached the edge of the curtain and stumbled, exhausted, into the large cavern that lay behind it. The place was set up as a workshop, with benches and tools, fuel and oil drums. It had the familiar smell of a motor pool.

A number of Chinese were in the cavern. They burst into action as the intruders appeared, scrambling for weapons they had racked against the wall. They never reached them. James and Schwarz moved ahead of the others, laying down wide swaths of autofire, their MP-5s crackling fiercely, tumbling the Chinese to the floor.

"Cal, check out Pol," Lyons called.

As James moved to see to Blancanales, Lyons, his subgun reloaded, crossed to the edge of the curtain and peered out.

He could make out the shadowy figures of soldiers advancing toward the cavern. Behind them were both the tanks. Schwarz, close behind him, was calling up Grimaldi.

"Rise and shine, pal," Schwarz said. "You want some action, now is the time."

He detailed the situation and gave Grimaldi his coordinates.

"Don't hit the rock formation 'cause that's where we are. Anything else out there you can have. Especially those damn tanks."

"I hear you," Grimaldi said as he wound *Dragon Slayer's* power. "I should be with you in six minutes. Think you can keep them busy until then?"

"It'll be a struggle but we'll do our best. Over and out."

CHAPTER FOURTEEN

Jack Grimaldi eased back on the controls as the helicopter lifted off. The moment he was airborne he retracted the landing gear, turning the combat chopper in a tight circle and poured on the power. The black machine clawed its way through the rain and wind, quickly attaining operational height. Grimaldi readjusted the controls and leveled out. He checked his time. He was within his estimated arrival window.

He had the weapons array on-line, his slaved helmet locked in. His scanner monitor showed him the picture below, ghosted in a misty green. As he came quickly up on the combat zone, Grimaldi was able to see the figures moving on the ground. He could also see the two lightweight tanks. One was motionless, the other moving up to join it.

"Okay, let's see what you make of this," Grimaldi muttered into his throat mike as he put the chopper into a shallow run, skimming the treetops. His fingers caressed the trigger of the missile launch, waiting until he had the moving tank in his field of vision. Grimaldi adjusted his aim by a slight movement of his head. The tank was in direct line. He touched the trigger, and a heat-seeker missile sprang from one of the weapon pods leaving a thin trail of smoke in its wake. Grimaldi watched in silent fascination as the missile burned through the darkness, then impacted against the hull of the tank. The resulting explosion sent a white-hot burst of fire into the night, and the tank vanished in a maelstrom of fractured steel and flame.

As *Dragon Slayer* overshot the stricken target, the ammunition inside the tank exploded, adding another ball of flame and smoke. Debris was hurled in every direction, much of it causing injury to the troops following in the tank's tracks. For an instant the scene was starkly lighted by the blast, which faded quickly, drawing a merciful cover of darkness over the bloody result.

Kicking back on the controls, Grimaldi arced the combat chopper in a return run and repeated the missile strike on the remaining tank. By the time he made his run and released his missile, the tank crew and the troops huddled behind it had gone. They were seeking cover before the surviving tank was destroyed. Their fears were justified when Grimaldi released another missile and took out the second tank in another flash of fire and crackling explosions.

With his initial task accomplished Grimaldi gained height and circled the area, checking out what lay below. The only spots of light were the burning hulks of the two tanks. Fuel had sprung from ruptured containers, flash-igniting as it rained over the earth around the shattered hulks of the tanks. Surviving troops let loose wild, inaccurate bursts from their weapons. The shooting was in anger, with little sane thought to more important matters. Grimaldi returned, sweeping in low, and opened up with the chain gun. The awesome power of the machine gun, cycling its rounds at a terrible rate, cut through the Chinese troops, decimating their numbers in an instant.

Hitting the night sky again, Grimaldi took the combat chopper out of the area, swinging it back on a return course to his landing zone where he put the helicopter down and cut the power.

Opening his radio, Grimaldi contacted Schwarz. When the Able Team commando came on, Grimaldi heard the commotion in the background.

"You guys okay?" the flier asked.

"We're getting there.

"Your little problem outside has been taken care of. Keep your eyes open for some ground troops still on the prowl."

"Thanks for the assist," Schwarz said. "Over and out."

A trio of Chinese had breached the camouflage cover and engaged the Stony Man team. The cavern rang to the chatter of autofire, slugs striking equipment and flying in all directions. A stray slug, angling off a steel cabinet, gouged a hole in a drum of fuel. As the liquid burst across the floor of the cavern, other shots reached the same area. Sparks flew from impact with steel and the fumes from the spilled fuel ignited. Flames swelled and grew, rising swiftly, curving in to hit the roof of the cavern, then rolling down to floor level again.

Retreating to the rear of the cavern, the Stony Man team reviewed its fading options.

"If we go out front, they'll cut us down," Manning said.

Despite the expanding curtain of smoke, the soldiers were moving deeper into the cavern. Lyons tossed one of his last two grenades. The projectile blew with a loud crack, taking out two of the Chinese troops. The survivor backed off quickly, coughing from smoke inhalation.

"Now what?" Schwarz asked.

"Check this out," Manning shouted. He had been inspecting the rear wall of the cavern and had found a steel door.

"You think it leads into the base?" Schwarz asked.

"I'd say so," the Canadian said.

He checked the door and found it opened onto a steel landing at the top of a metal spiral staircase. Manning ducked through the open door, peering down the stairs. He could see various levels below him, with step-off landings.

"Let's go," he called over his shoulder.

Schwarz and James helped to support the injured Blancanales. James had strapped him up as best he could. The Able Team commando had a bullet lodged in his right hip, grating against the bone. He was in considerable pain, his face set and pale, but he refused to give in.

Lyons was the last through the door, fighting against the surging smoke that was being sucked toward the open door. His eyes were stinging, his breath catching in his throat as he followed his teammates. As he paused on the landing, the big ex-cop pulled the pin of his last grenade and rolled the bomb across the cavern floor, the smoke concealing its presence from the Chinese who were advancing cautiously. On the landing Lyons eased the steel door shut. He had taken his first step down the staircase when he heard the grenade detonate, the sound and force blowing back against the closed door as other fuel drums blew.

MANNING REACHED the first landing and stepped onto smooth concrete. A narrow passage led off, curving away to the right in the distance. With his back to the wall, Manning covered the passage as the others came down the spiral stairs.

"You hear that?" James asked.

They all listened and picked up the rattle of autofire from the far end of the passage.

"What do you think?" Manning asked.

"Wild guess says it's probably McCarter and the others," James replied.

"Leave me here," Blancanales said. He was still gripping his MP-5. "We need to keep an eye on these stairs."

"Go ahead," Schwarz said. "I'll keep him company. Leave him on his own, and he'll probably shoot himself again."

Lyons was about to protest but Blancanales prodded him with the muzzle of his H&K.

"Go with them, Carl. We can handle this."

The three moved off quickly, with James in the lead. They broke into a steady trot, covering the length of the passage quickly.

With only a few yards to go they came to a dead stop as the heavy crackle of autofire rose in volume. A uniformed figure stumbled around the bend in the passage. The soldier carried an assault rifle, and the moment he set eyes on the Stony Man team he opened fire.

The hail of slugs scored the passage wall, filling the air with dust and splinters of stone. The team was already down, hugging the floor, returning fire. The Chinese was caught by the triple blast, his chest shredded as he was slammed back against the wall.

Lyons gained his feet first, reaching the bend in the passage. He pressed against the wall and peered cautiously around the corner.

At the end of another length of passage the way opened up. From where he stood, Lyons could see a solid door with a window in it. The subdued clatter of autoweapons came from the other side of the door. Lyons beckoned James and Manning.

"Looks promising," James said.

They reached the end of the far passage, pausing to check the open area. It was clear. The door was set in a smooth wall that sealed off the area. James was about to examine the keypad set in the wall next to the door when his eye caught movement on the other side of the window. James took a close look.

"Hey, guys, you really want to see this," he said just before he rapped on the window with the muzzle of his H&K.

COLONEL LI CHENG made his way cautiously down the narrow steps that led to the lower level of the facility. The fact that he refused to allow his emotions to show in front of his men was the only thing that prevented him from throwing up. The sight of his control center being systematically destroyed by the assault team and their Chinese conspirators sickened him. Apart from all the work he and his teams had put in, the fact that his deadline would no longer be achieved angered him more than anything else.

Jun Wang's death, the result of a valiant, but doomed, attempt to stop the assault team, held his attention for a few seconds. Then he dismissed it outright. If Jun had only stopped to consider what he was about to do, he might still be alive. Throwing away his life in a futile gesture that was as empty as a drained water bottle profited no one. Especially Li. Jun's death had left a void in the colonel's organization that would need filling quickly. His dilemma would be in finding someone as good at the job as Jun had been.

Standing in his secure office, witnessing the destruction of his dream, Li had quickly considered his options. According to the garbled reports he had received from topside, his security force had suffered heavily. The assault team, aided by a sophisticated helicopter, had inflicted overwhelming casualties and was in the process of breaching the facility. Digesting the information, Li made his decision. Paramount in his mind was his own safety. If he was captured, or killed, then all his plans came to an end. If he retreated, which seemed the wise thing to do, he could get back to the mainland where he would be safe. There he could regroup and work on a new strategy. He still had in his possession the master computer disks containing all the data required to create the systems stolen from the Americans. At this moment they were at his home, in the hands of the Japanese Makura. The rogue computer expert was already hard at work developing the circuit boards and chips required to run the systems. Even if Li lost his island facility he would still be in possession of the disks, which gave him a winning hand because he could start again.

Reaching the bottom of the steps, Li followed his burly protector along the dimly lighted passage leading to the helicopter pad. Set in a deep depression behind the main bulk of rock that stood over the facility, the pad was concealed from anyone standing outside. A camouflage net that could be quickly drawn over the top of the crater was already being hauled back. Li's pilot was warming up the French-built SA 341 Gazelle, which was painted in military olive drab. Li had used the machine for a number of years since it had been put at his disposal. Although designated as a light observation helicopter, the Gazelle did carry gun and rocket pods.

The heavy-built Chinese sergeant crossed to speak to the pilot, while Li stayed under cover. The rain was still pouring from the clouded sky and above the crater, the wind was still blowing heavily.

The colonel refused to look back. What was done could not be undone. All that was left open to him was to look forward. To plan the resurrection of his scheme, because Li still believed he could make it work. As long as he still had the disks holding the vital information collated and entered by Djin Shu, then he still held the trump card. The project would be reborn.

He heard footsteps on the steps behind him. Whoever was coming down was moving quickly. He heard voices, faint but growing stronger, and they weren't speaking Chinese.

Moving away from the door, Li drew his pistol. He gestured at his protector and when he caught the man's eye beckoned him across.

Confirming Li's thoughts, the burly Chinese nodded and moved to stand on the opposite side of the door.

The colonel said one thing before he fell silent.

"I want them alive!"

THE REUNION WAS BRIEF. The time for backslapping would come later.

"Gary, you've got charges," McCarter said. "Go with T.J. He'll show you where the generators and fuel tanks are. Blow the whole area. Leave something here so we can make sure this lot can't be put back together."

"Sounds like you have something else in mind," Lyons said.

"Colonel Li was up there in that office a while ago. I want to find him."

"So do I," Mei added.

"Once you have the charges set, get everybody out of here and call Jack in. I want all our people on that chopper so we can get the hell out once this place blows."

"Don't you miss the ride," James said.

McCarter smiled. "I can't wait to get off this bloody lump of rock."

The Briton made sure his weapons were loaded then joined Mei and Tsu. They made their way out of the control center and found the stairs that led to the upper floor. The door to Li's office stood open. The office itself was empty.

"Damn!" Mei said.

She stood in the middle of the room, staring around in frustration while McCarter went through every drawer in the desk and the cabinets.

Tsu made a quiet, thorough inspection of the room. He drew their attention when he discovered another door on the far side, partly hidden by a Chinese flag draped across the wall. The door opened onto a narrow flight of steps that led downward. As they crowded in the opening, they felt chill air blowing up the steps.

"Clever boy built himself a back-door escape route," McCarter said.

He led the way down. As they neared the bottom they could hear the sound of the storm still raging outside.

"Sounds like a dirty night," McCarter observed.

The door at the bottom stood wide open. Across a flat area, under an open sky, stood a helicopter. The rotors idled slowly as the machine powered up.

"Could be we're still in time," McCarter stated.

He could see the dark bulk of the helmeted pilot sitting in the cockpit of the Gazelle, but no one else.

"Where is Li?" Mei queried, pushing forward, her caution forgotten in a moment of anger.

"Wait!" McCarter warned.

He was too slow. Mei stepped nimbly past him, peering around.

A bulky dark shape lunged at her, powerful fingers clawing at her shoulder. McCarter moved to intercept, shoving the hand aside. He received a heavy blow to the side of the head for his trouble. It knocked him off balance. Before he could recover, the big man moved again. His clubbed fist drove at McCarter's head, catching him across the jaw and putting the Briton down on his knees, dazed.

Mei yelled wildly; a gun went off.

As McCarter struggled to regain his feet, he saw Tsu Han step in front of Mei as the bulky Chinese went for her. Something curved and glittering caught the light as it slashed back and forth.

Mei screamed, and Tsu Han stumbled back, clutching at his body. Blood was bubbling from deep wounds, spurting between his fingers. The heavyset Chinese cut with the knife again, across Tsu's face and throat.

"Bastard!" McCarter yelled. He found he was still holding the assault rifle and he brought it up, turning it on the knife-wielding Chinese. He triggered the rifle and held it down, putting most of the magazine into the Chinese. The man tumbled back, his body punctured by numerous bullet wounds.

Mei was staring at him, shouting. McCarter took his finger off the trigger to hear her last words before something struck him a crippling blow across the back of the skull. He went down hard, Mei's cry still imprinted in his memory.

"...behind you. Li...."

And then his world turned black and deep and empty.

CHAPTER FIFTEEN

"Tsu Han is dead," James said. "We found him near a helipad. I'm guessing the chopper we saw take off had Li in it."

"What about David and Anna?" Manning asked.

"No sign of either of them."

"Let's get a search going," Manning said, but when he saw the expression in James's eye he paused. "What? You think Li has them?"

"Gary, I don't know. But I can't figure any other explanation. Anna wouldn't have walked off and left Han like I found him. Not the way she felt about him. If they're alive, where are they?"

Manning looked around, his eyes searching, hoping the answer might pop out of nowhere.

"And you know David wouldn't go off without letting us know. And where would he go, anyway? There was no way out of that crater where the landing pad was. We checked the facility. Nothing. They're not in there. Not outside. That only leaves Li's helicopter. Tsu Han's dead. So is a Chinese sergeant. That still leaves the colonel. I reckon he's got them in his chopper. If they were dead or wounded, we would have found them, Gary."

"This mission has been jinxed from the start. Everything that could go wrong did. Now this."

"Hey, man, relax. We got the result, didn't we? Things got a little hairy for a while, but we all got back together."

"Now David has gone missing? I don't call that together."

"Things happen. We don't plan them that way, but we deal with them. We always do."

James glanced at his watch.

"We've got time," the Canadian said. "My explosives go off on the button."

"I know. Just now I have a dent in my faith. So let's move, huh?"

They walked away from the facility, across the muddy ground and past the burned out shells of the tanks *Dragon Slayer* had devastated. The combat chopper was waiting for them, with everyone else on board. That included the rest of Mei's people who had walked in at the tail end of the conflict. They were brought up to speed, and stood in openmouthed amazement at the shattered wreck of Li's organization. The few survivors had already made their break, losing themselves in the stormy darkness, satisfied to be alive and offering no further resistance to the force that now had control of the area. Explosive charges had been laid under the massive fuel tanks and around the generators. They had also been placed in the control center and Li's office. Manning had allowed a generous time before detonation in order for everyone to get clear. Grimaldi had been called in, and he had landed the chopper a couple hundred yards from the facility.

James and Manning climbed into the passenger

compartment. With his passengers all on board Grimaldi secured the hatch and increased the power. The combat chopper rose into the dark night, the island dropping away swiftly. Once altitude was reached Grimaldi set course for Taiwan.

Three minutes into the flight the explosion lighted up the sky behind them. A ball of flame rose, blossomed, then faded and became a thick pall of smoke that hung dark and heavy over Li's island.

No one made any comment.

James sat next to one of Mei's men. He explained what they believed had happened to Mei and the man they knew as Clancy.

"Do you have any idea where Li might take them?"

"The colonel will want to keep the news of his defeat as quiet as possible. Saving face is important to him. I believe he will take them to his residence in Guangdong Province. It is about an hour's flight from the island."

"Is it well protected? Isolated?"

"Yes. Large house in its own grounds. High walls all around. From what we know, Li has his own people guarding it."

"If I find a map of the mainland, could you pinpoint the location?"

The man nodded. "Are you considering a rescue attempt?"

"We may. Right now I don't know."

"The island was one thing. But if you go into Chinese airspace over their territory it could become very awkward."

"I understand what you're saying. But look at it

from our point of view. One of our own may be there. We can't leave him. Or Anna.''

"We might not have any choice," Lyons said, turning in the seat where he was sitting next to Grimaldi. "I just got off the line with the boss man back home. The order came through. We stay away from any rescue attempt until we get the official word.''

"Hell, no," James fumed. "We don't go home and leave one of our people behind.''

Manning leaned over and gripped James's shoulder. "Right now we can't do a thing for them. We need intel. Time to review the situation. Breathing space.''

James nodded. He didn't speak for fear of saying things he might regret later. But it didn't stop him from having his own private thoughts. The trouble was, he didn't like what he was thinking.

Stony Man Farm, Virginia

"MAN, THIS IS BAD," Hunt Wethers said.

"Not the best news we've had lately," Carmen Delahunt agreed.

"Hold up, guys," Brognola said. "Look, I admit it doesn't look good right now. But we need more information.''

"How long before the President gets back to you?" Wethers asked.

Brognola shrugged. "Something like this takes time. It has to be discussed. All the options considered.''

"Hal, what's to consider?" Delahunt asked defensively. "If the Chinese have David and Mei Anna, we have to get them out.''

"How? Send in the Navy? Threaten the Chinese with retaliation if anything happens to our people? This is different from the covert operation on Li's island."

"I don't see why," Delahunt argued.

"It is, Carmen," Yakov Katzenelenbogen said quietly.

He had entered the Computer Room and silently crossed the floor. He sat in an empty chair, leaning forward as he chose his words.

"Up until now this has been a mission based on deniability. The Chinese will refute accusations of theft and the building of a facility intended to counter our own. Right now they are desperate to maintain a good image worldwide. All their diplomatic overtures are based on showing a more progressive attitude. When they embarked on the technology thefts, they were counting on it remaining low key. The U.S. would, they imagined, be reluctant to make too much of a public fuss over the losses because it would shake the faith of allies if they realized how easy it had been for the Chinese to help themselves to such sensitive material."

"But we didn't let them get away with it," Delahunt argued. "We sent in our teams to shut them down. And we did it. So why not continue that and send in a rescue for David and Mei Anna?"

"Because the rules have changed now," Katz said.

"Rules? You make it sound like a game," Wethers said.

"That's exactly what it is. A game that can have an effect on thousands of lives. The problem is that we have to play that same game in order to contain it."

"Look at it this way. How do we justify an armed incursion into Chinese territory? The world would see it as an act of war, and that is how the Chinese would play it. Deny all knowledge of a secret base. What happened on that island will be covered up. The losses concealed. Not hard for a closed country like China. And what could we say to prove anything? We destroyed the base ourselves. The Chinese would hold up their hands and say go ahead and prove it."

"And we would lose that argument," Wethers agreed.

"Exactly," Katz said. "So where does that leave David? In Chinese hands probably accused of being in collaboration with an active dissident responsible for illegal acts. Which also brings Mei Anna into the picture. The Chinese have a prize worth exploiting. They'll have a field day."

Delahunt shook her head. "This is all wrong. You talk like David and Mei Anna don't matter."

"Of course they matter, Carmen. All I'm doing is explaining the way it is likely to go."

"But what happens to them?"

"Most likely a show trial. Guilty as charged. Anna could be executed to set an example. I think they would keep David alive. Give him a life sentence and send him to some isolated prison. Or a labor camp. Knowing the way the Chinese government works, they would keep him alive so they could use him as a bargaining chip. He's someone they could use in negotiations when they want something."

"And all the time both sides would know the real truth," Wethers said bitterly. "Even us."

"Precisely," Katz agreed. "Hunt, there's nothing

new there. It's the way political bargaining has gone since day one.''

''I understand that, Katz, but I'm never going to accept it's right.''

''Hunt, it isn't right. I never said it was. We play with people's lives without question. Take away their freedom, their choice to decide whether they want to be used as pawns in a mindless game.''

''And that's what we've done to David,'' Delahunt said. ''Abandoned him to whatever the Chinese decide to do with him.''

''Think about it, Carmen,'' Katz said gently. ''Think about the situation. What can we do?''

Wethers sighed, shaking his head slowly. ''Not a damned thing,'' he said. ''Not a single, damned thing.''

AN HOUR LATER Brognola assembled them all in the War Room. From his manner everyone knew he wasn't the bearer of good news.

''You know the situation. We have contained the island problem. However, David and Mei Anna appear to have been taken captive and removed from the island in a helicopter under the command of Colonel Li.''

''Has this been proved conclusively?'' Barbara Price asked.

''It has been assessed by the team on the island and is the only logical conclusion. There was no reason or physical evidence to show David and Anna were anywhere else in the area. The timescale since they went looking for Li fits in with the helicopter lifting off and the rest of the team coming to find them.''

"All right, Hal, what's the bottom line?" Price asked. "If we assume David and Anna have been taken, what are we going to do about getting them back?"

"Nothing," Brognola said. "We do nothing."

He waited until the collective reaction had set in.

"This has come from the President himself. It was no easy decision for him. In effect, he is taking Stony Man off this mission. The teams will be ordered home as soon as the wounded have been dealt with."

"They won't like it," Price said.

"Jesus, Barbara, do you think I do? Do you think I want to abandon one of our people to the Chinese? But even I couldn't justify any kind of rescue attempt."

An awkward silence drifted between them until Brognola cleared his throat.

"I guess I was out of line there," he apologized.

"Hey, I forgive you," Price said lightly. "Now let's go and tell the guys before they invade Beijing."

"I KNOW WHAT you're saying, and I know why you're saying it, Hal," Carl Lyons said. "But I'm having a hell of a time accepting it. So are the rest of the guys."

"What option do we have, Carl?" Brognola asked, his voice sounding harsh over the line. "Hard-facts time. We just can't launch a raid on to the Chinese mainland and expect to get away with it. Logistics aside, there are too many negatives. Too much of a chance it could blow up into something that could take us all down with it."

Lyons went very quiet. His mind was weighing the

facts against his gut feeling, and no matter how he rolled it over there was no upside to the thing.

"Carl? You still there?"

"Yeah, I'm here."

"As much as we don't like it, we're going to have to step back from this. David is on his own. At least for the time being. The President has put his best people on this. He wants to see if they can come up with a solution."

"Hal, don't expect any of us to hold our breath waiting for that to happen."

"Soon as you can, get Jack to fly you out of there. He's been instructed to rendezvous with a carrier. The med unit on board can see to the wounded. Carl, will you tell them for me? If you don't want to, I'll speak to them when you're on the carrier."

"No. I'll tell them."

"No heroics, Carl. That's from me. They all walk away from it."

"I'll tell them."

Lyons closed the connection. He stared at the receiver in his hand for a moment, then threw it down and walked out of the communications room and went to find the rest of the Stony Man team. He wasn't looking forward to giving them the news about McCarter.

Not one little bit.

CHAPTER SIXTEEN

Aboard Li's Helicopter

David McCarter had been awake for some time, though he stayed where he was, slumped over in one of the seats in the helicopter. He had realized his hands were bound behind him in the first moments of regaining consciousness, so he knew the situation was far from satisfactory. Until he had a chance to assess the matter, he decided to remain still.

The ride was bumpy, which was due to the weather. Out the corner of his eye McCarter could see one of the side windows. It was streaked with rain. And the helicopter was being buffeted by the strong wind still blowing.

He had a bad headache, the result of being struck across the back of his skull. Dimly he recalled Anna yelling a warning just before he'd been clubbed. Someone had hit him hard, obviously not bothered by what damage he might do. As well as recalling Anna yelling, McCarter suddenly remembered what she had said.

Something about Li. Had he been the one who had struck him? McCarter made a note to check that out. If Li had been there at the time, it seemed likely that he owned the helicopter they were in. In that case, there was no knowing where they might end up. For sure, McCarter knew, they weren't being invited along for tea.

McCarter realized he was assuming Anna was on board as well. Tsu had been killed without deliberation. Would that have applied to Anna? He hoped not. He wanted to see the spirited young woman again. In the short, hectic time he had known her, McCarter had found he was attracted to her quite strongly. He refused to even contemplate her death.

The flight went on. It felt endless to McCarter, tied and lying facedown on a seat, with no way of knowing just what was happening. It left him feeling frustrated. The Phoenix Force leader liked to be in charge of his own destiny. At any given time in his life, McCarter was only happy when he knew what was going on around him. Denied that pleasure he started to get restless.

A sudden powerful gust of wind caught the helicopter. It sank, then veered off course, rolling with the drag of the wind. McCarter felt himself being jerked around, his body slithering across the narrow seat. He fell, twisting as he did, and landed hard on the floor of the cabin. He lay stunned, his left arm and shoulder aching where he had landed on them. The Briton struggled to right himself and finally managed to gain a sitting position, leaning back against the seat he had just fallen from. Now he was able to see the whole of the cabin and in one glance he experienced pleasure and disappointment.

The pleasure was in seeing Anna. Like him she had been bound and propped up on one of the seats opposite. Her eyes met his and she managed a weak smile. The left side of her face showed an angry bruise where she had been struck.

McCarter's disappointment came from seeing Colonel Li Cheng, seated beside the chopper's pilot. Li was watching his prisoners, a faint smile on his lips as he regarded them. He had a pistol in his right hand, and he rested his wrist on the back of the co-pilot's seat.

"If this was a commercial flight, I would be apologizing at this point for the uncomfortable journey," he said. "In this case, the harder it is for you the better I will like it."

"No point asking for a stiff drink, then?" McCarter asked.

"I considered killing you earlier. It would have been an easy thing to finish you both. Then I decided that would be unfair. Not to you, of course. To me. After what you have done, the punishment must be long lasting and extremely uncomfortable."

"Bloody hell," McCarter groaned, "you're not going to make me sit through one of your Chinese operas are you?"

"Levity in your position is hardly a sensible option."

"Why? You going to kill me for it?"

"You British never change. Arrogant and facile as always. The best thing we ever did was throw you out of Hong Kong."

"We should have kicked your arses all the way back to Beijing. You sat on the mainland and watched us build it into the best piece of real estate in Asia, then started whining about wanting it back. Worst thing we ever did, Li. I just hope I live long enough to see how quickly you screw it up."

"The days of empire are over. China is going to create its own destiny without overseers."

"Collectives and five-year plans? A nation held down by a few megalomaniacs like you? Wake up, pal, the new millennium is here. Time to put away your thoughts of Chairman Mao and get real."

Li almost fell out of his seat in his rush to reach McCarter. There was a terrible determination in the way he began to kick the Briton, aiming at McCarter's torso and head. If it hadn't been for the unsteady roll of the helicopter, caught by the battering wind, he might have continued until his victim was dead.

IT WAS SOME TIME before McCarter opened his eyes again. His entire upper body ached, and the left side of his face felt out of shape and numb. He spit blood from his mouth. Across from him Mei Anna sat slumped in her seat, staring at him. McCarter managed a lopsided grin.

Li was in his own seat, strapped in this time, his shoulders hunched as he spoke into a radio handset. He was speaking in his own language, and this time McCarter didn't even bother to try to translate. Just thinking about it hurt.

The helicopter seemed to be flying on an even keel now. The wind wasn't banging against the fuselage quite as strongly, but rain still peppered the windows.

McCarter winced after making a slight move. Dull pain reached up to make him groan. Li was too busy with his radio to notice. The Briton sat upright, pressing against the seat cushion at the back of his head. He became aware that the helicopter was descending, swinging around to a new course. Within the next few minutes their descent quickened. Despite the bad weather, the pilot put them down with barely a bump. He locked down the controls and cut the power. As the engine faded, the sound of the falling rain increased in volume, hammering away at the helicopter's fuselage.

Li turned abruptly, still brandishing the pistol.

"Just remember this gun is fully loaded."

"Manage it yourself did you?" McCarter asked breezily.

"Jim!" Mei snapped.

"You would be advised to warn this fool that he is doing himself no good."

"If I do, will things get better?" Mei asked with a mocking tone in her voice.

"Perhaps a spell in a labor camp will take the edge off your humor," Li said. "Think about that prospect. Both of you."

THE HELIPAD WAS situated in the grounds of Li's residence. The sprawling house, a mixture of modern design and Chinese classical, did nothing to bring comfort to McCarter and Mei as they were manhandled from the chopper by a number of Li's soldiers who had come out to meet them. They were marched across the landing pad and inside the house. The last thing McCarter saw before the door slammed behind them was a small fuel tanker being positioned beside the helicopter.

Li spoke to one of the soldiers and McCarter and Mei were directed along a tiled corridor, down a flight of steps into a cellar area. At the end of another, less pleasant corridor they were halted in front of a steel door. The door was unlocked. One of the soldiers freed their hands, and McCarter and Mei were thrust into the gloomy cell. The door slammed shut behind them, the lock clicking as the key was turned.

"Well, I don't think I'll be booking with this tour company again," McCarter muttered as he inspected the small cell. The walls and floor were rough concrete. The ceiling, painted white, was fitted with a light with a wired cover, embedded in the plaster.

"Jim, shut up," Mei said as she made her own inspection of the cell.

The light went out, plunging them into total darkness. McCarter felt his way across the cell until he found Mei. She gripped him tightly as they moved to the closest wall and sat with their backs to the cold concrete.

McCarter felt Mei shivering in the chill air. He drew her close to his body, feeling the soft caress of her hair against his cheek.

"This isn't how I planned our first date to turn out," he said.

"Oh? So this is a date?"

"Kind of," McCarter said.

"I have a rule about first dates."

"What?"

"I have to know your real name."

"Someone might be listening."

"Quietly."

McCarter leaned close and whispered to her. She was silent for a while.

"And?"

"I'll stick to Jim Clancy for now," she said.

"For now?"

"Until we have our first real date."

"Sounds reasonable to me."

THE LIGHT CLICKED ON. A key rattled in the lock and the door swung open. Two armed soldiers stood just inside the cell shouting at them.

"They want us to go with them," Mei said.

She and McCarter stood, blinking against the bright glare of the light. They were chilled and stiff from their night in the bare cell.

The guards took them back along the corridor and up the steps, along another hallway and up a wide staircase to the first floor of the house. Through a window on the landing McCarter saw that the rain had stopped and the day looked reasonably bright. They were taken along a wide corridor with delicate paintings hung on the walls. At the end, a double door opened into a bright, large room. As McCarter and Mei were pushed inside, Li Cheng turned to face them, smiling like some benevolent uncle. He was in full uniform, a pistol in a holster on his broad belt.

"Good morning," he said. "We have a pleasant day for you."

The guards closed the doors and stood rigidly to attention on either side of them.

McCarter took a quick look at the room and its occupants.

A tall, striking Chinese woman stood by one of the windows, staring out across the grounds. Dressed in a black, slim-fitting cotton suit, she had the appearance of a fashion model. When she turned her head and caught McCarter's eye, he sensed something evil about her.

A computer station stood in one corner of the room, and seated in a large, leather chair, his fingers busy at the keyboard, was a lean Japanese. He didn't look up, or pause in his work during McCarter's and Mei's entrance.

There was one more man in the room. He was seated in a comfortable chair across the room from where Mei was standing. She was watching him closely, an angry expression in her eyes, and Mc-Carter realized she knew the man.

Li Cheng had also noticed Mei's interest in the man.

"I believe you know Jiang Fu."

"I thought I did. Until now."

The colonel seemed to be enjoying the moment. He glanced at Jiang Fu.

"Our British friend seems to be at a loss. Why don't I explain?"

Li moved to stand behind Jiang's chair, resting his hands on the man's shoulders. McCarter watched Jiang's face and saw that he was sweating a little. There was an uneasy look in his eyes.

"Jiang Fu is part of Miss Mei's group. He joined them some months ago. What Miss Mei did not know was that Fu also works for me. His assignment was to infiltrate her little group and pass me all the information about them that he could. It took time of course, because he needed to gain their confidence, and it was only very recently he was able to start sending me that information."

Li paused, watching and waiting for reactions. McCarter looked at Mei, who was still staring at Jiang. McCarter could see her breasts rise and fall as her breathing quickened. He spotted a flicker of movement in her body as she prepared to move and he stepped up to her, gripping her arm.

"It's what they want you to do," he said. "So don't."

Mei's face was taut with anger as she looked up at him.

"You expect me to stand here and let that... that...miserable little traitor get away with it?"

"You have little choice, Mei Anna," Li said.

"What other little surprises do you have in store for us?" McCarter asked.

"Only one," Li said. "Jiang Fu is a talented individual. Not only did he infiltrate Miss Mei's pathetic little group, he also worked for someone you knew. One of your countrymen."

Neil Hallam.

The name sprang into McCarter's mind instantly, and he realized what Li was implying. He recalled Hallam's remark about his suspicions concerning an informant within his own organization.

"Jiang Fu has been working for the British, too."

"Meaning?"

"Your contact in Hong Kong? Hallam? He died recently. Shot on the steps of the hotel you met him at on your arrival, according to Fu."

It was McCarter's turn to feel the rising anger of betrayal. He looked at Jiang Fu, his immaculate suit and neatly brushed hair, the way he sat with confidence in Li's home. Yet behind the facade Jiang Fu did look a little uncomfortable. Perhaps because too much was being revealed about his identity.

"I'm surprised you allow a piece of garbage like that in your house, Li. There I was, thinking you were a man of culture and class, and all the time you're down in the gutter with this scum."

"There are times when people like Jiang Fu are useful," Li explained.

"The way I see it, Li, he can't be trusted. He's already betrayed two different groups. How can you be sure you won't be next?"

The colonel raised his hands in a sweeping gesture. "How indeed? We live in an extremely deceitful world."

He dropped his hands to his sides. "However, I am safe in the knowledge that Jiang Fu will never betray me."

McCarter's face remained impassive as he saw Li bring his hands into view again. In his right he held a knife. With a swift, sure move the colonel caught hold of Jiang Fu's hair and pulled his head up and back, stretching his throat. He reached over, laying the knife blade to the man's taut flesh. Li made a deep, severe cut, laying Jiang's throat open. Blood coursed from the massive wound. The man struggled, his mouth gaping as he tried to suck in air. He kicked out. His hands clawed at the arms of the chair. The front of his shirt and suit had turned a glistening red. Rattling sounds bubbled from his bloody mouth, then he became still.

Li released him, smiling. "Now we can all rest safe in our beds."

McCarter sighed. He was starting to get impatient with Li's tiresome games.

"Cut to the chase, Li. What do you have in mind for us? As much as I like standing around, I'd like to know."

"I would like to make you suffer for what you have done to me," the colonel said. "For the great inconvenience you and your interfering colleagues have caused me. The months of construction. The expense. The labor. The facility you destroyed would have become one of our most advanced weapons. We would have possessed great influence over this part of the world and even have been able to reduce America's capability to defend herself if the need arose."

"Did you expect us to sit back and let that happen?" McCarter asked.

There was movement by the window as the tall Chinese woman swung around suddenly. She snapped something to one of the guards. He came forward, took Mei's arm and led her to a chair, pushing her down on it.

Shun Wei went to stand behind the chair.

"Cheng," she said in English, "introduce me."

"Of course, my dear. This is Mr. Jim Clancy," Cheng announced. "He and Mei Anna are the ones behind all our difficulties."

"Has he said anything?" Shun Wei asked.

"Nothing of consequence yet. However, we will change that."

"Li, I don't have a thing to tell you. We've accomplished what we came for. Kick seven bells out of me if it amuses you, but don't expect too much information because I don't have any. I'm done here. And you are out of business."

"You think so?" Li pointed at the Japanese, still working at his keyboard. "Kobashi Makura. Despite your efforts, we will still succeed. Makura is already developing the first of the computer circuit boards required for the American Slingshot Program. I will rebuild the command center easily. The circuit boards are the heart of the machine, and I still have the master disks containing all the design schematics."

"You're not there yet," McCarter said. "It'll take more than a second-rate hacker to design those boards."

For the first time since they had entered the room, McCarter saw Makura react. He rose from his seat with a stifled yell. He was halfway across the room before one of Li's guards stepped in front of him, blocking his path.

"Touchy, isn't he?" McCarter observed.

Li stepped up to the Japanese. "Ignore him. He is only trying to provoke you."

"Trying?" McCarter said. "He gets any madder he'll blow."

Makura threw a murderous glance in McCarter's direction. He thrust a long finger at the Briton.

"I will kill you."

McCarter grinned, despite his aching face. "Get in line, mate. If you think you're man enough."

Even Li was pushed aside as Makura lunged forward, all control gone now. He reached the Briton in three long strides, reaching out with his long, lean arms.

McCarter seemed to be ignoring him. He stood motionless, as if he were inviting attack. Makura closed in quickly. At the last moment the Briton swayed to one side so that Makura's lunge missed by inches. The Japanese tried to correct himself, swiveling awkwardly, and tried to regain control. He failed. McCarter's right knee came up and slammed into Makura's stomach. The Phoenix Force leader put every ounce of power he could into the move. The impact bent Makura from the waist. He clutched at his body, gagging violently. Makura's hesitation gave Mc-Carter the time to step back and deliver an unrestrained kick that connected with Makura's jaw. The force spun the man back across the room, his arms flailing. He struck a chair and fell across it, rolling to the floor where he lay moaning, blood spewing from his crushed jaw.

One of the guards blocked McCarter from following up, jabbing the butt of his rifle into the Briton's side.

Li, his face livid, turned on McCarter.

"You can die here—now!" he yelled.

"Go ahead, Li, if you have the nerve. But remember I'm not Jiang Fu. I don't have my back to you."

Li snapped something at the armed guards. His instruction was too quick for McCarter to decipher, but he caught the look of alarm in Mei's eyes. She opened her mouth to warn him, but it came too late. Something hard thudded into the small of McCarter's back and he was driven to his knees. Shun Wei strode across the room to stand over him. She mouthed something, then hit him across the face with something in her hand. The blow knocked McCarter to the floor. He lay still, gritting his teeth against the pain in his cheek, his mouth clamped tightly shut. The side of his face burned with dull, aching pain. He could feel blood running down his face. Hard hands grabbed him and hauled him upright. Still on his knees, he stared up into the face of Shun Wei and saw her taut features, her mouth set in a tight line. He saw her tense and braced himself for a second blow. She hit him again in the same place, only harder. McCarter crashed to the floor again. The polished wood tiles were cool against his face.

The hurt refused to go away. McCarter lay still, trying to absorb the pain. The side of his face felt swollen. When he moved his jaw, it hurt badly. He could taste blood on the inside of his mouth where a tooth had torn the cheek. In the background someone spoke, and McCarter was pulled to his feet again. He was manhandled to a chair.

Li appeared before him. "Do we have an understanding now, Mr. Clancy?"

"The only thing I understand right now, Li, is that you have a bloody sick girlfriend."

Li sighed. "Mr. Clancy, I could have had you killed on more than one occasion today. Perhaps you still do not grasp the gravity of your situation."

"No? Look at it from my perspective, Li. I know what you've been doing on that damned island. Right now you don't know how much information I have on you. But you'd like to know. Pal, I'm going to tell you the same as last time. I don't have a bloody thing to say. Kick me all the way along the Great Wall it won't make any difference. So, as they say in the East End of London, up yours, Jack."

"This is not getting us anywhere," Li yelled.

"I'm not here to help," McCarter said.

"No!" Li thundered, losing control completely. "All you are here for is to destroy. To burn down everything I have built."

"What the hell did you expect? You steal our technology and believe we're going to sit back and let you get away with it?"

Li managed a smile. "But I have. I will rebuild the facility. When it is done, we will have the means to match the U.S.A. and anyone who threatens us."

"The Americans aren't going to sit back and let it

happen. They can change their operating controls. Alter codes and computer programs.''

"Intricate system programs are not so quickly changed. It takes time. While that happens we will still have access.''

"If you lose it, you'll have to steal some more,'' McCarter said dryly.

"If it is necessary. But it won't be. I still have my information. To help my country I will do what is needed.''

"Every thief has an excuse for what he's doing.''

"China needs this protection. We cannot allow the West to dominate us any longer.''

"Look around you for God's sake. No one is trying to dominate you, Li. Don't use that old excuse to cover up what you're doing. You bloody people are all the same. Power for power's sake. To hell with the poor sods out there who only want a peaceful life. Stop pretending you're doing this for China. It's for you, Li. A step up the ladder. A way of keeping in with the sad bunch in government who are running scared.''

"And you, Mei Anna? Do you see the world through this man's eyes?''

"Don't patronize me, Li. Your scheme is just another cause to empower your regime. It's correct what Jim says. This isn't about China's safety. That's your excuse to cover up your real agenda. And why we have to stop you.''

"Do you really believe you and your pathetic little group can do a thing to me?''

"We have got this far.'' Mei said. "Your base has been destroyed. The Americans know what you're doing.''

Shun Wei interrupted. "The Americans? You talk about them as if they can solve everything. If they are so great, how did we just walk in and take what we wanted? Right from under their stupid noses."

"Why?" Mei said. "Because they trust people. They give what they have. Perhaps too easily, but they share their knowledge and their discoveries."

"Then they can't complain if we help ourselves."

"For what? So we go back to confrontation? To the days of mistrust and hate?" Mei shook her head. "Ask the people if that is what they want. The *real* people of China. Give them hope. Give them a chance to build our country into something good. Don't take a step backward into the Dark Ages."

"The real people of China do not know what they want," Li said. "That is why we have to decide. Why we tell them what is right."

"Of course," McCarter said. "Your way. Make all the decisions for them. Convince them the rest of the world is their enemy. Keep control over everything so they can't get to the truth. Bloody hell, man, are you real? We're in a new millennium and you're still hanging on to the cold war mentality? That went out with the bathwater years ago."

"I suppose next you will give me an example," Li said. "The Soviet Union? Of course. We have all seen what has happened there since they rejected Marxism. You tell me I am living in the past. What incentive do I have to go forward if Russia is all you can offer? A nation in ruins. No money. No economy. Floundering without direction. Crime. Drugs. Breakaway states causing misery and destruction? Do you see this for China, Mr. Clancy? I do not think so. I prefer a strong China. A united nation with the capability to stand up to any threat.''

"Russia has her problems. I'm the first to admit that. But at least she's trying, coming to terms with a new way of life. The breakup was internal, not caused by outside influences. The old Communist ideas were over. Worn out. They weren't working, so they changed the rules. No one said it had to be easy. But I believe they'll make it work. It'll take time and they'll come out okay. But I'll tell you something for nothing, Li. It's a damn sight better than hanging on the way you and your cronies have. Small-minded men with outmoded ideas hanging on to something that's long dead, because given the chance, the people would throw you out tomorrow for a better deal. The only thing keeping them down is *you* with your tanks, guns and bloody military.''

"No!" Li shouted. "The people are behind us. They see the way forward. A powerful nation able to stand against anyone.''

"You sound like one of those bloody awful patriotic songs they play over the radio all the time. For God's sake man, talk like you have a brain not a government script.''

Shun Wei lunged forward, screaming in her fury and lashed out at McCarter. He tried to avoid the blow, this time seeing the black leather-covered cosh in her hand. His reaction was a margin too slow and the solid weight glanced off his cheek, splitting the skin. McCarter swayed but stayed on his chair.

"Insult the colonel again, and you will die.''

"Lady, I've been threatened with that ever since I came into this bloody room. Right now it doesn't even make me sweat, so shut up about it. And while we're at it, stay away from me. Hit me once more, and I'll forget my bloody manners.''

"You are like all the British," Shun Wei said. "Arrogant and stupid. Remember this. We threw you out of Hong Kong. Maybe that was just for starters.''

"Threw us out?" McCarter was unable to hold back a laugh. "Lady, I already had this out with the colonel. I think you read too much of your own propaganda.''

McCarter's taunt worked just as he had expected. Shun Wei lost control, coming at him with unrestrained ferocity. Her right arm swept up, the black cosh swishing as it was aimed at McCarter's head. He was more than ready this time, stepping aside as she moved in close. He reached out to grab her wrist, twisting hard and yanking her off balance. Shun Wei was pulled around to face him and McCarter backhanded her. The blow snapped her head around, blood smearing her chin from a split lip. The Briton used her own momentum to send her staggering into the closest of the guards, and as the man reached out to catch her, McCarter lunged off his chair and stepped around her. He elbowed the guard in the throat, hard, and snatched the assault rifle from his hands as the man clutched at his shattered throat, gagging. The Briton swung the rifle butt-first and whacked the guard under the jaw, stretching him out across the floor.

He turned the rifle, tracking the other guard across the room. He triggered a short burst, the 7.62 mm slugs knocking the man to the floor, spattering the surface with bloody spray.

"Jim!" Anna yelled.

McCarter heard the rush of sound and turned to

meet Li's rush. The man was fumbling for the pistol in the shiny belt holster he wore. He was still trying to pull it free when McCarter snapped the butt of the rifle into his face. The blow sent the colonel to his knees, and the follow-up blow to the back of his head slammed him facedown on the floor. McCarter removed the pistol and crossed the room to where Mei had already picked up the rifle from the other guard. She helped herself to the extra magazines, slinging the gun over her shoulder.

"See if you can find any computer disks," McCarter said.

He crossed to the door and locked it, then returned to where Mei was on her knees, yanking open drawers and scattering stuff across the floor. McCarter went to the computer and removed the disks from the drives, shoving them in one of his zip pockets. Then he ripped out all the cables and used the butt of the rifle to stave in the monitor and smash the drives.

"Are these what you want?" Mei asked. She had a stack of disks in her hand. The labels were all written in Chinese script.

"You tell me?"

She scanned the disks. "They refer to masters for various systems. I can't tell you anymore."

"Are there any others?"

Mei shook her head and handed the disks to McCarter, who stuck them in a pocket.

"Let's hope these are all he has."

"They must be."

"We'll look bloody stupid if they're copies of the latest arcade game," McCarter muttered. "Now let's see if we can get the hell out of here."

"Of course, Jim, we'll just open the window and fly."

"The window is the only way we can go."

In the distance they could hear shouting from somewhere in the house, and the clatter of boots on the stairs.

McCarter picked up one of the heavy chairs and used it to smash the glass of the room's window. He peered out. There was a wide ledge below the window, and to the left it ran some twelve feet to a parapet edging a flat-roofed section of the house.

"You scared of heights?" he asked.

Mei smiled. "Only when I'm falling from them."

"Funny," McCarter said.

He stepped on to the ledge, helping Mei outside. They flattened against the wall and edged their way along. Behind them they could hear thumping on the room's door.

"Jim, get a bloody move on," Mei urged.

"Language!"

McCarter reached the parapet and hauled himself over, then caught Mei's arms and dragged her over. She dropped beside him a scant moment before the crackle of an assault rifle told them they had been sighted. Bullets ground into the stone parapet, filling the air with stone chips and showering them with dust.

McCarter returned fire, his burst driving the shooter back from the window.

"Which way do we go?" Mei asked.

"I want to get to that helicopter down there," McCarter said. "It's our way out of here."

He led the way across the flat roof. They were near the far side when Mei lifted her rifle and fired. Her initial burst was off target, but she quickly readjusted her aim and caught the soldier who had emerged from a door set in the end wall. The man fell back, his chest bloody.

McCarter spotted another group, which had climbed a metal ladder that led from the ground. He triggered at the leader and caught him in the face. The man fell backward with a brief scream, crashing to the ground below. The others on the ladder were caught between the ground and the roof. McCarter stepped to the parapet and triggered another blast that made any decision worthless. The soldiers went down in a tangle of shredded flesh.

Yards away Mei engaged others who had used the roof door. They made the mistake of trying to crowd through at the same time, and her unrestrained burst cut them down. Their slumped bodies blocked the door and prevented others from coming through. She flattened against the wall beside the door and took what she could from the bodies. Extra magazines for the assault rifles and grenades from a web belt. McCarter joined her.

"Look," she said.

McCarter took two grenades. He pulled the pin on one and tossed the bomb down the stairwell beyond the corpses. The grenade clattered down stone steps before it detonated with a sharp crack. The explosion was followed by yells of pain.

He returned to where they had first climbed over the parapet and looked into the window to the room they had exited. There was movement just inside. McCarter pulled the pin and leaned out over the parapet, hurling the grenade with an almost lazy throw. He watched the projectile spin, then drop inside the room. Seconds later it exploded. Smoke and debris flew out the window. A bloody figure fell across the sill, suspended half in and half out of the room.

"This is all very well," Mei said, "but it doesn't get us off this roof."

"Just like a woman to mention the snag," McCarter said.

"Yes. So?"

"I'm working on it," McCarter said as he jogged across the roof to the far end. Peering over the parapet, he saw a sloping tiled roof some five feet below. "Let's go."

There was no time for debate, or hesitation. There seemed to be a lull from the opposition. McCarter couldn't know whether it was due to a lack of numbers or simply that they were regrouping. Whatever the reason, he and Mei had to take the opportunity to head for the helicopter.

They dropped to the tiled roof and ran along the apex, heading for where the roof sloped to a jutting outbuilding, which had a flat roof. They reached it without challenge and scanned the area before jumping to the roof, then to the ground.

McCarter checked the way ahead, aware that their next move would take them across open ground as they made for the helicopter. The first thing they did was to take out the partly used magazines and snap in fresh ones.

"Anna, when we go, run like hell. Not in a straight line. Zigzag. Makes a harder target to hit."

She gave him a scathing look, then said calmly, "I never would have thought of that, Jim."

They rose to their feet back-to-back, each taking an area to check for movement. McCarter pulled the

pin on one of the remaining grenades and held the
orb ready. Mei watched him and repeated his move.

"You ready?" McCarter asked.

She stared at him, her face immobile. Only her
eyes showed her true feelings.

"No," she admitted, "but that won't stop me."

"*Go!*" McCarter yelled.

And they went.

CHAPTER SEVENTEEN

McCarter ignored the aching pleas from his battered
body. He wanted to lie down and just relax, but knew
that if he gave in he wasn't going to reach the waiting
helicopter. The sight of Mei Anna, running with surprising grace and speed, made him cast aside his notion to quit. If she could make it, he wasn't about to
give in.

They were halfway across the grass when Mc-
Carter spotted movement near the helicopter. It was
the pilot who had flown them in. He came around the
front of the chopper, a stubby machine pistol in his
hand, and the moment he set eyes on McCarter and
Mei he raised the pistol and fired. His first shot kicked
up a gout of earth inches from the woman. She
swerved, slipping on the still-damp grass, and almost
fell. Her pause allowed the pilot to track in on her.
His pistol cracked and Mei gasped and went down.

McCarter slid to a stop, turning, and lined up the
pilot in his sights. The Briton fired from the hip, triggering a burst that opened the pilot's chest, spinning
him so that McCarter's second burst stitched him between the shoulders. The pilot fell forward, bouncing
off the side of the helicopter's canopy before he
thumped to the ground.

McCarter knelt beside Mei, reaching to turn her over. Black hair fanned across her face. He brushed it away, staring down at her.

"Anna?"

She exhaled, her eyes opening as she recognized his voice.

"It hurts like hell," she said.

Spreading blood marked her tunic just over her ribs on the left side. She pulled it up and exposed the ragged gash in her smooth flesh. It was bleeding and raw.

"Can you make it to the helicopter?" McCarter asked.

"Try to stop me."

She snatched up her rifle as McCarter pulled her to her feet.

Behind them the sound of a revving engine reached their ears. Over his shoulder McCarter saw an open-topped black car pulling away from the house. It swung off the drive and cut across the lawn, heading in their direction.

"Go," McCarter yelled and pushed Mei toward the helicopter. He turned to face the oncoming car. Two figures were in the vehicle beside the driver.

One was Li, his tunic tattered and bloody. One side of his face was a shredded mess where he had to have caught part of the grenade blast from the projectile McCarter had thrown in through the window. He was wielding an autorifle.

On the rear seat beside him was Shun Wei. She didn't appear to be injured in any way. Even at the distance he was from the car, McCarter could hear her screaming orders.

The Briton fired on the car, catching the front tires

with his second volley. Rubber shredded and the car lost some traction, chewing up swaths of grass and earth as it swept broadside. The driver struggled with the wheel, but the more he struggled the less control he had. McCarter raised the rifle again and took aim, touching the trigger and loosing a short burst that caught the driver in the side of the head. The man slumped sideways against his door, the car rolling forward out of control. The Briton followed it, firing at the rear, blowing the tires and peppering the body-work, coring through to the gas tank.

As the slewing car began to slow, Li kicked open his door and leaped from the vehicle. He landed in a crouch, then ran forward, firing.

McCarter faced him head-on, the pair of them trading shots. The Briton felt something clip his sleeve, scoring a thin burning line across his arm. He returned fire, saw Li stop short, the muzzle of his assault rifle sagging to the ground.

"Jim," Mei yelled from the helicopter. She had the door to the cabin open and was leaning out, her rifle resting across the top of the door. "Let's go."

McCarter backed off, ramming home a fresh magazine and cocking the rifle. Out the corner of his eye he saw Li struggling to stand upright. The front of his tunic was bloody.

A burst of fire came from behind McCarter. The long blast ripped into Li, from groin to throat. The colonel crashed to the ground, facedown, and McCarter knew he wouldn't be getting up again.

Reaching the helicopter, the Briton glanced at Mei as she lowered her rifle. The grass below her was littered with shell casings.

"Feel better now?" he asked.

"Tsu Han is still dead," she said. "So are a lot of good people."

He clambered into the pilot's seat and checked the controls. Mei, leaning over the back of the seat, read out various instructions, deciphering the Chinese characters. McCarter flicked switches and used his own familiarity with helicopters to fire up the engine. The rotors began to turn, slowly at first, but gaining speed as he fed more power, encouraging the engine to power up.

Mei moved to check out the grounds. She made out a few uniformed figures emerging from the house.

"Jim, we have movement near the house."

McCarter, increasing the power, eased back on the controls. He felt the chopper start to lift. Gaining a few feet, he turned the chopper toward the house, flicking open the fire control button for the machine-gun pods fitted to the side of the helicopter.

"Shun Wei," Mei said, pointing to a female figure running toward the house, waving her arms as she screamed instructions at the soldiers.

Autofire was directed at the helicopter.

"You shouldn't have done that," McCarter said, and touched the firing button.

The Gazelle vibrated as the machine guns opened up, sending twin lines of slugs racing across the grass. The blast ripped into and through the scattering soldiers. It continued on into the front of the house, pockmarking the walls and shattering windows. McCarter eased the hovering helicopter across the frontage, then gained height and swung it to roof level. He located the window of the room where he and Mei had been confronted by Li and Shun Wei.

McCarter was thinking about the computer station,

the possibility that they might have left some valuable disks behind. He backed off while he searched for the button that armed and fired the missiles housed in the pods. He armed the first set, fired and watched the slim rockets leap from the sides of the helicopter. They went straight through the window and a split second later the room blew in a ball of fire and smoke. Debris was hurled out across the lawns, and the explosion rocked the helicopter.

McCarter worked the controls and took the helicopter up and away from the house and grounds. He sat back, feeling the helicopter respond to his touch now. He glanced at the instruments, satisfying himself that they had ample fuel, then spoke over his shoulder.

"Anna, can you give me a hand with the radio? See if we can locate my people."

"Give me a minute."

He glanced around and saw she was binding her wound with bandage she had located in the first-aid kit.

"You okay?"

"Yes. I'm fine, *David*."

McCarter settled in his seat, a satisfied smile on his face.

MEI JOINED HIM awhile later. She dropped into the copilot's seat and reached for the radio handset, slipping the spare headphones over her dark hair.

"Check through the incoming signals. Could be there might be a locator transmission being sent. Knowing my mates, they won't have given up yet."

Mei stared out through the canopy.

"Where are we heading?"

McCarter tapped the map clipped to the board in front of him.

"Taiwan?" Mei said. "Oh, well, I've always wanted to visit."

Taiwan

CARL LYONS WANDERED out to where *Dragon Slayer* sat on the concrete. He carried a mug of steaming coffee for Jack Grimaldi. The Stony Man pilot had refused to leave the combat chopper in case McCarter managed to locate them. He was constantly monitoring the radio frequencies, hoping he might get a response to his transmitted signal.

"Hey, Jack, let me take over."

Grimaldi took the coffee as Lyons climbed inside and passed the mug across.

"I'm fine," he said. "How are the guys?"

"I spoke to Encizo a while ago. They're okay. The medics on the carrier have looked after them fine. They operated on Pol earlier and took the slug out. He'll be off his feet for a while, but he'll make it."

"That's good news."

Lyons indicated the radio. "Anything?"

"Nothing."

"Jack."

"Don't say it, Carl. I know all the arguments. But, dammit, if any man can get himself out of a mess, it's David. I won't walk away from this."

"You think Stony Man was wrong making us stand down?"

"Yes. No. Christ, Carl, I can see both sides. The guys don't want to leave a pal in the lurch. I know every single one of them would go storming into

China right now if they decided it was the thing to do. But I know Hal's position, too. He sees it from the other side. We don't have any idea where they took David. What could we do? Take the chopper and go flying up and down the country looking for him? Take on the Chinese army? The air force?''

Lyons didn't reply. Grimaldi was right. Brognola was right. But none of it made up for the fact that one of their own was lost. On his own with no backup, no rescue attempt imminent. It didn't do a great deal for Carl Lyons's peace of mind.

When Grimaldi leaned forward, adjusting the settings on the control panel, Lyons didn't pay all that much attention. He figured the flier was making sure he had his radio on-line.

''Son of a bitch,'' Grimaldi said suddenly.

''What? You got something?''

Grimaldi put the sound on the speaker, and Lyons heard the voice he had believed might be gone forever.

''...up your signal. We're on a course for Taiwan. You want to confirm? Come on somebody. If I can't see your bloody ugly mugs, at least I can listen to that awful American slang you bums call English.''

Grimaldi was grinning like an idiot. Even Lyons had a smile on his face.

''Jack, don't you lose him. I'll go get the others.''

EPILOGUE

Hal Brognola sat in the War Room, scattered papers on the table in front of him. He had just read through the final report on the interception of the *Blue Water* by the Navy sub, recalling the event as it had come through on Kurtzman's computer....

Aaron Kurtzman had jerked upright in his chair as a warning beep from his computer alerted him to a message coming through. He swung around, almost knocking over his mug of long-cold coffee, and keyed in the response that flashed the information on his screen. He read it as the details filled the large screen, and a smile creased his bearded face.

"Go, Navy!" he boomed, startling everyone in the com room.

There was a sudden rush as Kurtzman's exclamation galvanized the team into action. They crowded his wheelchair, staring over his shoulder.

"Damned if they didn't do it," Kurtzman said. "Stopped *Blue Water* and put a Marine team on board before the ship's crew knew what was happening."

"Did they find what they were looking for?" Wethers asked.

Kurtzman enlarged the text so they could all read

it. At the same time he asked for a printout. "According to the submarine commander, they located computer hardware in the hold. In crates marked Domestic Goods. Computers manufactured in the U.S.A. Tracking and monitoring devices. Enough to equip a substantial facility. And they located master disks in the captain's safe. The sub's computer guy checked them out and they have data that matches material taken from U.S. sources."

"Good result," Barbara Price said. "Aaron, what did they do with the equipment?"

Kurtzman swung his chair around to face her, a wide grin on his face.

"Guess," he said.

"Okay, smart-ass. Any casualties?"

"There'll be a couple of Chinese seamen with sore heads tomorrow, is all. According to the report, resistance was minimal. These were just ordinary Chinese crew members. Not hard cases."

That had been welcome news, something to ease the tension that had been building as they had all waited for news about the combat teams. The situation hadn't been as good. Missing personnel. The mission starting to come adrift. It was at times like those that the people at the Farm could do very little except wait and hope. All the electronic marvels they had at their disposal couldn't do a thing to pull a mission back on-line if some natural occurrence interfered with it.

The sudden storm. The sinking of the junk and then the news that there were members of Phoenix Force out of contact, possibly lost. All those incidents left Stony Man out on a limb. Words of comfort were no help to anyone in those circumstances.

Brognola never lost faith. He knew his people. Their strengths and their ability to overcome setbacks. He was also a realist, and he accepted there might come the day when one of his people might not come back alive. They were good. The best. But they weren't immortal. If the time came when one of them died out in the field, they would all mourn the passing, but they were strong enough to go on. To step beyond personal grief and to carry the fight forward.

This mission had generated some difficult moments. Even when it had come together, as during the conflict on the island, the teams had been united again. Until the moment when McCarter and Anna Mei had vanished.

That, more than anything, had created problems. With scant information on McCarter's whereabouts, the teams had wanted to go into China and bring him out. Brognola's command had never felt so isolated as when he had been forced to order their standdown. He had wanted to let go. Even knowing it would have been futile, and possibly might have created one hell of an international incident. Thankfully, the teams had taken his decision. The wounded had been flown out to the Navy carrier while the others had remained in Taiwan, monitoring the airwaves in case McCarter managed to get through.

When he did, it had seemed like a miracle, a reprieve for all of them.

Brognola had breathed easy for the first time in hours. After the cheering had died down he had collected his paperwork and made his way to the War Room where he sat in semidarkness contemplating the ramifications of the whole affair, which had started the day Djin Shu had been murdered in San Francisco. A great deal had happened since then.

It wasn't over yet; Brognola knew that. There would be a lot of recriminations. Behind the scenes the Chinese would raise the roof, and so would the U.S. Accusations would fly like snowflakes in a blizzard. Threats and counterthreats would be made. In the end, though, nothing would come of it because there was no real proof.

Li's island base had been destroyed. The Stony Man teams had retrieved much of the stolen information, with proof on paper that the Chinese had gained their technology illegally. China wasn't going to make too much of a fuss by going public, nor was the U.S. administration. The affair had revealed loopholes in security that would have already been sealed. In the end they would all be back where they had started.

Except for the people who had died. And there were always those caught in the cross fire who shouldn't have been involved. It was par for the course. Innocents suffered along with the guilty.

Brognola pushed at the papers on the table. In the end it always came down to that. Reports. Statistics. Information that would be filed away. Life and death pared down to a few words on a sheet of paper.

An official stamp stating that the case was closed.

The big Fed knew there was more to it than that. His people were more than rubber stamps on paper. They were real.

They existed, lived and breathed and carried the memories of the things they had seen and done with them. As long as he was in charge of Stony Man, they would stay real. He would worry over them, sweat when they were out in the field and carry some of the grief they had to bear.

The reason was simple—they all cared.

The day any one of them stopped doing that, they were all in trouble.

James Axler

OUTLANDERS®

DOOM DYNASTY

Kane, once a keeper of law and order in the new America, is part of the driving machine to return power to the true inheritors of the earth. California is the opening salvo in one baron's savage quest for immortality—and a fateful act of defiance against earth's dangerous oppressors. Yet their sanctity is grimly uncertain as an unseen force arrives for a final confrontation with those who seek to rule, or reclaim, planet Earth.

Gold Eagle brings you high-tech action and mystic adventure!

THE Destroyer™

#121 A POUND OF PREVENTION

Created by

MURPHY and SAPIR

Organized crime lords are converging in the East African nation of Luzuland, for what looks like an underworld summit. Remo—with his own problems—is just not in the mood to be killing his way up the chain of command in East Africa. Chiun has gone AWOL, and unless he can beat some sense into his pupil's skull, Remo's bent on nuking a mob-infested Third World city to deliver a pound of prevention to wipe out a generation of predators....

Available in October 2000 at your favorite retail outlet.